BEST

LESBIAN

EROTICA

2009

BEST
LESBIAN
EROTICA
2009

Series Editor

TRISTAN TAORMINO

Selected and Introduced by

JOAN LARKIN

CLEIS PRESS

Cleis Press Inc., P.O. Box 14697, San Francisco, California 94114.
Printed in the United States.
Cover design: Scott Idleman
Cover photograph: Celesta Danger
Text design: Frank Wiedemann
Cleis logo art: Juana Alicia
First Edition.
10 9 8 7 6 5 4 3 2 1

"Hard To Get" © 2008 by Rachel Kramer Bussel first appeared in *Purple Panties: An Eroticanoir.com Anthology* edited by Zane (Streber Books, 2008); "Lipstick on Her Collar" © 2008 by Sacchi Green first appeared in *Lipstick on Her Collar and Other Tales of Lesbian Lust* edited by Sacchi Green and Rakelle Valencia (Pretty Things Press, 2008); "Spike" © 2007 by Jodi Payne first appeared in ebook format (Torquere Press, 2007); "Dream Date" © 2007 by Radclyffe first appeared in *In Deep Waters: Erotic Excursions 1* edited by Karen Kallmaker and Radclyffe (Bella Books, 2007); "Tough Enough to Wear a Dress" © 2007 by Teresa Noelle Roberts first appeared in *Crossdressing: Erotic Stories* edited by Rachel Kramer Bussel (Cleis Press, 2007); "Velvet" © 2008 by Lisabet Sarai first appeared in ebook format (Eternal Press, 2008); "Stuck at Work and Late for a Date" © 2008 by Chelsea G. Summers first appeared in *Yes Sir: Erotic Stories of Female Submission* edited by Rachel Kramer Bussel (Cleis Press, 2008).

CONTENTS

FOREWORD

Tristan Taormino

In 1995, I began work on my first edition of *Best Lesbian Erotica*, and here I am writing the foreword for *Best Lesbian Erotica 2009*, the last volume I will edit. Fittingly, it feels like the ending of a sex-filled affair. I'm sad, I'm satisfied, I'm nostalgic, and I'm ready for the next adventure.

In fact, as I read the stories for this collection knowing it would be my last, they reminded me of a steamy affair I had some years ago. I was in San Francisco speaking at a gala evening honoring Joan Nestle in the fall of 1998. I stood on the stage of the Victoria Theater with literary luminaries like Dorothy Allison, Jewelle Gomez, Carol Queen, and Alison Bechdel, and I was the youngest woman asked to read the work of one of my heroines. I chose a passage from "My Woman Poppa," one of Joan's signature pieces of erotica that was first published in *On Our Backs*. It was about butch/femme power dynamics, strap-on sex, the politics of penetration, and passion.

My woman poppa who knows how to take me in her arms and lie me down, knows how to spread my thighs and then my lips, who knows how to catch the wetness and use it, who knows how to enter me so waves of strength hit us both. *

After the event came to a close, I was standing on stage talking with the other readers and audience members. I spotted a hot butch in the audience making her way toward us. Actually, it looked like she was making a beeline for me. She had on a sharp gray suit and tie and well-shined wingtips. Her hair was sculpted into a perfect pompadour. She had a retro cool about her as she swaggered up to me and introduced herself. Her icy blue eyes were warm underneath her macho gaze. I admit it, I was pretty taken with her. I told her I was only in town for a few days. I invited her to a book reading the next night at A Different Light in the Castro. She showed up at the store, hung back in the travel section while I read from my latest work. This time, she was dressed in dark blue jeans with thick turned-up cuffs, and a plain white T-shirt peeking out from a vintage bowling shirt. And she had that pompadour, perfect again.

I don't remember if we went out after the reading or not, I just remember ending up at her apartment in the Mission. It was filled with mod furniture and a fluffy gray cat the same color as her suit from the previous night. She was a gentleman, as if she'd gone to a school for gentlemanly skills or something, and we talked on her couch. It turned out that we both used to ride horses when we were younger, so we compared notes. We swapped stories about hours spent at the stable and waking up at four a.m. to go to horse shows.

"Why did you stop riding?" she asked.

I paused, looked her right in the eyes, and the words tumbled out of my mouth before I could stop them.

"I lost my nerve," I said quietly.

"Yeah," she nodded. "I know what you mean."

I had never told anyone that before. I had never even said those words out loud. Who was this stranger and how did she unearth such a revelation from me? My stomach fluttered. I felt cracked open. Part of me wanted to dart out the front door. She leaned in to kiss me before I had the chance to escape. And I surrendered…to her mouth on mine, to her hand on the back of my neck, to her thigh pressed between my legs. When she slipped her hand under my skirt and slid two fingers between my slick lips, it was obvious: I was smitten and soaked and *hers*. Seduction has never felt so easy. I have never felt so easy.

She pushed her face through my tangle of curls and pressed her mouth to my ear.

"I'll be right back," she said, and disappeared.

I heard water running and realized she was in the bathroom. The water kept running and soon I wondered what she was doing in there. But I kept still on the couch, exactly where she had left me, and waited. She finally emerged in boxers and a silk smoking jacket with gold-colored lapels. I saw a bulge in the boxers. I smiled. She sat down on the couch, and I didn't need any more of an invitation. I slipped my hand inside the opening of the blue fabric and found her cock. I tugged at it to guide it through the slit and that's when it hit me: she had a really big dick. I mean, big like a porn star replica…big like, well, bigger than I was used to. I wrapped my lips around it anyway, decided to give it my best try. It hit the back of my throat and there were still several inches left to go. I put my hands around the base and pressed down on it with each bob of my mouth. She moaned like she was turned on and mad about it at the same time. It was music to my ears. As I leaned back over her to continue working her with my mouth, she fingered my pussy. She touched my chin and brought my mouth back to hers. We kissed and I think my nose started to run, probably from deep-throating her one too many times, and that gray cat. I was allergic to the cat.

We made our way to the bed in the other room where she climbed on top of me. She sat up between my legs and reached for the bottle of lube on the bedside table. She poured some in her hand and started to stroke her cock with it. The robe fell open slightly, and I saw a flash of black leather against her chest. She moved my hand between her legs and put it over hers and continued to stroke. With my other hand I traced my way up her chest over the robe's silky fabric. I looked at her, wanting to know if it was okay to go under. She tipped her head down slightly.

I found my way to her chest and the leather harness that encased it. Her nipples were hard cylindrical points, thicker than mine and twice as stiff. I followed the black leather down the front of her chest and realized it was connected to the harness underneath her boxers. I was trying to picture how it all fit together in my head when I felt her hand move underneath mine. She spread my legs and the cock was hard against my inner thigh. I felt the tip at my opening. The lube had warmed up with her stroking, and it felt good. She pushed in slightly and my legs fell open farther. Then her entire body covered mine as she went all the way inside. I felt the smooth silk of her robe against my chest with the stiff leather just underneath it.

She fucked me like that for many months, with steamy cross-country phone calls and emails in between. Then, I came to visit her and realized that she and her girlfriend—she'd had one all along—had gotten very serious. Her girlfriend was no longer happy and gracious when I came to town, although she wouldn't say so. Sometimes, a femme just knows when another femme is grinning and baring it, and I knew. So, I sat down with my San Francisco sweetheart in my friend's apartment and I told her good-bye. Her butch ego took a hit, and she wasn't happy. But she didn't stay mad for very long. The beautiful thing about the whole affair is that it never had the time (or perhaps the inclination) to get ugly or mean or bitter. It was perfect in that way. My time with her filled me with sexy memories, without the sting of a bad breakup. It had run its course, and we had to go our separate ways. To this day, when a butch excuses herself to the bathroom and I hear the sound of running water, I think of her.

And that's what it's like leaving *Best Lesbian Erotica*, a series I created and nurtured for sixteen volumes. No temper tantrums or messy phone calls, just a bittersweet ending to a wonderful affair.

I will miss the saucy femme who wrote a brilliant personal ad, the woman who had a hysterectomy and feared she'd never ejaculate again, the mom who was in love with a knife sharpener, the Muslim sisters-in-law with depilatory wax, and the surfer girl who became a boy. I'll never forget all the horny hitchhikers, cheating wives, unconventional vampires, pervy professors, and leather daddies. Or the yoga teachers, dyke superheroes, butch bakers, kinky sex machine inventors, queer strippers, and lesbian escorts. I'll miss how writers managed to work Queen Elizabeth, Little Red Riding Hood, Rita Hayworth, Salome, and Monica Lewinsky into their lesbian erotica. I'll miss all the words writers use to describe swollen clits, wet pussies, stiff cocks, hard nipples, muff diving, blow jobs, hand jobs, finger-fucking, cunt-banging, and ass-reaming. I will miss sex in parks, office cubicles, bathrooms, taxicabs, subways (and subway tunnels), national monuments, Italian villas, and trailer-park brothels; at tranny boy pool parties and on carnival rides. I'll miss revenge sex, make-up sex, anonymous sex, fantasy sex, love sex, hate sex, and public sex. I'll miss genderfucks, mind fucks, power fucks, and first-time fucks. I will miss reading a new story by the most published author in the anthology series, Peggy Munson. I'll miss reciting snippets of erotica to my partner before bedtime. I'll miss the thrill of accepting a piece and receiving the author's bio with the line, "This is her first publication." I'll miss meeting writers all over the country and reading in bookstores and bars and backyards. I'll miss proofreading the galleys and jerking off.

I'm happy that the series will continue in the capable hands of Kathleen Warnock, who has contributed stories to many volumes herself (writing under a pseudonym). I'm honored to have been the keeper of this collection for so long, and I can't wait to see what the next fifteen years bring!

Tristan Taormino
New York City, 2008

*Joan Nestle, "My Woman Poppa," in *A Fragile Union: New and Selected Writings* (Cleis Press, 1998), 151.

INTRODUCTION:
IMMERSION COURSE

Joan Larkin

"Mm!" My friend has a sly, knowing look. "So, when I read this collection," she teases, "I'll know what you like to do in bed."

"Don't assume anything," I say sharply. "You won't have a clue what I like to do. You'll know what I like to read, what I like thinking about. You'll get a good look at some of my wildest, dirtiest fantasies—and a few sweet, romantic ones, too. You may guess at some language I enjoy in the bedroom. You'll know a whole range of scenarios, any one of which turns me on just thinking about it. You'll know words and mental pictures that ignite my feelings and arouse my flesh. But what I *do*—? That," I tell my friend, "stays private." I insist on the boundary. You know what Robert Frost said about good fences making good neighbors.

Here's the thing. Having just read and reread this stack of shamelessly delicious, varied, unpredictable stories and felt the effect on my pulses of their thrilling details, I've never been more convinced than I am right now of this truth—I'm sure of it: the *brain* is the wildest sex organ of all. Just remembering an image from one of these stories—a pair of ripped panties, say—or a spiked heel, a nylon cord, a strap-on under an Edwardian dress, the sound of a zipper, or of lube quietly gliding over silicone—one image is all it takes to make my skin blush and my muscles tense. It's *thinking* that shortens the breath, raises the temperature, and quickens the blood. Let's hear it for the imagination!

These stories are full of objects you may or may not have used: latex, rubber, silk, and silicone; clamps, collars, harnesses, plugs, floggers, camisoles, scented candles; and yes, one outrageous enema bag. You may be inspired to go shopping. I was. But in truth all you really need is this book and some light to read by. I read many of the stories in manuscript format, at bedtime, in a supine position, and I can enthusiastically recommend that you do, too. This is not an academic exercise.

As for what the fabulous women in this collection like to do in bed—well, I'm here to report that very little of the dramatic action takes place in beds, and almost none of it is horizontal. Bars, clubs, kitchens, a tattoo parlor, a famous public park, a concert hall, a diner, a war zone, a librarians' conference, an art gallery, a cruise ship, a beach, a balcony or two. And what happens there, at a depth, under these many surfaces? Themes of power, self-knowledge, self-revelation, love, and even spirituality run through scenes of domination and submission, the inhabiting of old and new roles, sudden turnabouts, the intensity of repression, and the wild exhilaration of freedom.

From teasingly playful to darkly cruel to hilariously inventive, I was riveted—as I know you will be—by the sophistication and power of these writers—and by what they exposed of me to myself.

I began reading these pieces convinced I was the same vanilla romantic I'd been since prehistoric times—the '70s, when all feminists were expected to sport construction boots, femmes were suspect, bisexuals were out-and-out traitors, and trans persons had no voice. But reading these stories has been an illumination. Not only has this immersion course expanded the scope of my erotic imagination and shaken off old, limiting ideas of political correctness, it has made me hungry for more: more pleasure, more life, more connection to myself and to others. In awakening my lust, these stories free the life force in me.

Yet another revelation: the better written the story, the more erotically powerful it is. Writing itself is an erotic art, ruled by rhythms of desire and release. These stories are written by women who know how to tease, gradually unfold, and prolong our interest, or how to pull us into their worlds with an immediate shock and hold us there, breathless, watching a sometimes dangerous drama unfold. Their rhythms are as compelling as their voices are different. The variety of scents and flavors made me swoon. I won't forget the outrageous baby talk and undercurrent of incestuous fantasy in Thea Leticia's "The Christmas Gift," the hilarious/serious revelation of the eternal holy feminine in Jean Casse's "The Virgin of G," the unabashed fetishism of Jodi Payne's "Spike," the melding of dominance and class in Jean Roberta's "The Placement of Modifiers," nor the dark, anonymous coupling in Jessica Swafford's "Golden Gate." I'll read Radclyffe's "Dream Date" over and over, reveling in the drawn-out fantasy of the considerate escort who's thought of—well, *everything*—and I'll keep coming back to savor the danger of loving a merciless park ranger in Anna Watson's "Beneath the Carpet Is the Floor." And these are only some of my favorites. You'll have favorites, too, worlds you'll savor and want to return to. But I promise that nothing between these pages will disappoint you.

So turn the page. Let's get the party started.

THE VIRGIN OF G

Jean Casse

"You sound like my grandmother!" She turned on the light and sat up.

"No!" This was both a denial and a protest because I wasn't some religious old lady muttering prayers in Spanish, or maybe Latin, in the corner.

I still knelt between her legs, my head lifted, lips moist from her. "Just let me get a mirror so you can see, too. She shows up really clear in this light. Let me take a picture."

"No way." She brushed me aside as she got out of bed. "You did not see anybody in my cunt. You are not going to talk crazy like my grandmother, seeing the Virgin in an apple core, San Francisco in a half-eaten Baby Ruth bar, I don't know what-all. All the time. No!"

"Listen, Lupe..."

"No."

But I knew what I saw. We'd been lovers for a year, but it took all that time of looking to see it, and it took a candle she'd bought as a joke in a bodega the day before.

"Look," she'd laughed. "Just like my grandmother has all over her room. Let's get one for our flat."

We'd just moved in together. We hadn't even unpacked the boxes yet when she carried that candle upstairs and set it on her old steamer trunk in the bedroom.

The picture glued to the glass was of the Virgin of Guadalupe, Lupe's real name, though she never used it. "Merciful Virgin Mary of Guadalupe, show clemency, love, and compassion to those who love you and fly to your protection. May your intercession, like the sweet fragrance of roses, ascend to your divine son..." I read in English from the back of the candle, while Lupe read the same words in Spanish. We cracked up laughing because Lupe was the opposite of an innocent virgin: more scary than merciful, more apt to tie me to the bed and tongue me just to the edge of coming before she stopped than she was to show love and compassion. Lupe was exciting, not protective, the rose thorn rather than the scented bloom. She kept me alive on the blade of her own brand of love.

I looked at the picture, at the sweetly simpering face of the Virgin surrounded by the pink and black folds of her robe, a crown on her head. There were rosebuds along the bottom edge, with a strange little boy peeking out from the lavender underskirt of the robe.

"Who's the kid?" I asked Lupe.

She rolled her eyes. "Baby Jesus. Don't you know anything?"

"No. I'm Jewish, remember?"

By the next evening, we'd unpacked the sheets and blankets

from Lupe's old trunk, made the bed, and set things around the bedroom. Lupe's belts and ties hung from hooks on the wall over the bed, lace curtains draped the windows, and the Virgin of Guadalupe rested on the bedside table.

"Maybe I should put her back on the trunk under the window, what do you think?" she asked.

I hesitated not only because she so rarely asked my opinion, but also because I'd developed a strange attraction to this candle. "I like it by the bed."

She shrugged. "If you want. But I think it would look better over by the window."

To her it was a work of art to be placed like the pictures she was lining up against the walls so she could decide which ones to hang.

"It might be useful by the bed. For a bit of light," I said.

"Right," she answered with a sideways smile.

Did I find the Virgin attractive? I'd never been drawn to purity before. Sweet women didn't attract me. Was this a religious vision of love and compassion? Not likely, because I was raised by Jewish hippies whose true religion was anarchist politics.

Though my arms still ached from carrying boxes up to the third floor, I felt my clit swell at the sight of Lupe's smile. My exhaustion disappeared along with my philosophical questions.

"Praise the Virgin," I said as I fell on the bed. "Let's light the candle."

Twilight was slowly darkening the room. The picture on the candle glowed, seeming to expand, its image pulsating in my brain when I closed my eyes and let Lupe tie my wrists to the headboard with bands of silk. She ran her tongue down my neck, sucking lightly, then continued to slide it between my breasts, circling my navel before descending to grab my clit lightly between her lips.

I was floating, close to coming, the Virgin for some reason throbbing along with me at the back of my eyelids, when Lupe slapped my face until my cheeks turned bright red, saying, "Play fair! Let's turn this around." As if she'd read my mind, as if she knew the Virgin was stuck in there, and she didn't want the competition. She untied my wrists and guided my head downward to her cunt while she stretched out on the bed.

"My little sex slave," she murmured, ruffling my short hair.

How many other women had she said this to? As far as I knew, I was the only one she'd ever wanted to live with. My heart began to pound as I parted her legs to look at her slit, something she always liked me to do first.

"How perfect is it?" she whispered, loudly enough to be heard in the back rows of a large theater.

"Unbelievable," I responded, holding up the Virgin candle for a closer inspection.

And that's when I sucked in my breath, because there it was: a perfect oval, a dark fringe of hair, pink outer lips, fuchsia inner lips, a dark fold in what looked like robes, a clit like a crown at the top, and the rosy asshole smiling like a small boy's face.

"O," was all I could say, my mouth circled around the sound of it. Ever since Lupe and I had been together, I hadn't noticed I was fucking the Virgin herself.

"What are you doing?" She was cross because she didn't like me to deviate from our script. I was supposed to tell her how perfect her lips were, how neat each crease, how erect the clit, and then sink my face into her until she started coming, when

I had to stuff exactly three fingers in her cunt and pump slowly back and forth until she told me to stop.

Then I would have my reward: she'd thrust one of her vibrating dildos deep inside me, pushing against my womb until I exploded. She always let me pick the dildo as long as it was her favorite green silicone Jolly Giant. He pleased me as well as any, so I didn't object.

But this time I couldn't go on as though nothing were different. I had to tell her.

"I see the Virgin from this candle in you." I held the candle aloft, the better to see her with.

That's when Lupe snapped the light on, blinding me, and accused me of being crazy like her grandmother. She got up and paced around the room with her arms folded, then lay back down, flinging one leg over my shoulder, pushing her cunt almost into my face. "Okay, look at it in the light. Sniff it, come on. Take a deep drink. This is what's real."

But in the brightness I saw in the dark circle of Lupe's hair the rosy folds of the Virgin's robes, crowned by orange shafts of reflected lamplight radiating from Lupe's clit. There was the scent of roses, too, which must have been soap or powder still clinging to her fur. Her black cat jumped on the bed and came to stick his nose in, but immediately backed off, hissing. Lupe had named that cat Lucifer, so whatever put him off must have been divine.

"You're right," I lied. "The vision is gone. I don't see it anymore."

"Good. Now let's get back to business," she said, switching off the light.

I blew out the candle.

That I did still see the Virgin would be my secret. I didn't see her in the rolls at breakfast the next morning; I didn't see her in the peach we split and fed each other, the juice running down our chins. But I saw her in my mind, and knew she was still in Lupe's cunt. I wanted to take pictures for proof. I had my cell phone; I had a camera that fit in the palm of my hand. I'd photographed her cunt before, so I figured she wouldn't suspect what image I wanted to capture if I waited a few days so she'd forget my vision.

We visited her mother and grandmother. The old lady looked up at me from the corner where she spent her days in prayer and slowly closed one eye. Was that a wink? What did she know?

The first time we'd gone over to their apartment, she'd asked Lupe, in a Spanish that sounded hopeful, though I didn't understand a word of it, if I was, perhaps, a boyfriend.

"Her name is Rebecca. Not a boy!" she'd shouted at the old lady in English, before translating her grandmother's remarks for me. "And she's quite deaf, so we have to shout," she'd explained.

"I keep telling you shouting won't help because she doesn't speak much English anyway. Nobody ever listens to me," her mother had sighed.

On this visit the old lady smiled flirtatiously at me when I helped her to the table and pulled out her chair. Maybe she still thought I was a boy, or maybe she sensed I was a fellow visionary. We all sat down to a lunch of homemade tamales. Lupe and her mom began a loud conversation as if they meant to include the grandmother, which they clearly didn't because most of the talk, all in English, was about her: the pains in her knees ("From kneeling in church every day, I swear it!"), the rash that was developing on the backs of her hands ("A stigmata, you think?" "Oh, shush, don't give her ideas."), the way she kept calling Lupe's brother's second wife by the name of his divorced first wife. ("I think she does it on purpose to embarrass him because she doesn't believe in divorce. I swear it!")

I felt right at home with these people because their intense voices and waving arms reminded me of the way my parents would debate politics by the hour, their shouts blending into what became for me a comforting background, a discussion that could be about anything, or nothing. Lupe's grandmother kept praying, though, and giving me quick glances, which was disturbingly unfamiliar.

When we left, Lupe ranted about how worried she was that the grandmother was driving her mother crazy. "But even though my mom doesn't go to church anymore, she still has that Catholic sense of guilt and duty, so she'll never put her in a home. *Abuela's* mother, my great-grandmother, lived to be 101, so we've got a good twenty years of this ahead of us. But if my mom goes first, I wouldn't have any problem putting her away."

By the time we got home, I realized this was not a good time to try to get a picture of Lupe's cunt.

Lupe usually fell asleep after sex. She couldn't help herself; an orgasm would put her right out, typically with her body flung carelessly across the bed, legs sprawled open for my continuing admiration. I'd photographed her before in this Sleeping Beauty state. I still had some old shots of her cunt in my camera, but as I clicked through them, I could find none that reflected the image of the Virgin. Now Lupe took to sleeping curled up, her fists held protectively between her clenched legs, while I sat and waited for her to relax. But the few times she did, she'd roll over on her stomach, hands still between her legs, as if she knew my little camera was ready for her.

Maybe there was something to be seen in the curves of her hips, in the breasts squeezed between her arms. I ran my camera over her body, my eyes fixed on the monitor, but I didn't see any saints or virgins. I clicked pictures of the licorice cleft between her breasts, the browned loaves of her ass, the sweet crescent of her back as she curled around herself.

Nothing was going to happen. She would never unfurl herself to me again. We'd make love in the dark, and after she curled up to sleep, I'd light the candle to watch the flame flicker behind the image of the Virgin.

One day when the candle inside the glass was half gone, Lupe threw the whole thing in the trash.

"We need new candles," she announced. "Plain ones. No pictures. No more damn saints."

She went out that afternoon and bought silver tapers that she stuck into glass star candleholders and placed around the flat. For me she bought an old menorah she found in an antique shop on McAllister Street, whose little candles—all nine of them—she lit every night.

"I thought you'd appreciate this, Beck," she said when I protested.

"I do, it's lovely, but it's not Hanukkah, and you don't light all the candles every night even then. It's like, well, you don't keep your Christmas tree up all year, do you?"

"We could. We could get a plastic one, like my mom's." She shrugged. "Why not? Who cares about all that religious stuff? If it's pretty, light it all year. If you can see the Virgin in my cunt whenever you want, I can light your menorah every night."

My skin jumped. This was the first time she'd mentioned my vision since the night I'd had it. Was this an unfolding? Or was the whole thing still eating at her, keeping her on guard?

"You never let me see your cunt anymore," I reminded her.

She stood before me with her legs apart, hands on her hips, as if daring me to push her down on the bed. But I knew that if I did, she'd scratch and bite because *she* should be the one to do the pushing, not me. I put my hands on her shoulders anyway and shoved. Something had changed; instead of protesting, she fell back on the bed, legs apart, smiling up at me. She unzipped her jeans and wriggled out of them, threw her black panties on the floor, and spread her legs wide.

"Come on," she said. "Give me proof."

And I saw, in the bright sunlight streaming through the thin curtains, the rosy folds that made up the Virgin of Guadalupe: her face so dark I couldn't quite see it, the throbbing crown on top, the child's face below. I grabbed my phone out of my pocket and nosed it in there. She jumped when she heard the buzz of the flash, but said nothing. I looked at the picture I'd just taken, and there it was, even more clear than the real thing.

"Here," I said, thrusting my phone at her.

She held it, studying it, saying nothing. And then she asked, "Did I tell you about the time my grandmother saw the Virgin in a banana?"

"You mentioned it, yes. You laughed at her."

"It happened more than once, actually. The Virgin must like bananas as much as *Abuela* does. But the first time, my mom was pregnant with me when my grandmother cut that banana lengthwise down the middle, and opened it up, and there was the Virgin of Guadalupe. My mom said the banana was all black inside, like rotted from the middle. But *Abuela* said it was a sign that I was going to be a girl named Guadalupe. And I was going to do great things.

"'Like what?' Mom asked. 'Make us all rich? If she stays a virgin forever, how can she marry money?'

"But *Abuela* just shrugged. 'Virginity has nothing to do with sex or marriage,' she answered. 'It's in the soul.'

"Mom thought she was loony, but she went along with it because she thought Lupe was a cute name. And then she made banana bread out of that banana. My grandmother was livid— it was a saint! How could she? *Abuela* wanted to preserve that banana forever. Now the baby—me—would be cursed! I'd lose my soul. I'd never know who I was. Besides, *Abuela* wanted to show the neighbors, like she always did with the saints she found in food. She says you can find saints anywhere if you know how to look. Me, I have a good imagination. I can see anyone anywhere if I put my mind to it. Anna Nicole Smith in an ear of corn. But I've never seen a saint spontaneously. I guess I'm just not on the saint hotline, or something. Maybe *Abuela* was right. I'm doomed to never know myself."

Lupe sighed. Was she really sad about this, or was it some trick to make me relax before she called me a delusional idiot?

"And you know what?" she went on, looking at the picture again, "I'm not even sure I see it here. It's like figure and ground, you know, in a psych textbook. First you see the vase, then it's two women nose to nose, then it's the vase again, flashing back and forth. I think I maybe see the Virgin of Guadalupe in this picture, but then it's just my cunt, like a trick, fooling me. And maybe you're even more fooled. You're a Jew, Beck; if religion has any logic, you should be seeing Moses spreading the Red Sea of my cunt, or whatever."

"I'm not religious—I just believe what I see. And if I saw the Red Sea parting, I'd believe that, too. But I think my vision, if you want to call it that, comes from you."

"I want to believe." Her voice was small. "But I can't. It just doesn't make sense."

"What? Religion, or wanting to believe in it?"

"None of it. Hold me. Kiss your Virgin."

She wasn't being ironic. With my lips on her folds, I was too close to see what exactly I was licking as I lightly tipped my teeth to her crown, my tongue to the baby Jesus. I bathed her rosy robes in my saliva until she began to sing in a way I hadn't heard her do before, a high-pitched, pure wail descending to a melodious growl, a wordless language I understood completely, a language that nudged me to all the right spots around her crevice until she quivered into silence and fell immediately to sleep, leaving me to pull back and watch the Virgin's throbbing crown as I stuffed my own cunt with my fist, my silent mouth open as I came.

Lupe began to sing with a band, all women I hadn't met before. I'd never heard her sing until that afternoon, but now she sang all day in her terrific range, from soprano to growl. She sang Mexican songs, old Beatles tunes, and all kinds of ballads, ancient and modern, from "Barbara Allen" to KT Tunstall and Norah Jones. But when she practiced with her band, it was always her own original wordless shrieks and howls, the sounds she originated every night now in our bed. Her voice was the only instrument she played.

She bought another candle of the Virgin of Guadalupe, and kept it lit day and night, and when it burned down, she put another candle inside the glass to keep it going. Poor Lucifer would hide under the couch when she sang, and would fly out the door whenever the band arrived to practice. After a while, that cat didn't come back at all, but Lupe didn't seem to miss him. She spent more time with her grandmother, who always, Lupe said, sent me her very best wishes.

"*Abuelita* knows your soul," she said with a nod.

Anybody's soul, or just mine? I was afraid to ask.

Her band started performing in clubs; they called themselves the Virgin of G, with Lupe as G, dancing to the rhythm of her own rising and falling cries. I usually went along to watch their act. First the band would play to warm up the audience, and then Lupe would come out into the spotlight wearing the shortest skirt she had, and begin to wail in that wonderful, wordless voice, up and down the scale, making my spine and quim quiver together. I wondered jealously if she had the same effect on the rest of the audience as they danced wildly, twisting and flailing their arms like no dance I'd ever seen. Lupe's dress and the music the band played were like a cover for the purity of her voice, which shone like a candle illuminating her soul.

"G!" The audience shouted. "G! G! The Goddess!"

I could tell they didn't see the vision. Even when the audience was all women, or Mexican, they didn't get it. I don't think the band understood, either. There were two black women on bass and guitar, great blues players who loved to weave their music around Lupe's voice, and a drummer with long blonde hair that she tossed back and forth as her drumsticks flew, and this really hot French dyke named Severine on piano, who wore dark green leather straps around her wrists and ankles. They were in the groove with Lupe, and yet not. Their music was rhythmic sex, while Lupe was something deeper, silent at her core even when she sang. Only her *Abuelita* and I could see her soul.

At the end, Lupe would bend over and flash her twat at the audience, but it was so dark and she was so far away no one could see the Virgin within her.

When we got home, she'd lie on the bed, spread her legs, and ask me what I saw, and I would say, "The Virgin is blushing pink tonight and her crown is sending out rays of light. The baby Jesus is hiding behind a bouquet of red roses, no, there he is, popping out now."

"Get me a mirror," she'd order, and then she'd look closely. Sometimes she'd exclaim, "Yes! It's just like you say tonight. Perfect!" and other times she'd sigh, "I don't see it. Suck my clit hard; make me come. I see more clearly then."

And after, when she'd look in the mirror, she'd call out, "Yes! Yes! There she is, she hasn't left me," and begin to sing her chorus of moans and growls.

She printed out the best of my pictures, the ones where even she could sometimes see the Virgin, and hung them on the bedroom walls, where I would often find her standing before one, inspecting it closely, sometimes smiling, other times shaking her head, murmuring, "Figure. Ground. Figure. Ground," as she tried to call up the Virgin.

I had a theory the Virgin lived in the cunts of all women as an eternal self-possession nothing could deflower. We held the mirror to my cunt, but neither one of us could see anything, not even figure and ground.

"Just Becka's delicious cunt," she said, licking me from clit to asshole. "But just because we can't see, that doesn't mean the Virgin's not in there."

Once she snuck up behind me while I was cleaning out the tub, my tail in the air. "Nice pussy," she murmured, pushing her Virgin against me. "Nice little cockerel, too," she added, putting her finger to my clit as she crowed.

I began to take pictures of women's cunts, claiming to be doing a book of feminist erotic photographs. I did the band; I took shots of everyone I knew. Nobody else had the Virgin in them. "You're special," I whispered to Lupe every night before going down on her. "And I am so privileged."

"No," she answered one night. "My *Abuelita* says all women are the Virgin. We'll see when we're ready."

"But why do I only see her in you?" I asked.

Lupe shrugged. "*Abuelita* says beginnings are slow, understanding takes time. She says we're on our way."

These days, Lupe prefers to visit her grandmother while her mother's at work. "Mom isn't ready," she explains solemnly. "I can't talk to her yet."

When she takes me with her, I sit silently while she and the old lady talk in Spanish. Sometimes they moan together, almost like Lupe's singing, but more sedately, like praying. Often Grandma smiles at me, putting her warm hands on my head, smiling and nodding like she's reading my mind.

"I always tell *Abuelita* how you see the Virgin in me," Lupe explained the first time she took me along. "I say I feel the Virgin of Guadalupe grow stronger within me every day. I tell her how my singing helps me. She says singing always clears your vision, and orgasm can make you see because it's your body singing. My *Abuelita*, she's really all right." And then she continued in Spanish, translating for her grandmother.

Grandma nodded and smiled until Lupe went to the

bathroom, when she pulled me closer to her. "You have an old soul," she said. "You are man and woman both. That's why you see. That's why you can help our Lupe find herself. She was born for great things, you know. But for a long time, I lost her."

Her English was perfect.

She tapped her forehead with one finger. "Me, I understand. I know you do, too. All women contain the essential world inside, clean, perfect, virtuous. It's up to us to help them see."

"Why...What..." I stuttered, but then Lupe flushed the toilet, and Grandma drew back, a finger to her lips.

"Shush," she whispered. "When you learn to be silent, all languages and ideas will come to you."

I'm not sure I understand as well as *Abuelita* thinks, but I believe if I continue to worship Lupe every night, I'll get there. She still likes to tie me up sometimes, but then she holds me in her arms, her fingers on my cunt so perfect and gentle that I come in seconds, the Virgin of Guadalupe quivering in back of my eyelids. Gentle and merciful, Lupe lets me come again and again as we pray together: "...wipe away our tears and give us comfort and assistance as we search for you in our bodies and our souls. Amen."

THE DINER ON THE CORNER

Zaedryn Meade

As soon as we walk into the diner on the corner, I visualize fucking Shanna on the counter. Or behind the counter, or against the counter, hell, I don't care—but I am certain the curve of the metal edge, the bar stools, and that old-fashioned silver milkshake machine would go perfectly with her rockabilly-femme style.

This is our first date. She picked me up at the dyke bar last weekend while letting me think I was picking her up, and me being enamored with her immaculate femininity—the tattoos on her shoulders, the shade of pink her nails were painted, the faint flowery scent I wanted to lean into her neck to inhale, the low-cut dress and perfectly curved cleavage, the vibrant hair with streaks of dark purple and red—I didn't notice until halfway through the evening that, though

I thought I was warming her up to ask for her number, she was secretly rolling her eyes, thinking, *Get on with it already*. She had control of every detail, but let me think I did.

Tonight, I've picked everything out precisely: black button-down shirt, my favorite sleek red tie, black slacks; solid black freshly polished shiny wingtips; plain, simple black fedora on top, because it may rain tonight.

And because she likes them.

We meet at the movie theatre. She looks incredible: four-inch heels with small straps over the arch of her foot, a little buckle on the side; dark hair down over her shoulders and touching her neck; stockings and a fifties dress that comes just above her knees, with a slightly flared and layered skirt, and low-cut, again, showing off the lovely curves of her breasts. I don't stare. *Don't stare*, I tell myself. *You're being an asshole*. I try not to stare. Talk to her face, not her tits.

"I like your...hat," she giggles, dark eyes lowered, looking up at me through those lashes, slyly, shyly, from the side, that glance of submission.

I don't blush, but my cheeks get a little warm. "Thanks." I rarely wear hats. I love the way they look, love the tough butchness they play into, but I get self-conscious about what it's doing to my perfectly messy hair—my singular vanity. As soon as we get to our seats, I balance the fedora on my knee and run my fingers through my hair to see how it's holding up. (A little smashed. I try not to care.)

I don't remember the film. Something about music, Dublin, and falling in love. I remember thinking that there should be more sex in it. And that I forget how crowded and bright movie theatres are here in New York City—I miss being able to mess around in the darkest back row.

I do remember the way she laughed, the way she got teary once or twice, the way she kept stealing glances at me. Her hand on my thigh and the—oops—accidental brush against the bulge in my pants. The way her lips circled and sucked the straw in her soda, slow.

After the film, we walk to the corner twenty-four-hour diner. I slide into the booth and she slides in next to me, stockings on vinyl. Her left thigh touches my right, and I feel the brush of her leg against my slacks.

There are a few other diners scattered at tables, but it's late. There's one old man gumming through chicken fingers and reading the newspaper, and one table of teenagers blowing straw wrappers and eating fries off each other's plates. The waitress comes over, and I order a vanilla milkshake and a slice of apple pie, heated. "We'll share," I tell them both.

We chitchat. I toy with the sugar packets and crunch ice cubes from my water glass. She eases her leg over my thigh, which catches my breath, stirs my cock. I gently put my hand on her knee and let myself finger the thin, silky fabric of her stockings. She's still chatting as if nothing is happening. She liked the film, she's saying. The male lead was cute and sweet in a butch sort of way. "Do you think men can be butch?" she asks me.

My fingers are crushed against her thigh, seeking her creamy skin. I try to pull my consciousness from between her legs to say something intelligent.

"Well, I think that's complicated," I start, "because...while I think the gender identities of butch—and femme, too—are inherently queer by definition, I also notice some men with a particularly *female* flavor of masculinity that is closer to butch than any other word or description...."

"Yeah!" She has an eager and excited edge to her voice and presses her leg farther into my lap, twisting her torso a little to look more directly at me, opening her thighs. "I know what you mean—but if men begin to have a butch identity, does that invalidate it for the women who have to fight so hard to claim it?"

The layers of her dress are pushing up her thighs and I can feel the edge of her stocking under my fingers, lace and elastic, the line of ribbon up her thigh to her hip: a garter belt. I brush my fingers against the rough edge and press them into her inner thigh, just a little. I wonder how far she'll let me go.

I want to find out how far she'll let me go.

The teenagers clear out and the diner quiets. She leaves her hands on the table but parts her lips. She's looking at me, gazing at my mouth; I bite my tongue and feel it swollen.

Shanna leans in slightly, slowly, ever so subtly, tilting her head without realizing it as my grip on her thigh strengthens. Neither of us notices as we do this, we only notice the space between our bodies crackling electrically.

I find the crease of her hip with my fingers, that line where her thighs meet her pelvis.

Her mouth gets closer to mine, inches away. I can feel her breath. She doesn't move any closer but is begging me with her whole body to make a move. To kiss her. To keep moving my fingers up her skirt. She lets me think it's all my idea. She is shifting, something is happening in her body and mind, an intentional submission, an offering up of her mouth and cunt and hungry body. We can both feel it, but it is nearly imperceptible.

"You want...this, okay?" I whisper, fingers getting bolder, brushing against her cunt, the swollen outer labia. I can feel the air between our mouths stirring. The movement of my lips makes them touch hers, briefly, softly. I can nearly see the swirls of her breath, hot and heavy.

She bites her lip at the touch, nods, without moving her head; submits a little deeper with explicit permission.

"One vanilla milkshake—" The waitress clears her throat and sets it down in front of Shanna, who jumps, but I stay exactly where I am, smiling, amused, then turn my head slowly without moving my hand.

"One apple pie." The waitress sets the small white plate in front of me.

"Thanks," I say, taking a fork with my left hand, my right still between Shanna's thighs.

The waitress raises her eyebrows. "You two okay here?"

"Yep." I say. Shanna's cheeks are hot and flushed. She examines the milkshake, stealing a glance at me. My fingers are quiet but persistent, still on the softness of her cunt.

The waitress raises her eyebrows at me again and I can't quite tell, but I think she winks. She's cute, the waitress. Dyed black hair, thick tattoo of a faery on her left bicep, those chunky black glasses. She's the only one working, but it's dead in here, so after a round she goes back to reading her book at the counter. She's not paying us any attention.

I twist and shift in the booth and adjust so I can flatten the palm of my hand against her cunt, slowly, cupping it. She's not wearing panties. She knew she could have me. She's controlling every detail.

She inhales and can't look at me, tongues her lip gently. "Are you...will you...?" she begins, but can't finish. She wants me to kiss her. I want to ravage her, thrust her up against the vinyl. Want her hands gripping at the sides of the booth as she comes against my hand.

I grin, that sly cocky grin that says I know what she's asking, I know what she wants, and I'm taking my own damn time giving it to her. She knows she'll get it from me, so my only power here is how and when she'll get it. She offers me her neck and I take it, leaning in, kissing her shoulder, her collarbone, exposed in her low-cut dress. "You have to be quiet," I say. "We're not alone."

"We almost are," she breathes, closing her eyes and tilting her head so I can get to her neck. My fingers run lazy circles around her clit and inner lips, slick already. I dip two fingers inside and feel her muscles pulsing, slide them in and out while she begins to pant. I circle her clit again, flick it gently and feel her body contract and respond.

"Anybody could walk in at any second," I say. "Anybody could see my hand under your skirt, if they looked for just a second." She shivers and presses her thighs open, presses her cunt against my hand, grips my forearm in one hand. I'm working her clit a little harder, a little faster, and her breathing is coming heavier, her body is tense. She's trying to keep her face still.

"You haven't even touched that shake," I say, nodding toward it. She shoots me a look like she wants to tear me apart with her eyes and attempts to move the tall milkshake glass toward her with one hand. She still wants me to kiss her and I am not letting up with my fingers on her cunt, on her clit, swirling, flicking against the hood, finding that sweet spot where her pelvis tenses and her limbs go limp.

Shanna's eyes don't leave my face as she opens her mouth for the straw and sucks the milkshake into her mouth. Cold. I can see it hit her tongue and explode in creamy sweetness; her eyes roll a little and her pussy responds, presses harder into my hand. She takes another sip, and I work two fingers against her clit.

She bends her head back—just a little, just the slightest bit, she wants to be able to throw it back and scream but she can't, she's in a diner, my hand against her, fingers circling, working, flicking, pressing, and her whole body shudders, and she grips my forearm in her fist, gasps a little, just a little, and her thighs contract to grip my wrist and she comes, with no sound at all, her body absorbing the noise she wants to make, and I don't let up, don't let up at all, until—she gasps, inhales deeply, and pulls on my hand to back off.

I grin and watch her face. She's trying to keep her features together and make it not look like she's just come. Trying to regain her composure. She looks at me a little shyly and em- barrassed, unsure how loud she was, how obvious, and she glances around quickly but there's no one in the diner any- more, the few patrons have all left. It's just us, and the waitress at the counter.

"Holy. Shit," Shanna says softly, still breathing hard. I still have that stupid grin on my face, that power-top grin.

I lean in and kiss her, gently, soft, on the lips. Her mouth is cold and creamy, tastes of vanilla. Sweet. She's a fantastic kisser, all supple and slow. We kiss for a moment and I pull away, still smiling, and she tilts her chin down and looks up at me through her lashes.

"Want some pie?" I ask. I gather a bite on my fork, she nods, and I slip it between her lips.

"Oh," she says, chewing, warm apples and cinnamon on her tongue. "It's good. Want some shake?" I take a few sips. It's partly melted now.

The waitress comes over as we are giggling. "Would you two

mind—?" She starts. "I'm out of smokes. I'm just gonna run to the corner, be right back."

"Sure," I say. The waitress nods, gives us another quick once-over glance, and spins on her heel. The diner is deserted. It's just me and Shanna. I watch the waitress walk out, the bell on the glass door ringing softly, and turn to look at this gorgeous femme. She's smoothing her hair, already watching me, watching my face, and she slides out of the booth and holds out her hand. I take it and slide out behind her.

"Your turn," she says. Crossing the diner floor, her heels click against the hard linoleum, and I watch her ankles as she walks, her calves, her knees. She keeps her legs tight together, crisscrossing like a model. My mouth waters.

She stops at the counter and raises her arm, guiding me back behind the bar as if we're on the dance floor. I grin and nearly flush, a little embarrassed, flustered to be somewhere I'm not supposed to be, seeing the clutter of dishes, rags, coffee mugs, silverware, napkins, salt and pepper shakers, ketchup and Tabasco bottles. And, of course, the gleaming, polished silver milkshake machine.

I slide behind the counter and she spins on a stool, crossing her legs at the ankle. She leans over, spilling out of her dress. I lick my lips, run my thumb over them, position myself behind the bar. I grip the handle of the milkshake machine and run my hand over it, stroking.

"So," I say. "Can I get you something?" I'm having trouble keeping my face straight. It feels a little silly, but it's also hot. What will she do? Let me fuck her, here, really?

Shanna purses her lips. "What do you have back there?" She leans over the counter and shifts her hips, then reaches for my belt.

I grab her wrist and hold it for a moment, surprising her. I bring her hand to the package behind my fly and make her feel my hard-on. She *oohs* a little, still in character, and lifts her ass onto the counter, swings her legs over it, opens her knees. She grabs my tie and pulls me to her, kissing me hard, running her fingers along the short hairs on the back of my head, wrapping her legs around my waist.

"I want…" I say between kisses, "I want you, I want you to…suck me. Would you do that?"

She nods yes and closes her eyes, just for a second, tips her chin down, and slides off the counter. She kisses me again and, palm flat against my cock, fingers on my fly, she unbuckles my belt, unzips, and pulls out my packing strap-on. Swiftly. Expertly.

She kisses me while she does this, hard; kisses the corner of my mouth, my cheek, my jawline; my neck, next to my collar; and she sinks to her knees.

The tip of my cock touches her lips and it feels tender, sensitive. As though I can feel her, sucking it into her mouth, working her tongue down the shaft. This is the thrill of the borrowed cock, the filling of it, the way it becomes mine. It is hitting my clit perfectly and her mouth, oh, god, her mouth feels exquisite. I want to release into her—want to grab her hair and work her against me, push down her throat.

I hold on to the counter instead. The metal edge cuts into my palm. She works her tongue on the underside of the head of my cock and my hips buck, pelvis tightens. I tip my head back, hips forward.

"God," I groan, aware that it is what would give this whole thing away, should someone walk in the door. My expressions. I keep one eye toward the door but my eyelids keep closing. God, her mouth feels fantastic.

Shanna looks up at me, eyes wide and shining, cheeks taut, hands on the thighs of my black slacks. I want her, want to fuck her. I look around—where? We can't have much time, but I already feel close to coming. She sees me glancing around, my stance has changed.

I groan as she sucks me hard, particularly deep, and pull my cock from her mouth. "Wait," I say, "somewhere...else." I offer my hand and she takes it, rises off her knees back onto her feet.

I have a perfect sightline into the kitchen, and notice the huge walk-in freezer right behind the doorway. There may be people back there, a line cook, a busser, but they wouldn't notice us. We could sneak right in. Shanna sees where I'm looking and waits for me to take a step.

Tiptoeing, almost, once I move she follows and we reach the door in a few quick strides. My cock bobs from my fly. I pull on the industrial handle, somewhat thick in my hand and satisfying to grip. I let her go in first.

She turns to face me and brings her shoulders up. "Brr." The air is cloudy and it burns my throat a little to inhale.

I survey the situation. A few boxes, milk crates, stacked up in the corner, filled with some heavy containers, jars, lidded plastic. Some of the boxes have been peeled open, others are still wrapped and sealed. Shanna's face reads skepticism.

I sit perched on the edge of the crates and boxes and say, "Come here."

She frowns a little. "What, here? I'm not sure—"

"Oh, hell yes." I stand, take a step toward her, reach out and wrap my arm around her waist. She fits well against me this way. Her arms go up around my neck somewhat instinctively.

"But—" she says, a little too sweetly, batting her lashes at me. She has control of every detail.

"Mmmhmm." I lift her skirt and she gasps at the cold air, it contracts her thighs a little. I take her left knee to the crook of my elbow, and bend my legs to get underneath her, gripping my cock in my fist, sliding inside her slowly but easily. She moans and it is a lovely sound. She's not holding back, begins working her hips against mine, thrusting and circling in S-curves, figure eights. She hooks her foot behind my back and I bend, balancing the weight of our bodies, taking a few steps backward again to lean against the boxes for support. Perfect. Perfect—my shoulders lean and my hips thrust freely, deeper and a little harder, my cock already so hard and her lips on me, on my neck again; I can see my breath hanging in the air as I exhale, hard, groaning every time she presses against me, and she kisses me, lips full on mine, tongue softly fierce, mouth open, open.

My hands are on her hips, pressing against her hard. I can feel every place our bodies collide, the heat in such stark contrast to the frigid air. She arches her back and presses me deep; I thrust harder and lose myself in the rhythm, hard, and again, again, against her as my muscles contract, face tenses, pelvis thighs ass tense, hard, harder...and then shuddering release, still thrusting and vibrating against her, getting softer, slower, coming down.

I hold on to her and breathe into her neck, her hair, for a moment. We kiss, giggle, weave that sex haze, gather ourselves.

Shanna exits the freezer first and returns to our table, and I follow. I pull my wallet out of my back pocket and the bell on the door jingles, the waitress tosses her cigarette into the street after she's opened the door, and then turns to see me tossing a few bills onto the table.

I pick my fedora up from the table and set it on my head,

run my fingertip over the rim, and slide my wallet back into my pocket. Shanna has one knee on the vinyl booth and takes another mouthful of vanilla milkshake.

"C'mon, doll," I say, offering my hand. She takes it and the sound of the milkshake glass on the table echoes. "Let's blow this joint."

She laughs. I'm being a bit ridiculous. Ah, well, why not? I circle my arm around her waist, wink over my shoulder at the waitress, and we walk out of the diner on the corner.

OPERATION BUTCH AMBUSH

Tawanna Sullivan

Hip-Hop Soul Night was in full swing at the Blue Gator. From her place at the bar, Charlie could take in all of the action on the floor and survey the new women filing in. It didn't take long to find a target. They began an intricate eye tango: stare, lock eyes, smile, look away, repeat.

During the third round, Charlie noticed that her Coke had dwindled down to ice cubes. She turned to flag down the bartender. A few minutes later she felt a hand on her shoulder. The young Latina woman demanding her attention was in full Mack Daddy gear, from her snug-fitting baseball cap to her fresh-pressed jeans.

Though she was scowling, there was no real menace in her voice. "Stop staring at my girl. We came out to have a nice time, why you got to be disrespectful?"

Charlie took a sip of her refreshed drink before responding. "And you are?"

"Anna."

Charlie looked over Anna's shoulder at the lady in question. Her overly painted face was a mixture of pride and embarrassment. "How would she know I was looking over there, if she wasn't looking over here?"

Anna turned the scowl up a notch. "Back off, okay?"

It could have ended there, but Charlie was feeling mischievous. "If you came all the way over here to defend her honor, you wasted your time."

"What the fuck are you trying to say?"

"Let's not play this game." Charlie put her glass down. "You know I was looking at you."

"Hell no!" Anna looked dumbfounded. "You ain't got no business looking at me like that. Do I look like some kinda femme to you?"

"Even the hardest woman has a soft spot, and I want to play with yours." Charlie gently caressed Anna's forearm.

Stepping back, the young stud almost knocked a drink out of someone's hand. "I don't know where you come from—"

"Charlie. I'm Charlie."

"—but we don't do that butch/butch stuff up here." Anna struggled to find the right words. "That's just too gay."

"Well, you don't have anything to worry about because I'm not a butch...."

Five minutes later, they were in the back of Anna's Jeep. "We're not supposed to be doing this," she whispered as Charlie nibbled on her earlobe.

"If you feel uncomfortable, tell me to stop."

Once Charlie's lips found their way to the sweet valley

between her neck and shoulders, Anna's inhibitions melted away. She unbuttoned her denim shirt and allowed access to her pierced nipples.

Charlie pulled and twisted the silver rings with her teeth. Discovering the bulge in Anna's jeans, she began to gently tug it. Anna moaned as the strap-on rhythmically rocked against her clit.

Before Anna could protest, Charlie had unzipped her pants, unsnapped two of the leather clasps of the D-ring, and was directly strumming her clit.

Then, the phone rang. Charlie would have ignored it, but it was Toi's ringtone. Reluctantly, she drew back. "Be chill, sweetie. I have to take this." By the time she got to the phone the ringing had stopped, but she had a brand new text message: *My house. 15 min. Toi.* Any time Toi was home on a Friday night, something had to be wrong. Either El had managed to get arrested again or Denny had returned from her latest straight-girl escapade with a broken heart.

Anna had come back to her senses and was hurriedly trying to fix her clothes. The dildo didn't want to snap back in place so she kicked it under the driver's seat. "Don't tell anybody about this shit, okay?"

"I won't." They exchanged numbers, and Charlie gave her another kiss before heading back to her car.

Latoya "Toi" Bennet, Elsa "El" Sparks, Denise "Denny" Franks, and Charlene "Charlie" Boyd were the original Fierce Fucking Four. It was a silly name they had given themselves after their ouster from the Butch/Femme Preservation Society. Their motto was simple—no matter whom you find yourself attracted to, be fierce enough to admit it and act on it.

As word got around about how much fun they were having, others wanted to join in. Since four had grown to over twenty, a new name was in order. Playbois, Hardy Bois, and Lost Bois had all been suggested and thoroughly ridiculed. Since all the meetings were held at her house, they'd settled on Toi Bois for the interim.

Charlie recognized the motorcycle in Toi's driveway and felt her blood pressure rising. It belonged to Ruth Carson, president of the Butch/Femme Preservation Society. When Ruth began purging undesirables from the group, she hadn't expected Toi to leave with the expelled. She was obsessed with bringing the wayward femme aggressive top switch with a bondage fetish back into the fold.

Ruth was on the sofa fidgeting with a cup of coffee. Charlie immediately went on the offensive. "What the fuck are you doing here?"

"Stand down, soldier." Toi greeted her with a kiss and steered her toward the recliner. "I know this is awkward, but we need to put our personal issues aside." After Charlie settled into the chair, she continued. "You know the show 'Butch Ambush'?"

"Of course, I do." Charlie rolled her eyes. "A so-called lax butch gets snatched off the street and offered ten thousand dollars to take a week of butch lessons from gracious hosts Rocky and April."

"Some contestants have disappeared." Toi turned to Ruth. "Tell her about the BRC."

Stripped of vitriol, Ruth's normally boisterous voice was flat. "They haven't actually disappeared. When you sign the contract to appear on the show, you basically enroll in the Butch Reformation Institute and agree to stay until you are a fully functioning butch. If Rocky and April aren't satisfied with your progress after the first week, you get sent to the Butch Reeducation Center. If a femme tries to raise hell about her missing girlfriend, the 'Butch Ambush' lawyers come out in full force."

"So," Toi cut in, "if you don't conform, you don't go home. Police are useless because, technically, no one has been kidnapped."

Charlie picked at a loose thread on a pillow cushion. "Ruth, I think you're full of shit. On the off chance that everything you say is true, it still doesn't explain why you're here."

Averting Charlie's gaze, Ruth ran a hand through her salt and pepper locks. "The BRC is actually the basement of the 'Butch Ambush' studio. We have an ally on the staff, but security is very tight. We need you and Toi to pose as applicants, get inside the building, and raise hell. While you are the center of attention, our agent will help us break in."

Her patience wearing thin, Toi was more direct. "Ruth thinks there is a spy on her team."

"We've tried to send decoys before, but they were turned away at the gate. No one knows that I've come to you and I've tapped a few trusted friends for the raid." Finally, Ruth couldn't resist a dig. "Besides, you're the perfect candidate for the Reeducation Center."

"Fuck off, Ruth." Charlie went into the kitchen. Instantly, she was upset with herself for letting the old bulldagger's words sting. She felt better when Toi's cool lips brushed against the nape of her neck. "I still think this is a setup. Since when do couples apply together to be on the show?"

Toi gave her a hug. "That's the way it works, baby. The ambush is just a theatrical way to start the show. No one is really surprised when that van shows up."

Charlie thrust her hands in her pockets. "I'd feel better about this if we could get the rest of the bois involved."

"Letting anyone else know about this collaboration beforehand could jeopardize it." Taking out her compact, Toi refreshed her mascara. "After they finish with the butches, who do you think they will ambush next?"

"Fine, I'm in."

"A producer will be out to speak with you in a few moments." The receptionist took their application and smiled at them. "Three others couple have already been in today, but I think you two really have a shot." She buzzed them into the lounge.

Charlie wasn't sure they could pull this off. Ruth hadn't exaggerated about security; they had to go through two metal detectors and a pat down to get in the door. Hidden by a dense wood, the building itself was completely surrounded by an electrified fence. It was the perfect place for some crazy cult to make its last stand.

Toi pulled Charlie close and began playing with her ear. "Don't be nervous," she whispered between nibbles. "You are Diana, I'm Tara, and we're just here because we need that ten thousand dollar prize money to go on a cruise."

Taking the hint, Charlie relaxed and tried to get in character. "Easy for you to say. No one is talking about fixing you."

"That's because I'm perfect."

A mousy looking production assistant appeared with clipboards for them. "Your applications aren't complete," she said. "Neither of you signed the waiver."

It was more than a waiver. It was three pages of archaic language written in miniscule print. "We'd have no problem signing the waiver if we were actually chosen for the show," Toi said. "After our attorney has vetted it."

The woman was visibly shocked. "You can't move forward in the interview process—"

"I think we can make an exception in this case," said a husky voice from behind. It was Rockalene Shea, the host and executive producer of "Butch Ambush." Next to her was April Gorey, the femme half of their production team. The pair began circling Charlie like hungry sharks. "Sister," Rockalene began, "you look like you've lost your way. Tattoos and piercings everywhere—you look like a perpetual beach bum. Is that makeup?"

Seeing as Rockalene looked like a football player turned mortician, Charlie decided not to take the criticism personally. "I like following my own path."

"Are you really following a path or just letting the cards fall where they may?"

"I bet she doesn't open doors for you," April said to Toi. "Does she cater to you or does she take your femininity for granted?"

"We do all right," Toi responded.

April put a sympathetic arm around her. "But that's just it, sweetie. If you wanted to settle for just 'all right,' you wouldn't be here."

Toi sighed. "I guess."

The production assistant cleared her throat. "Okay, then. You will have one-on-one interviews with Rocky and April. If they decide to take on the project, we will need to get your signatures."

Charlie was ready to follow Rocky into the hallway when the elder stateswoman shook her head. "I know deep down inside you are eager for some of this wisdom, but I'm interviewing Tara. She needs to learn how to recognize a good butch when she sees one." With a grand gesture, she offered Toi her arm and escorted her away.

"Come on, Diana," April said. "I get to give you a full evaluation and suggest a course of treatment."

"Whatever you say, Dr. Gorey." On their journey Charlie made note of the restroom and utility closet.

The tiny office actually looked more like an interrogation room. There was a desk, two chairs, and a small window overlooking the trash compactor. The worn folding chair creaked and groaned as Charlie tried to find a comfortable position.

They spent the first few minutes in silence while April poured through the application. Occasionally, she stopped shuffling papers to make notes. "I see you two have an open relationship. You don't mind if someone else fucks Tara?"

Charlie grinned. "Nope, and I don't mind if she fucks someone else. Not everyone is meant to be monogamous."

"Why are you really here, Diana?"

"For the money, of course."

"Do you really need money?"

"T wants to go on this cruise—"

"Do you want to go?"

"Well, I don't really—"

"So, you let your girl bully you to get a makeover you don't want and go on a cruise that you don't want to be on."

Charlie shrugged. "People who love each other compromise."

"And what has Tara ever given up for you?" April didn't give her time for an answer before going in for the kill. "You are spoiling her—and that's not what she wants. A femme doesn't want to run roughshod over her butch; she needs boundaries. She wants to be put in her place."

Examining the scuff on her sneakers, Charlie appeared to be in deep thought. Ruth had briefed them on the pitch April used to suck in potential contestants. "T wouldn't see it that way."

"Maybe not consciously, but she did turn you in." April switched to a more sympathetic tone. "Let us help you become the woman she needs."

"Whatever. If she's not satisfied with me, she'll tell me. Y'all can ambush someone else."

"Now, your girl would be pretty upset if you walked away from this without even trying. It's just seven days."

"Okay. What would it take for you to reject our application, to tell Tara that I don't qualify for butch lessons?"

April partially drew the blinds and sat on the desk. "Tara's application says that you need to learn proper table etiquette." She opened her legs to reveal a well-coiffed pussy. "Let's see if you can eat this sweet poontang without making a mess."

This wasn't in the script, but Charlie didn't hesitate. "No."

The femme hostess extraordinaire frowned. "Don't tell me. You're the type that can't fuck without some false extension of manhood?"

"I didn't say I wouldn't fuck you." Charlie retrieved a safe sex kit from her back pocket and snapped on a purple glove. "I'm just not going to eat you, no extensions needed." She put April's left foot on her shoulder. Gentle tongue strokes made the tightly toned legs tremble.

A salty-sweet aroma greeted Charlie as her cheek glided along April's thigh. Spreading open the glistening lips revealed a fat little clit that had thrown off its hood. She stroked it gently with her gloved thumb. "Do you like that?"

"Yes," April whispered between labored breaths.

A chill went through Charlie's body as manicured nails raked lightly through her short afro. Pulling April to the edge of the desk, she stood up to relieve the pressure on her own throbbing clit. "Hold on tight, baby. You're about to go on a ride." The thumb didn't break its stride as one and then another finger slid into the eager pussy.

Now, face-to-face, it was evident that the femme taskmaster had disappeared. The new April was radiant and vulnerable. "You feel good," she said. She pushed the straps of her dress down and, arching her back, offered her newly exposed breasts.

Charlie's tongue flicked over the hardened nipples as she massaged April's walls with slow, measured strokes. Legs wrapped tightly around her waist. Suddenly, April's quick breaths turned into moans.

The quivering started at Charlie's fingertips. Charlie watched entranced as the waves of orgasm quietly spread out to the surface. Fighting the impulse to scream had forced tears from April's eyes. With one last shudder she went limp. "Don't move," she whispered. "Please."

"So, do you still think I need lessons?"

"No," April said before laying her head on Charlie's shoulder.

Charlie was awash in sexual energy. She wanted to drop her pants and rock her clit against April's lavender-painted toes. Instead, she gently lowered April to the desk and announced she was going to the bathroom. She was glad that no one was there to see her scramble out of the room disheveled. Summoning the image of Ruth was enough to put her own fire out and get her back to the business at hand.

Before putting the second phase of their plan into action, Charlie checked in with Toi. She walked into Rockalene's executive suite to find her sitting behind a large mahogany desk. "Girl, you should have knocked," Toi said. "I was ready to hurl this phonebook at you." She pointed at the purple glove and smirked. "So, did you handle Ms. April?"

As much sex as she'd had in her life, Charlie couldn't understand why talking about it still made her blush. "Yeah, you could say that." She tossed the drenched glove in Rocky's recycling bin. "What happened to your host?"

Toi pointed at the empty sofa. "She said some stupid shit about wanting to put me between a rock and a hard place."

Charlie found the butch guru on the ground tied up with phone cord. It wasn't needed—she was out cold. "So you knocked her out?"

"It's not my fault Rocky's got a glass jaw." The computer beeped and ejected a disk. Toi replaced it and clicked the mouse a few times. "I'm copying her hard drive. We need to know everything she knows. Ruth is concerned about her crew, but we need to see the big picture."

"Okay, finish up. We'll be running out of here soon."

Toi waved her away.

According to Ruth's spy, the bathroom shared an air duct with the security office. Charlie's first stop was the utility closet where she found turpentine and paint thinner. Bolting the door to the ladies' room, she removed the grate over the vent. This time she put on a pair of gloves and soaked a bunch of paper towels in the turpentine. They were dropped down the shaft first. She poured paint thinner down behind them, making sure it flowed down the sides and didn't splash.

The fumes were giving Charlie a headache. She splashed water on her face before tossing down two lit rolls of toilet paper and her gloves. Though flames had spread quickly through the duct and had spilled over into the bathroom, she walked out as if nothing unusual had happened. An assortment of alarms sounded and the sprinklers came on.

The noise brought both Toi and April into the corridor. Toi gave Charlie a high five. "Excellent," she said. "Our part is over, let's get out of here." Then, Toi turned to April. "You better wake your girl up and get her out of here."

April looked from them to the smoke billowing from under the bathroom door. "What did you do? Who are you?"

Charlie blew her a kiss. "We're Poontanganistas, baby! Liberating the world one pussy at a time!" Just then, the lights went out. She grabbed Toi's hand and ran.

Once they were far enough away from the compound, Charlie took out her binoculars. Fire engines had started to arrive and the employees were out on the lawn. In the back, Ruth and friends were leading a group of disoriented butches away from the BRC.

After learning about Operation Butch Ambush, the rest of the Toi Bois were extremely unhappy. El and Denny felt as original members of the Fierce Fucking Four they should have been consulted. Several Bois hated the idea of helping a rival organization.

Except for reminding everyone that it was a spur of the moment, do or die situation, Toi sat grim-faced through the tongue-lashing. By the third round of beer the conversation had turned congenial and all had been forgiven.

Toi again took center stage. "While Ruth was busting up the BRC, we decided to do a little digital Dumpster diving.

I haven't parsed all of the data yet, but 'Butch Ambush' was just the tip of the iceberg. We may have made a powerful new enemy." She paused to let the statement sink in.

Denny yelled, "I guess we'll just have to keep kicking ass! Who are we?"

"The Poontanganistas," the others cheered in response.

Charlie felt the familiar vibration in her pants and checked her cell phone. The pleasurable tingle had come from Anna. "I think we've got a new recruit."

BAIT AND SWITCH

Nairne Holtz

After paying La Passion's entrance fee, my lover Kirsti and I were stopped by the coat check girl and informed that there was a dress code or, rather, an undress code. I slipped the long loose cotton shirt I was wearing over my head—the garment had disguised the sluttiness of my camisole and silk shorts on the subway—and handed it to the coat check girl while Kirsti waited silently, arms crossed over her chest. She was wearing dark green cargo pants and a black T-shirt and had no intention of removing them, although ahead of us we could see other patrons were considerably more *déshabillées* in bikinis, lingerie, short skirts, and halter tops. Was Kiss My Passion, the monthly women-only night at Montreal's premier swingers' club, the right place for a butch? Kirsti had joked that if we succeeded in picking someone up, I, the femme, would be the bait, while she, the butch, would be the switch.

I placed a reassuring hand on Kirsti's arm, although I, too, had begun to wonder if this was a good idea. When I turned forty last year, I hadn't thought much about it. But a few months ago when Kirsti had accidentally taken one of my blood pressure pills because my pills had gotten mixed up with hers, I had thought to myself, "Nothing signals middle age like matching pill boxes." And I admit it depressed me. But a red sports car and a trophy wife were out of the question since I didn't drive, loved my girlfriend, and preferred to be the trophy.

"Are you coming?" Kirsti looked over at me, and I followed her long stride down a dark hall to a swanky lounge. The club was in an old bank so the ceilings were high, and the ornate columns and moldings from the bank's Art Deco days had been maintained. The lounge had a stone floor, and lined along it were a series of white leather chaises and pouffes on which women sat together holding drinks. Pink string lights dangled from a crossbeam; their dim wattage made the cavernous space seem more intimate.

"I'm getting us some drinks," Kirsti announced after I sat down on one of the pouffes. She made a beeline to the center bar where a woman in a black bra and tuxedo jacket was serving alcohol.

While I waited for Kirsti to bring me a cocktail, I glanced around. Many of the women were in groups and seemed to know each other. Kiss My Passion was known for attracting suburban bisexuals, whom I had hoped would be bolder than lesbians. But a flat screen television mounted on the wall showing amateur lesbian porn was the only action going on. There weren't that many women, perhaps sixty or seventy, which wasn't all that surprising. It was a sticky summer night, and the air, the streets, everything in Montreal was more still than usual. Residents had fled to the country or a beach while those with less money hung out on their wrought iron balconies, beer or wine in hand.

In the city of Montreal, sin was conducted with an insouciant Gallic shrug. Whatever you wanted could be found. What we wanted was discretion, and the tacky reputation of a swingers' club was a draw; we weren't likely to run into our friends, although it had been a friend that inspired the fantasy Kirsti and I hoped to act on at La Passion. When my old friend Annabelle had moved back into the city and started holding play parties at her loft, Kirsti had been impressed with her. We didn't go to her parties, but Kirsti, marveling at Annabelle's lush figure and naughtiness, said, "She's like Bettie Page come to life." "Would you believe we had a fling?" I replied. Kirsti's mouth dropped open, then she chuckled. "You two? You're both femme." She paused. "So, uh, what did you guys find to do with each other?" I was appalled. "I fucked her with a dildo. God, you're sexist." I had been so busy being offended I hadn't thought about the implications of Kirsti's question. But I did later when Kirsti laughed about a male friend of ours whose girlfriend had once been a lesbian. "I'm sure he'd love to have a threesome, but she'd probably bonk him over the head if he suggested something like that. Why are guys so into that?" I had smiled. "You tell me. The only time you ever wanted to know what I did in bed with someone was when it was another femme."

Busted. It wasn't every day that I made my girlfriend blush.

Kirsti pressed a drink into my hand, something white and frothy with a cherry and a slab of pineapple pierced by a cocktail umbrella. "I brought you a piña colada."

"Perfect." I sipped my drink while Kirsti gulped down a beer. When she had almost emptied the bottle, she set it on the floor. Then she reached over and tucked my slightly damp, freshly washed long hair behind my ear and whispered, "You look lovely, by the way." Her tone was gentle, and I realized that she had gotten over some of her nervousness. The alcohol probably helped, especially since she wasn't much of a drinker.

"Thank you," I whispered back. She surveyed me for a moment, then her hand caressed my waist, sliding the black silk material of my camisole over my pale skin. The sensation was slippery-soft, leaving a wake of relaxation that twisted into excitement when her hand slid around to my buttocks. When she fingered the strings of my thong, which reached just above my black silk shorts, I inhaled sharply. In anticipation of this evening we had not had sex for two weeks.

Kirsti withdrew her hand. "I think it's time for you to go fish."

"Where I grew up, as long as you were in the right place, the fish would come to you," I said. I had been raised in Nova Scotia in a cove by the sea. If you rode your boat to the shoals and ledges where the water was warmer, you could always catch something. Mind you, you never knew just what you were going to get. The trawl line could deliver an ugly wolffish or a live crab trying to pinch you.

Kirsti laughed. "The only fishing I did in Thunder Bay was ice fishing. Most times you would sit there for hours in the cold on a windy lake and nothing happened."

"Okay, okay." I surveyed the room. It was like being at a supermarket; a few women were good-looking, some were decidedly not, most were ordinary. If you got to know them, they might become beautiful, but that wasn't what this night was all about. "I'm going to get another drink."

As I waited for my drink at the bar, I heard Kirsti call my name. I looked over at her and she tilted her head in the direction of a woman who sat by herself on a sofa. She was pretty and plump with a shiny tumble of black hair that was shampoo-commercial perfect. Her skin had an ivory-olive tint that suggested she was maybe Greek or Lebanese, which was a plus. It meant I wouldn't have to do this in French or apologize for my crappy French.

I left all of my change as a tip, picked up my drink, and sauntered over to her. "Hi," I said. "I'm Ramona."

"I'm Sara."

"Can I buy you a drink?" It was a line that got the message across. I didn't feel like wasting my time making inane conversation about our jobs or where in the city we lived.

"Sure," she said, standing up.

I suddenly remembered that Kirsti was the only one of us wearing clothes with pockets and consequently was carrying our money. "Actually, my girlfriend will be buying you a drink," I said.

"Where's your girlfriend?" Sara asked.

I pointed out Kirsti, who immediately looked at the floor. Sara peered at her, taking in Kirsti's tall, rangy body, short silver-blonde hair, and slightly scrunched up face.

"You're lesbians?" Sara asked.

"Yeah."

"I used to have a girlfriend, but now I'm married with a kid." A large wedding band and engagement ring encircled Sara's fingers.

"And you're a little bored?" I asked.

"Oh, yeah," she said with a grin.

There was a promising recklessness in that smile, and she had these adorable freckles across her nose and cheeks, little flecks of light. My attraction to femmes was more sensual and aesthetic, but I figured if she was more of a top, we could be a tag team, bossing Kirsti around, telling her to get on her knees and service both of us. And if Sara was a bottom, well, telling girls what to do got me wet.

After introducing Sara to Kirsti, I took some more money from Kirsti and went to get Sara a glass of wine. When I returned, I found them engrossed in a discussion of their pets. In best let's-get-this-party-started mode, I waited for a break in their conversation before handing Sara her drink and saying, "It doesn't seem like the women here are doing anything besides talking."

Sara looked me in the eye. Hers were a deep brown with thick lashes. "I don't know if I could have sex with a complete stranger. But I could probably make out with complete strangers. At least if I have another drink. Um, the action is happening downstairs."

Two drinks later, Sara gave us a tour of La Passion. While jazz had played in the upstairs lounge, deep house music pumped through the downstairs. A bank vault had been turned into a dungeon where we found a few women whipping each other. Beside the dungeon was a special bedroom for exhibitionists, which had mirrors on the ceiling and cameras on the walls. The porn shown in the lounge had been a live recording of two older women whom we could now see in the flesh using vibrators on each other. Kirsti turned away first, suggesting we go into a cubicle.

The cubicles had privacy; a curtain could be drawn across the door. They were, however, cramped. In fact, they were like prison cells. Cheap tiles covered a floor that held only a futon mattress covered in easy-to-clean plastic. Remembering that this place was usually patronized by men as well as women, I felt a bit disgusted.

Sara and I sat down on the futon while Kirsti kneeled on the floor beside us.

"So what would you like to do?" I asked Sara.

She smiled at both of us. "I like other people to decide. Surprise me."

A twinge asserted itself between my legs. "I want to put on a show for Kirsti," I said. "I want you to lie back and let me touch you."

Kirsti stood up and grabbed some white towels that were hanging on a hook in the wall. "Here, this will be more comfortable for you two." She laid the towels out on the bed, and Sara stretched out on one. She was wearing a crimson dress with a plunging neckline, and Kirsti reached over and fondled one of Sara's breasts.

"I've wanted to do that since I saw you," Kirsti said.

Kneeling behind Kirsti, I put my hands on her hips. "Hey, we're not at the switch part yet."

"Sorry about that," Kirsti said, sounding completely insincere. Our relationship, both in and out of the bedroom, was an ongoing struggle for power. But she got out of my way, and I crawled on top of Sara. She smelled lovely, her perfume musky but subtle. I tucked away her hair and began to nibble on her neck. When she moaned, I pulled my mouth away.

"Close your eyes," I told her. I felt nervous. It had been a while since I had had sex with someone besides Kirsti, and Sara was femme. Femmes were always scarier than butches.

She shut her eyes, and I kissed her. Wet, glossy lipstick smeared across my own, and she cupped the back of my head with her hand, bruising my lips with a hard kiss and candy-sweet lips. I lightly slipped my tongue in and out of her mouth, under and over her lips, tasting and teasing her until I felt her large breasts push against my small ones, felt her wide hips pump against my leaner ones. It was all quite delicious, but I wondered what to do next. If Sara just wanted to make out, should I be stopping? I turned around to see what Kirsti was doing: nothing except looking at us with a dazed expression.

"Tell her to take off her dress," Kirsti said. Her voice sounded tight—I realized she was enjoying this.

"Roll over, Sara," I said. She complied and I unzipped her dress. Then she turned over, sat up, and pulled it over her head. Her bra and underwear were foam confections of nylon and lace, a pleasing contrast to the tone of her skin, the voluptuous surface of which was flawed only by a caesarean scar. I ran my hand along the slope of her stomach, her dark ribbon of scar, and then bypassed her panties for her inner thighs, which had the hot and slippery feel of freshly ironed cotton sheets. As my hand skated across the smoothness, I let my thumb graze the crotch of her panties. Every time I did this she moaned. When she started wriggling around, trying to make me touch her more intimately, I turned my attention to her full, round breasts. After reaching around and undoing the back of her bra, I began pinching her puckered nipples. Although her skin was damp with heat, she shivered.

Kirsti came over and half-sat, half-lay on the bed, her head propped against the wall. "Very pretty." She reached over for a moment to run her hand through Sara's hair while I sucked on Sara's nipples. "You two make a very pretty picture," Kirsti said as she drew her hand back and began to unbuckle her belt.

Sara opened her eyes. "I've changed my mind."

"About what?" I asked, although I had a good idea.

"Fuck me," she said.

"Well, Kirsti's going to do that," I said. "But first I want you to do something for me."

"Anything," she gasped.

"Touch yourself." I lifted myself into a kneeling position and peeled off Sara's underwear. I was a little surprised to see she was completely shaved. It was a look I always thought I would find creepy, infantilizing, but I suddenly realized shaving could also be a gift—easy access to a wet, aromatic pussy. Sara began to rub her first two fingers over her clit, careful to poise her sharp red nails upward. I slapped at her hand.

She looked confused. "I thought you told me to..."

"I've also changed my mind about something," I said as I pinned both her hands above her head. Before she could ask about what, I slid down and started eating her. This wasn't an act I had thought I was going to do, but suddenly I just had to. I didn't want her to come though, so I did her in a lazy way, just inhaling her—I love the way girls smell—and letting my tongue meander along her lips, into her opening, back and forth across the hard bud of her clit. Sometimes I paused for a moment to clutch Sara's hips and push my mouth and chin into her cunt and dig my now aching clit into the bed. My efforts seemed to be appreciated by Sara—her juice kept trickling down, and she was making these sounds, like *uh, uh, uh.*

A higher-pitched moan broke through Sara's noises. Out of the corner of my eye, I saw that Kirsti had both of her hands in her boxer shorts and was frantically jerking off. I lifted my mouth from Sara's pussy (although I kept a finger in her) and glanced over at Kirsti, who stopped moving her hands (although she didn't take them out of her underwear). I was about to admonish her when Kirsti said, "Ramona, I'm sorry, but I'm so excited, I have to come, okay?"

"Fine," I said. "We'll watch you." I slid my finger out of Sara.

"No, just keep doing what you're doing," Kirsti moaned. "Just ignore me."

Sara lifted herself up on her elbows. "I think you should do what Ramona says."

"I'm embarrassed," Kirsti muttered. But, after closing her eyes so she wouldn't have to see us staring, she continued masturbating until she orgasmed a minute or so later. She lay back on the futon for a moment, breathing heavily, then opened her eyes. She looked a little sheepish.

I moved away from Sara and Kirsti and slowly removed my own clothes. When I finished, Kirsti approached me on her knees, then ran a finger down the line of my cleavage, over my belly to my clit. "I see you're just as turned on as I am," she said, stroking me.

Kirsti was angling for control, but I wasn't quite ready to hand it over. (That would happen the minute she went down on me.) I did find myself panting a little as Kirsti knowingly, expertly fingered me. "I want you to fuck Sara."

"All right," Kirsti said, withdrawing her hand from my body.

"But you need to ask me first," Sara said, although she was already lying on her back again.

"I thought you liked surprises," Kirsti teased.

"Believe me, this has all been a surprise." Sara giggled. "Would you believe me if I said this isn't the sort of thing I usually do?"

"It might not be the sort of thing you do with women," Kirsti said, crawling on top of Sara. "But," Kirsti paused to stroke Sara's shaved mound, "maybe it's what you do with men."

"It's not," Sara said, looking annoyed, but she angled her legs wider for Kirsti's hand.

Kirsti began by toying with Sara's clit, and Sara responded by reaching around and lightly running her long fingernails across Kirsti's back. I almost found myself saying, "Kirsti likes having her hair pulled," but then I remembered this night was about new discoveries, not just doing what already worked well. And besides, Kirsti was focused on pleasing Sara. I watched Kirsti bang her knuckles against the rim of Sara's cunt for a few strokes before pushing her hand in and out of Sara, listened as Sara's moans rose and fell, a continuous note that echoed and reverberated in my own cunt. My nipples were pinpoints; my pussy was soaked. I rubbed myself, trying to hold back. But when Kirsti flipped Sara over and started spanking her, I felt my cunt start to clench. I had to take my fingers away from my clit to watch the rest: Sara lying on her stomach coming, her fists punching the futon, the core of her seized by Kirsti's hand.

There is only so much control a girl can hold on to. I barely gave them a chance to recover before asking them to please, please, make me come as well. Kirsti crawled between my legs and began flicking her tongue over my clit while Sara sucked on my nipples, her long hair draped across my belly. I felt like one of those party poppers being tugged at both ends until it explodes, and I did in a bang of bliss and wetness.

Afterward, Kirsti and Sara held hands, and for the first time since we had all met I felt a pang of jealousy. In my fantasy Kirsti and I were going to show a bi-curious girl just what it is lesbians really do; in reality we might have brought a closeted lesbian back into the fold. But that's the way it goes. When you bait a hook, you never do know exactly what you're going to catch.

GOLDEN GATE

Jessica Swafford

Late night, Golden Gate Park, propped back against a tree feigning boredom. I've heard that bois cruise here hooking up like guys.

The prospect of anonymous sex with a hot butch has me wet. I'm beginning to think that it was baseless rumor when you arrive striding through the darkened park. From a distance we cruise each other like guys: face, chest, ass, bulge.

I shove my hands in my pockets, pretending to be real interested in the toes of my boots, while you swagger over. As you come close I glance up. You mesmerize me with your hard gaze. I feel the heat from your body as you step closer. I put my hand on your crotch, hoping you're packing. I'm not disappointed. I stroke your hot cock. I shiver.

Our eyes lock as you shove me down to my knees. I fumble with metal buttons, ready to suck you off. Moist grass dampens my pants as I kneel before you. Opening my mouth, I touch the head of your cock with the tip of my tongue.

Growling "Don't tease me, bitch!" you shove your cock all the way into my throat. I begin sucking, mouth working up and down the shaft as I shove the base back against your clit.

As you fuck my mouth you say, "I could tell that you were a nasty little cocksucker. You wanted it from the minute you saw my big bulge, didn't you? What a sweet little mouth to be such a scuzzy nasty hole." You watch as I suck you 'til you cum, grasping my head as you buck wildly, head thrown back, eyes shut. Moonlight on your face, which is sweaty and twisted.

As your breathing slows and you regain composure, you grab my shirt in both fists and haul me to my feet. I fly backward, shoved against a tree.

You kiss me rough, painful, grinding your exposed cock into my crotch. I'm spun around, cheek pressed against rough bark, arm pinned behind me. Your pelvis rocks against me, cock rubbing ass through denim.

Working your hand down the front of my pants, you stroke my clit and I imagine it's a dick, blood surging to my crotch. You plunge farther downward, drive two fingers into my gushing cunt and begin massaging me inside, touching my core. I gasp and jerk, twisting my trapped arm uncomfortably.

Suddenly as they were there your fingers are gone, leaving me vacant. You deal deftly with the snaps and buckles. Cool night air brings the nerves of my bare ass to attention. I feel you move behind me, kicking my legs apart. Then you're in, pumping against me, thrusting hard and deep in smooth fluid strokes.

My face scrapes into the bark. The pain's so good, jolts to my clit. You're in my ear growling, whispering how I'm a good boi and how you really enjoy fucking me. You ask me if I like it and I stammer that I do. "Tell me," you hiss, "tell me you love it when I fuck you." I quietly moan, "Oh, god, I love it when you fuck me."

"Want me to stop?" you tease coldly. I shake my head no, as you begin shortening your strokes, teasing my hole, giving me just the tip. "Fuck me! Please fuck me," I beg. "Fuck me hard,"

You bite my neck as you shove in deeper and harder. I writhe against you as I come in a series of jerks and start riding the waves. You let go of my arm. I grasp the tree as you reach around and begin jacking my clit, while you continue to fuck me and gnaw at my shoulder.

I close my eyes and surrender, limp and powerful all at once; impaled on your dick, putty in your hands, riding your cock to ecstasy. I feel colors, warm red and orange, as I surrender completely. I'm floating, as I lose track, fading in and out.

Still gasping for breath, you slump forward, head on my shoulder, breath in my ear. And we're faggots and dykes and neither and both.

SPIKE

Jodi Payne

They'd been little more than a fleeting glimpse in her periphery, but Samantha felt a very familiar hitch in her breathing. She was sure of what she'd seen, picturing them in her mind so clearly that the image alone pulled her up short, stopped her where she stood, and compelled her to retrace her steps.

It didn't happen often, but when Samantha's desire took hold of her in this manner, it was shockingly intense and its force was as undeniable as gravity. The longing could overcome all reason, preempting everything she'd planned for the hour, the afternoon, or even the remainder of the day.

Lisa laughed at her sometimes in their more intimate moments, teasing her about what she termed a "fetish," but for all her teasing Sam's lover had never complained. She was a willing and eager enabler.

Sam moved back to the window and stood staring, captivated by the shine of patent leather and the allure of six inches of steel. The shoe was pure sex, cunningly crafted to fit the contours of a woman's foot. There was a glare on the glass and Sam put her hand up to shade it, leaning in for a closer look.

The stiletto pumps were standing in a pool of pink satin that was draped artfully over a tall, clear dais. They basked in the glow of a single spotlight, the black patent leather polished to perfection and reflecting the light into Sam's eyes. She was captivated, and she traced the line of each shoe with her finger against the glass, from the tip of the pointed toe, up its length and then down the ever-narrowing steel support to the impossibly tiny tip of the spiked heel.

Samantha longed to touch them, to put her nose to the leather. She swallowed hard, feeling an aching need rise within her, welcoming the arousal and the gentle flush to her skin. Lisa would taunt her with these, oh, yes, taunt and tease until Sam begged.

The profile of the shoe reminded Samantha of the contours of a woman's body, of Lisa's body, with its gentle slopes and enticing curves. The black leather vamp was lined with a smooth, white fabric that seemed soft enough to cradle a delicate foot but contrasted starkly with the commanding leather. Black leather for the public side and soft white for the private, the side that would caress Lisa's foot like a lover, holding on tight.

Samantha had to have them.

She entered the shop. She, in her torn jeans, T-shirt, and beat-up leather jacket. She, fresh off a job site with her rough and dirty electrician's hands. Her desires being what they were, Samantha had grown accustomed to being stared at in places like these, upscale boutiques with trendy clientele.

Women could be so judgmental.

And yet Samantha moved from the door to the window where the stilettos were on display and reached for them as if reaching for the Holy Grail itself, far too entranced to care if she looked out of place.

"Can I help you?" a voice said behind her in a sharp tone. It was nasal and impatient and Samantha fought the urge to tell the woman to go away and leave her alone.

"I'd like to buy these." Samantha listened to her own voice. It was sultry and awed, and she barely recognized it.

The woman gave her a sour look. "They're very expensive."

"I'm sure they are." Sam touched one of the stilettos, running her finger up the heel to where it joined the shoe.

"What size?"

"Six and a half."

Samantha ignored the woman as she glanced at Sam's feet. Sam was tall, five foot ten with a solid build, and her feet were a size nine at minimum. The last pair of running shoes she'd bought were tens.

"Six and half?"

"Go get them," Samantha ordered. "Wrap them in something feminine and pretty." Sam didn't even look back over her shoulder; she just fondled the shoe in her hands and did her best not to drool. She didn't give a damn what the woman thought of her; she only had thoughts of Lisa, of Lisa's delicate feet in these killer heels.

The saleswoman returned with a box wrapped in pink and

white polka-dot paper. That was perfect for her femme, and Sam nodded her approval. She handed over her credit card and ignored the whispers and stares from the other women around her. There was no way they were going to get laid as well as she would tonight.

The wrapped box went into a shopping bag and Sam left the store quickly, hurrying for home. It was coming up on five-thirty, and Lisa ought to be just getting back from work. She was probably sitting on their couch right now, sipping a glass of wine and flipping channels on the TV.

Sam rounded the corner and approached their building, her pulse racing. A casual observer would assume she was winded from her walk, but that was not so. One flight of stairs, then two and she was at her door, fumbling for her keys. She dropped them on the ground.

"Shit."

As she crouched to pick them up, the door opened. "Hey, sweetie," Lisa said, smiling down at her.

Sam shifted from crouching to kneeling and smiled back. "I have a present," she told Lisa solemnly. It used to mean just a present, but at some point in their five-year relationship it had become code.

Lisa slipped into Sam's game easily, her body taking on a bored posture as she leaned on the doorjamb. Her expression turned coy. "A present? For me?"

"Yes. For you." Samantha offered up the shopping bag.

Lisa turned abruptly and headed into the apartment. "Bring it," she ordered, and Samantha bit her lip and moaned. God, how she loved this.

In the living room Lisa sat on the couch and picked up her wine. She was still wearing a gray business suit from work and

Sam watched her hike up her skirt a little more than would have been appropriate for general business encounters, showing off the decorative band of her thigh-high stockings. Sam grinned and knelt again at Lisa's feet, pulling the wrapped shoebox out of the shopping bag.

"Oh, such pretty paper," Lisa said, praising Sam. Lisa looked down on her. "Open it for me."

Samantha nodded, setting the box on the floor in front of her and slowly pulling the ribbon loose.

"You're taking too long," Lisa chided sweetly and sipped her wine.

Sam let the ribbon fall into the shopping bag. "I'm sorry," she said, but she didn't move any more quickly despite the apology. Gingerly, Sam lifted the top off the box and set it aside. The shoes themselves were partially hidden from view by bright pink tissue paper, like a lover half-hidden by satin sheets. Sam bit her lip and whimpered softly as she peeled the delicate paper away.

"Show me," Lisa ordered. Her voice wasn't so much that of a mistress but of a dominant lover, encouraging and somewhat strained by her own arousal.

Sam nodded and lifted one shoe from its box, holding it reverently by the instep and careful not to get fingerprints on the fine, shiny leather. Her eyes were glued to it, and she took in a deep breath.

"Oh, Samantha," Lisa said, reaching forward to run a finger up the fine, silvery, stiletto heel. "Oh, my."

"I couldn't resist them," Samantha confessed, agreeing with Lisa's sentiment. She ran her nose along the insole, inhaling the scent of shoe polish and leather. "I imagined them on you and I felt fire, Lisa. Fire."

Lisa crossed her legs, dangling one stocking-covered foot inches from Sam's nose. "Put it on me."

"Yes," Sam said breathlessly, slipping the shoe onto Lisa's waiting foot. She tucked Lisa's toes in first and then seated the heel, licking her lips as she let it go. She shifted where she knelt, her cunt slick and warm and wanting.

Lisa didn't let her fantasize for long, offering her other foot, and Sam quickly slipped the second shoe into place. Lisa rolled her ankles, admiring how the shoes clung to her feet.

"Do you like them?"

Sam nodded again. "Fuck, yes. May I...?" Her fingers reached out.

"No." Lisa moved her foot away.

Samantha gasped. "Lisa!"

"Were they expensive?" Lisa asked coyly.

Sam nodded.

"Were they worth it?"

"Yes, yes," Samantha whimpered. "Please. May I touch them?"

Lisa nodded, running her fingers up the stem of her wine-glass before taking another sip. "You may touch." She lifted her foot, resting the heel of the shoe on Sam's shoulder. The heel dug in, hitting bone, and Sam imagined the bruise coming up. She turned her head and sniffed as far up the shoe as she could manage, then ran her fingers up Lisa's calf, under the hem of her skirt to her thigh until she encountered the warm skin above Lisa's thigh-highs. Lisa gasped lightly and Sam swallowed hard.

"What do you want, Sam?" Lisa asked in a whisper of offering.

Sam gave the front of Lisa's panties a snap.

"Ah," Lisa laughed softly. "And what's your hurry?"

Sam could only whimper in answer.

"Very well. Take off your shirt and jeans," Lisa told her. Sam tugged her shirt off over her head without a moment's hesitation, but her jeans took a bit more effort to remove without standing. She liked where she was on her knees; she liked that Lisa liked it. So she shoved her jeans down and rocked back on her heels to push them down to her ankles. She unlaced her Timberlands, then rocked forward again to tug the boots off so the denim could slide easily over her feet.

She felt vulnerable in nothing but her bra and boxers, and Lisa smiled down at her. "Bedroom," Lisa purred.

Sam sat back to watch as Lisa stood up in the stilettos, unzipping her skirt as she walked slowly toward their bedroom door, letting the shoes put that sway into her hips that Sam loved to watch. The extravagantly high heel made Lisa's calves tight and made her ass flex as she walked, and Lisa took careful measured steps partly to show off the shoes, but partly, Sam suspected, to make sure she kept her balance.

Lisa dropped her skirt in the doorway, stepped out of it, and turned to face Sam again. She took a moment to make love to the bedroom door, pressing her body along the edge and lifting her knee along its face, showing off. The black leather and her stockings stood out against the white paint of the bedroom door.

Sam stared at her; every move Lisa made felt like foreplay. "Undress?"

"I won't take orders from you, Samantha. You know that."

"Please?" Samantha begged shamelessly. "Please. I need to see you."

Lisa laughed. "Oh, Sam. You're so easily seduced." Lisa

turned to face Sam again and started to unbutton her blouse. Her thong was pink and her bra matched; both were edged in feminine lace and hugged Lisa's curves in all the right ways.

Sam got to her feet, not at all surprised to find her thighs trembling with anticipation. She could feel her pulse beating inside of her, bringing on a hot and damp desire between her thighs, and she followed Lisa into the bedroom, lost in a kind of lust-fueled trance.

Sam wanted to taste her lover, make her scream, send her soaring with tongue and teeth and hot breath while the cold, sharp, steel tips of the gift she'd given her lover dug mercilessly into her skin.

Lisa dropped her blouse, and her bra a moment later, on the floor at the foot of their bed. She turned in a circle, putting first one foot and then the other on the edge of the bed and stroking long fingers over her calves for Sam's benefit before climbing up and seating herself on the edge of the bed, legs dangling enticingly over the side.

Sam's knees turned to jelly and she sank to the floor in the doorway where she stood, crawling the rest of the way to her lover. Lisa allowed her to worship without restraint.

Samantha sniffed and licked the leather; she bathed the spike heels with her tongue and sucked on their length. Sounds escaped her, moans and gasps, hungry grunts and whimpers. Lisa remained silent and still, indulging Samantha's darkest, most secret desires without judgment or reproach, with nothing in her eyes but love, and a hot, burning lust.

Sam pushed a hand into her boxers and rolled her hips against her own trembling fingers and still Lisa watched. Then Lisa started talking softly, offering hot, encouraging words to feed Sam's already aching need. "That's it, my lover," Lisa said to her. "I love to see you like this: consumed, entranced, lost...."

Sam cried out, rolling her clit between her fingers. She lifted one of Lisa's stiletto-clad feet and placed it against her chest, nestling it right between her breasts and leaning her weight against the sole. She let her head fall back and moaned darkly, her climax so, so near—so very near as she slipped two fingers inside herself and rode them hard, nearer still as her clit bumped and rubbed deliciously against her wrist, and then suddenly she was coming. Muscles expanded and contracted, nerves fired and tingled, and her cunt pulsed as her orgasm rolled through her body.

"Oh, yes, Samantha. Yes," Lisa whispered above her. Lisa remained still until Sam's breathing evened out, but they both knew what was coming next. Even as Sam returned to herself, her breath grew tight again and her body rebounded energetically, filled with anticipation.

Lisa cleared her throat meaningfully and then shoved Samantha with the foot already resting against Sam's chest. Sam fell back, landing hard on her ass, and grinned up at Lisa from the floor.

"Who do you think you are?" Lisa asked in a haughty tone, eyes flashing at Sam with just a hint of a grin tugging at the corner of her mouth. "You can't buy me with expensive presents."

"Oh, yes, I can," Sam answered in a low tone as she climbed to her feet, the barest hint of a growl following her words. "Oh, yes." The shoes were, perhaps, Sam's fetish, but Sam knew well how much Lisa enjoyed the power they brought her and how aroused she became by the unfettered enthusiasm with which Sam brought herself off—every single time.

Lisa crawled farther back on the bed, but her eyes were locked on Sam's. "I do like the shoes," she offered tentatively.

"Yes, I know," Sam said, with more than a hint of sarcasm. "I can see that."

"The metal heels are kind of—" Lisa gasped as Sam interrupted her, reaching for Lisa and sharply tugging her panties down over her hips. "Kind of kinky," Lisa finished, breathlessly.

"Mmm-hmm. Very."

Lisa lay back on the bed, looking flushed and beautiful, and Sam crawled over her, forcing her legs apart with a knee. Lisa's long legs were still sheathed in her smoky-colored thigh-highs, and the stilettos gleamed despite the half-light in their bedroom, brighter and bolder than Dorothy's ruby slippers, and so much sexier, too.

Sam felt the hard steel of the stilettos scrape along the backs of her knees as Lisa opened for her. They kissed deeply and for a long while until Sam started to rock against Lisa, making her break the kiss to gasp and groan.

"Yes, Sam, yes," Lisa said softly, grinding her clit into the smooth strength of Sam's thigh.

Sam cupped one firm breast in her hand and lowered her lips to Lisa's stiff nipple, winning another gasp as Lisa arched up to meet her mouth. Lisa's nipples were sensitive and it didn't take much attention to get her going. Sam kept after them until Lisa started to pull back a little, and Sam knew she'd had enough. That was Sam's cue to move.

She bent at the waist, pulling her hips away from Lisa, and Lisa whimpered. "Sam, Sam…"

"I'm right here, baby." Sam slid down her body, peppering Lisa's skin with soft kisses and gentle nibbles, and Lisa apparently caught on because she settled down and seemed to let herself relax.

Sam thrust out her tongue and teased through Lisa's dark curls and then lower, dipping into the warm heat of Lisa's pussy, soaking in Lisa's sweet scent and finally tasting her.

Lisa gasped. "Fuck, Sam! Please, don't tease," she begged and raised one stiletto-clad foot, bringing it to rest on Sam's shoulder, just beside her ear where the shiny steel heel could not be ignored.

Sam moaned, the shoe taunting her out of the corner of her eye. "That's not playing fair."

Lisa laughed.

Sam turned her head and licked the leather where she could reach it, and then Lisa's other foot came up to join the first, perching on Sam's other shoulder. "Fuck, Lisa."

"Do it, Sam," Lisa ordered, and Sam pushed her tongue back into Lisa's folds. "Oh!" Lisa cried out and Sam took control, rubbing her tongue across Lisa's clit over and over until Lisa's hips started to rock. The heels dug into Sam's shoulders and she loved every little pinch and stab and burn, knowing Lisa was losing control, knowing she was sending her lover over the edge.

She slipped two fingers inside and Lisa tightened around them with a moan, using the leverage she'd won to lift her hips slightly off the bed. Sam kept after her clit hungrily, working the sensitive nub between tongue and teeth, sucking and rubbing and sucking again, keeping the rhythm deliberately sporadic.

"Sam!" Lisa shouted. "Oh, fuck, Sam! Don't...please...I need more!"

Sam relented finally and devoured Lisa with purpose, giving her the constant friction that Lisa was begging for.

"Yes, yes!" Lisa moaned and arched. "Sam! Oh, god, Sam!"

Her body twisted and writhed as she worked against Sam's mouth, pumping her hips harder and faster until Sam gave in and let her take over. Seconds later Lisa came hard, her lovely, curvy hips jerking and spasming as Sam continued to lick and suck. "Oh, Christ, Sam...enough...fuck...enough!"

Sam pulled away, panting and licking her lips triumphantly. "Fuck, I love those shoes."

Lisa nodded from where she lay, still breathlessly spent on the bed. "Hell yes, they're definitely keepers." She shifted and crossed her legs so they could both get a good look at the stilettos, then bent and turned her ankle around until the silver metallic heels were caught in the streetlight that shone in through their bedroom window. Spiked heels, patent leather. "They're beautiful."

Lisa could call it Sam's fetish, but Sam knew so much better.

PUNK LOVE

Victoria Gimpelevich

The concert is in a tight, dark little punk venue. Layers of graffiti scrawled over everything
in sight, toilets you can get an STD from, and
a ground-level stage for the band with only a
duct-taped half-circle to separate it from the
rest of the floor. Half the audience is also playing tonight, or dating members of the bands.
It's the kind of place I'd spent most of high
school in, sneaking out at night to catch the
latest show, blending into the studded crowd,
proudly bearing the symbols of local bands and
patchy dye jobs. Now the show just makes me
feel old, nursing the beer that most of the kids
here would need fake IDs to buy.

"Let's blow this place. I want a venue with
a bar," I say—I'm down to the last beer I
smuggled in. Kids in painted leather jackets are

flocking to an open box of cigarettes, hoping there are enough to go around. "The band members are the only ones even old enough to buy cigs here."

"Chill out. We always go to bars, I'm sick of them." Miles is my date for the night, my gay boyfriend, the cornerstone of a relationship neither of us can mess up with the complicated emotions of sex. He's a convenient partner for family events where lesbianism means the end of financial support those months where minimum wage doesn't quite meet both rent and student loans. "Besides, I wanted to see where people like you come from"—a jab at my tendency toward Doc Martins, faded band shirts, and pants that should have been thrown out three holes ago.

"Fuck you. I'm sexy and you know it."

"Only lesbians think that work boots and flannel are an attractive combo."

"You're not exactly fresh from Abercrombie & Fitch yourself, speaking of stereotypes."

"That's because I have fashion standards, not fashion obsessions. Now, is this next one done setting up yet?"

The average time between punk sets is half an hour, but the next band is late, and we are starting to push forty-five minutes of the same Clash-era mixed soundtrack on loop. The band finally starts to tune their instruments, and for some reason I'm drawn to the guitarist. She's the only female in a band of four—singer, bass, guitar, and drums. She has bright blue hair, the kind that leaves your bathtub streaked with color long after it's faded out of your hair, that she brushes out of her eyes while tuning the guitar. The gesture is casual, speaking of comfort in her skin. I like a girl with confidence.

The lights dim, and people drift from outside back into the

room. The guitarist plays with her legs spread wide and the instrument swung low, using the none-too-subtle phallic imagery of her male counterparts. Her entire upper body rocks back and forth to the beat of their first song, torso moving to the harsh beat so that straining against a fitted shirt I can tell—

"Oh, shit, she's not wearing a bra," Miles says. "That's great."

"Yeah, it is." She's pretty, soft features clashing against rough-hewn fashion. "Do you think she's a dyke?"

"Only one way to find out," he says. "I hope she is; you haven't been laid in ages, and you're such a downer when you're not getting any."

I roll my eyes at Miles and move in closer to the band. A small mosh pit has formed, full of punks ramming into each other and singing along to what lyrics are understandable over the static of bad speakers. The guitarist is absorbed in playing, and what strains of her instrument I can hear are reminiscent of Sleater-Kinney, or maybe that's just wishful thinking. They're not bad, but they're probably never going to have a following outside this state.

I move in closer, hoping for a better look. Like, maybe her nails are short or something. An indicator would be nice. The overlap between dyke and punk fashion sense has gotten me into trouble before. I think someone bats for my team, but then no, I've just got one pissed off straight girl on my hands.

I like the edge to her motions: jerky, like she means business, like she'd know how to fuck. So I chug what's left of my beer, toss it toward a corner, and join the fray. It's been a year or two since the last time I joined a mosh pit, and a clip to my jaw reminds me very quickly what it's like. Being lighter than most of the guys I'm moshing with, I get knocked around a lot. But rearing back and slamming into them is exhilarating. The mixture of pain and adrenaline puts me back in my body, giving a high much more active than the sluggish alcoholic joy I've gotten hooked on.

The song ends and my arm is aching, in a good way. I'm closer to the "stage," so I have a better view of the guitarist. She's thin, with the kind of perky tits that let you get away with going braless. Her eyes match her hair, and she lacks the usual thick, black mascara that punk girls favor. The unpainted face looks good on her, and the creeping feeling on my clit reminds me that it has been too long since I've been with a girl. The feeling spreads, and I know I'm wet, probably leaving a dark stain in my boxers. I imagine the guitarist's hand in my crotch, helping me along, returning the favor for her. She should have strong fingers, calloused from the firm strings she plays. I like it a little rough.

The singer tells about their next song, but I'm not listening. I'm staring hard at the guitarist, wondering if she can feel my gaze, if the thoughts of what I want to do to her are sending a chill up her spine. I'm wondering if she's single. A metal ring wraps around her asymmetric bottom lip. I imagine the cool metal contrasting with the warmth of her lips. It gives me the determination to plow to the front of the pit as they begin to play again.

A boy with checkered bleach squares on his head knocks me farther than I intended, and I crash straight into her. The guitar riffs stop for a few seconds as she regains her balance, but this is a punk band so she's not too surprised, and soon picks up again as though nothing has happened. I get back up and flash an apologetic smile, but her focus is back on the music.

Miles is laughing at me when I get back to him, so I hit him in the arm.

"Ow! Don't take your shortcomings out on me, Casanova. I can't help it if you're a klutz."

I wander outside as her band begins loading their instruments up into a trailer. The guitar is packed away quickly, but the drummer is left running back and forth, carrying the awkward parts of his drum set. She leans against a wall, watching him work. She fishes a cigarette out of her pocket. A hand rummages through another pocket, not finding what she wants.

"Need a light?" I walk over, lighter proffered.

She looks up, bright eyes showing recognition. "Sure." Her voice is even, confident like her movements, with a slight forced huskiness that tells me she's trying to act tough tonight.

"Just wanted to apologize about trying to kill you earlier."

She lights the cigarette, sucking in as she holds up the flame to get the tip to catch. "Don't worry about it." Her nipples are visible through the T-shirt, tempting little pebbles just begging to get sucked.

I realize too late that I'm staring. She has an eyebrow cocked, more amused than angry. "It's usually the boys who stare."

I should mumble an apology and go back to Miles, but I'm horny and that makes me brave. "You've got beautiful breasts; it's hard not to stare."

She laughs, the badass body language gone for a second, as she's caught off guard. It's not what I was expecting, but her face softens and there's an impish humor hidden in it. "Well, that's an honest answer at least. None of that 'my mind just wandered and I wasn't really looking' crap."

"What can I say? I'm a straightforward kind of gal." I've

got one arm next to her, leaning against the wall doing my best James Dean. Muffled voices and untuned instruments drift out from the other end of the wall. "What's your name?"

"Kat."

"Do you happen to like girls, Kat?" I ask, leaning in more so I can feel her breath on my neck, hoping I'm not pushing too far.

"Depends on the girl. I don't usually come to shows looking for a date." Her mouth is barely open and I move in closer, lick her bottom lip, teasing, asking, waiting for permission.

She grabs my head and pulls my mouth onto hers, fully covering her soft, strong lips. That's all the permission I need. I slide my tongue past her teeth and fill her mouth with it, rough. The cigarette drops to the ground, and a hand clamps on to my ass as her tongue fights for control of the situation.

She sees something, and her lips retreat to mouth an insult. At first I think it's for me, but then I follow her gaze to the bandmates watching us, making obscene gestures.

"Fuck off, guys," she says, jerking her head at them.

They laugh and don't move, saying things I can't make out.

"You wanna blow this joint?" she whispers, tongue flicking over my earlobe.

An image of Miles leaps, unbidden, into my mind. But he's a big boy and can get home by himself. "Sure."

She pulls me into her truck, the trailer full of instruments still attached, and we take off. The stereo is on too loud, and she cranks it up more as she drives. I slide a hand up her thigh until I've reached the crotch of her jeans and firmly stroke her clit through the fabric. Her breathing gets heavier and the car accelerates. Her hips grind against my fingers, and I can smell that she's wet. Or maybe that's me.

After a few sharp turns we're in an alley, slamming the doors of the truck behind us. This time she's got me pushed up against the side of the truck with icy fingers climbing up the back of my shirt and undoing my bra. There's no fumbling with the clasp, just one fluid motion that speaks for years of practice. She jams two fingers into my mouth, then three, and when I suck on them, she flashes a predatory smile.

"I'm going to fuck you 'til you beg me to let you come," Kat says, wiping my spit down the front of my pants.

"Awfully cocky, aren't you?" I grin and pull her shirt up revealing the pale breasts I've been wanting all night. I lick one nipple, drawing my tongue up slowly over the hardened nub then drawing the whole thing into my mouth, biting, sucking. I cup the other breast in my hand, massaging it and pinching the nipple. She lets loose a sharp exhalation and forces my head closer to her chest.

Soon my shirt's off too, and the freezing metal door presses against my back. My fly is undone and Kat's fingers are trying to find the gap in my boxers. She gives up and pulls them down with the pants. There's no trouble finding my clit, and I moan from all the pent-up sexual frustration being released.

Circular motions bring me close, and I know if she penetrates me I'll come. But it's too soon for that, and too one-sided. I yank down her pants, and now we're both standing here in the cold with our pants down around our ankles, like four-year-old boys learning to pee. I explore, tug gently on her pubic hair, dig into her folds until our scents mingle. Without warning I push in, sticking two fingers into her cunt. She gasps and jackknifes forward, one hand balancing on the truck and the other holding my crotch. She slips a finger in, pushing all thoughts out of my mind, and the first wave of orgasm hits. It's a literal wave, starting at her fingers and spreading to encompass the rest of my body.

She starts pumping in and out. Both of us are inside each other, doing the same things. It's too difficult to keep a different rhythm going when my entire body is focused on the one she's giving me. I want her to force me over the edge, take away any choice my mind has over my body feeling good. "Harder." I hook my finger so it hits her G-spot, pulling her closer to me from the inside. "Just fucking *fuck* me."

Kat smiles and pushes on my wrist, removing me from her soaking cunt. "You got it."

Machine-gun hits leave me gasping. I try to spread my legs as far as the denim shackles allow while Kat bends down for better access. Strands of blue hair fall into her face, covering one eye. My muscles clamp down around her fingers as they pump me, but she's going faster than I can and I'm reaching the point where my entire body spasms while I'm occupying every inch of myself, feeling the orgasmic rush expand to encompass all parts of me while still focused completely on the feeling in my cunt; it's verging on pain from too much sensation until it is pain and pleasure and every other physical feeling wrapped into one hulking entity that somehow forces guttural sounds from my throat, into the air, letting my new lover know that I'm there. The blasts from her hand, her entire arm, slow to a gentle rocking until finally they cease completely and she draws her fingers out, letting them brush my clit and giving me a final jolt, before exiting completely.

"My knees are going to buckle." I slide down the side of the trunk and breathe. She smiles, the pride in her skill visible.

"Follow me," she says after I've had time to regain some of my composure. She kicks off her pants and walks around to the back of the truck, jerking open the bed. I try to follow, but boots don't come off easily, and I'm still shaking and weak in the knees, so instead I trip over my jeans trying to waddle after her. She laughs.

"Fuck you. I'm sexy, and that's just part of my charm." The pants finally come off, shoes still on, and I jump in the back. There are blankets, making me realize the temperature has dropped while we were having fun. We get in the center of a makeshift cocoon, pressing freezing digits into each other's exposed flesh, the cool night still chilling our faces.

My hands finally thaw enough for me to place them on her breasts. "It's your turn now."

"Yeah? Are you gonna seduce me?"

"Hell yes I am." I lift her arms up over her head, pinning her wrists with one hand. She's just small enough for me to get a good grip. Then I kiss her, tongue deep in her mouth, licking her lips on the way out.

I have to let go of her wrists to move down, but she keeps them there, letting out a soft moan as I play with her nipples. This time around I take it slow, licking all around her areolas before letting the actual nipple enter my mouth, biting a little before I lick them. I move down, keeping the casual pace, using my mouth to appreciate the contours of her body, teasing her until her hips rock back and forth, trying to thrust into my mouth. I lick the crevice between her lips and her thighs, working my way into her pubic hair, and finally lick the leaking slit.

"You want it?" I ask.

"Yes." There's that edge in her voice that I liked so much, this time with a hint of desperation.

"How bad?"

"Fuck you."

I lick her slit again.

"Bad."

I plunge in, playing with her labia, her clit, finally tongue-fucking her vagina and hitting her clit with my nose. I take in all the salty moisture until all I can taste is my own spit and her hips buck against my face, strong spasms that start slow, reach crescendo and back off with a finale of baby spasms. Her hand reaches the back of my head, and she pulls me up, kissing her taste out of my lips.

We hold each other for a while, avoiding the inevitable nude run outside the truck to collect our clothing strewn around the concrete. The afterglow makes me lazy; I'd much rather stay under the blankets, skin touching skin. Kat leans over and kisses me on the mouth. "What are you doing next week?" she asks.

I cock an eyebrow.

"We've got another show on Friday. A house show. In my house. Kind of more like a party with music."

"Count me in." I nuzzle deep into the space between her neck and her shoulder. "Next time we can try a bed."

LIPSTICK ON HER COLLAR

Sacchi Green

The DC-7 burst from clouds over the South China Sea at an angle so steep VC rockets had no chance at a target. My breath caught and my butt clenched. At the last possible instant the plane leveled off, touched down, and came to a jolting stop.

I'd seen the same thing too often to be seriously alarmed. But I wasn't on board. And I wasn't Miss Maureen O'Malley from the *Boston Globe*, getting her first taste of the adrenaline-mill that was Vietnam in 1969. I wondered whether Miss Maureen's panties were still dry—and how long she'd last at this war correspondent game. If she couldn't handle the heat, the sooner she headed back to the ladies' pages, the better.

She wasn't hard to spot on the tarmac. Miss

Boston's dainty sandals, blue plaid skirt, and matching jacket
were about what I'd expected. The fine legs beneath the short
hem, however, exceeded expectations.

I wasn't the only one looking her over, but I was a lot more
discreet about it than the guys. Any overt attraction to women
could have landed me, if not in the brig, at least back Stateside
with a dishonorable discharge.

She showed the strain of flying halfway around the world.
Sweating in the sudden, brutal heat of Tan Son Nhut airfield,
lipstick blurred and tendrils of dark hair curling damply on
her cheeks, she seemed absurdly young. I'd have been all encouragement with a nurse or WAC just arriving in-country,
but the orders to ride herd on a journalist were really chafing
my chops.

"Miss O'Malley," I said firmly, seizing her attention, "I'm
Sergeant Hodge, your driver. Let me get that bag." I bent to
the heavy suitcase. Yes, very fine legs, and naked. No panty
hose. "C'mon in under cover while they unload the rest of your
baggage."

She focused on me hazily. Probably hadn't slept for at least
twenty hours. I felt just a smidge of sympathy.

"Oh...thanks...this is all there is."

Well, that was a point in her favor. "Okay, good, but I still
have to pick up a few packages." I was about to offer to show
her the rudimentary ladies' room when she blurted, "But...I
was expecting a woman driver."

"And I was expecting Maureen O'Hara," I said, amused.
Passing for a teenaged boy often comes in handy. "Southeast
Asia needs more redheads." I shed my helmet and brushed back
my russet forelock. My short hair didn't tip her off, but my
grin did the trick. She surveyed the rest of me more closely.

"Oh! I'm sorry." Her face flushed from more than the heat. "That's WAC insignia, isn't it? I still have a lot to learn."

No kidding. I silently steered her into the terminal, aiming her toward the restroom, and leaving to retrieve packages I'd promised to pick up. It wouldn't hurt to let her stew in a bit of embarrassment for a while.

Not for long, though. She emerged looking tidy and composed, makeup freshened. As she stepped up into my jeep she caught me admiring the nice rear view, and her deliberate wriggle as she settled into the seat made me wonder with a touch of paranoia just what this reporter had come to 'Nam to cover. A juicy scandal about dyke WACs would put women in the military back decades, just when we were needed most.

Through the dust and traffic I kept my attention on the road, weaving around troop transports and the occasional heavily laden water buffalo. I could feel her assessing gaze on me.

"Miss O'Malley," I said, when the traffic diminished, "my orders are to take you to WAC headquarters at Long Binh. The captain will sort out what happens next. Apparently you have authorization to bunk in our compound, unless you'd rather check into a hotel in Saigon. Some of those places the French built are as ritzy as anything in Paris."

"I can't afford a hotel," she said frankly. "It was all I could do to get here. Three papers gave me accreditation, which just means they'll consider printing what I write. None of them are willing to pay my way until I prove myself. Which I will!" Her face looked suddenly less cheerleader pretty—and more dangerous.

"I heard you wanted to write about the women serving over here," I said casually.

"Just for starters. I had to use that line to get anywhere. WACs, nurses, Red Cross workers, maybe some orphanage scenes."

"Look, Miss O'Malley," I said sharply. "You won't get far assuming the women here are just 'soft' news for the Sunday Supplement. Or the orphans, either."

She looked startled. "Sorry, I didn't...Well, thanks for reminding me to stay open-minded. I'll need all the help I can get to learn the ropes. But just call me Maureen, won't you? Should I call you Sergeant?"

"Not as long as you're a civilian," I said. "I'm Marjoe to just about everybody." I darted a quick glance at her. "Pleased to meet you, Maureen."

"Nice to meet you, too, Marjoe. And my apologies for not being Maureen O'Hara." Her teasing smile produced an all-too-charming dimple beside her mouth.

I looked her over. "Actually, you remind me more of Miss Connie Francis. That's just fine."

"Wasn't she here last year?"

"She was, and I have the autographed picture to prove it." A little casual conversation wouldn't hurt. "I wasn't a big fan before that. 'Who's Sorry Now' and 'Lipstick on Your Collar' aren't my style—I'm more of a 'Born to Be Wild' and 'Light My Fire' kinda girl." I gave her a wide grin. Let her make what she wanted of that. "But Connie Francis sure got my respect. She went places Bob Hope wouldn't, hopping flights in Hueys and Chinooks to give the boys in the boonies a look at what they're fighting for." I wouldn't admit it to anyone, but I'd even sung along at Can Tho when Miss Francis led the crowd in "God Bless America."

Maureen sat up straighter. Her sweat-dampened blouse

showed the distinct contours of her nipples. I managed not to stare.

"That's what I want to do! Get to see the real war, meet the guys and tell their true stories. I'm going to get out to the front, after a few weeks behind the lines learning my way around."

We were within the outskirts of the town by then. I jerked the wheel abruptly, pulling off into an alley. Miss See-All-Tell-All would have seen plenty of mortar craters already if she'd been paying any attention.

"You want to learn something?" Anger sharpened my voice. "Get out right here for a minute." *Don't let her get to you... keep your cool...*But I wasn't listening to myself. She *was* getting to me. In too many ways.

Maureen stared for a few heartbeats, then stepped down onto the dusty ground. I kept my eyes strictly away from her enticing backside this time.

I grabbed a lug wrench from the rear of the jeep. Maureen looked me right in the eye as I approached, holding her ground, hands on her nicely curved hips.

"Behind the lines?" I asked. "Lady, there *are* no lines. See the chicken wire on the windows of that bus going by?" She nodded, but her gaze didn't leave my face. "That's to deflect grenades." I drew a groove in the dirt with the wrench halfway around her. "The only line in 'Nam is the one you pull around yourself to keep your shit together!"

She seemed to grow taller. I suddenly knew what was meant by that old cliché "flashing eyes." How had I missed noticing how green hers were?

"Sergeant Hodge," she said icily, "if you *ever* call me 'lady' again in *that* tone of voice, I'll have those stripes off your sleeve, and the sleeve off as well!" She looked me up and down with disdain—until a hint of a smile made her dimple flicker. She dropped the briefly assumed British accent. "And quite possibly the whole shirt."

I closed my gaping mouth, then opened it to take a deep breath. "Wal now, Miss O'Hara," I drawled, regaining some control, "yuh shore are purty when yer angry!"

"Thank you, Mr. John Wayne," she said primly, and relaxed into a giggle. "Just never forget, I'm no lady, I'm a journalist!"

"Thanks for the warning," I said. Some woman! It was going to be damned hard to think of her only as a reporter, but her mental tape recorder was probably spinning right now.

Back in the jeep, I kept up a running commentary on bombings and mortar attacks by VC infiltrators, usually targeting troop transports and the bars and restaurants favored by American servicemen. Maureen reached into her shoulder bag for a notebook and did, in fact, start jotting down notes.

"Was that during the Tet offensive last January?"

So she *had* done some homework. Could be more to her than a pretty face, a knockout body, and a wicked sense of humor.

"It goes on all the time at some level, but yeah, that was the worst of it. I was up north at Nha Trang back then. Never seen anything like it, and hope never to again."

"I hope you won't. Just the same...Don't get me wrong," Maureen said quickly, leaning toward me so that I couldn't help noticing her breasts pressing against her blouse, "but if a major offensive like that did come again, I wouldn't want to miss it."

"No chance it'll miss you." I didn't bother with trying to squelch her voyeuristic instincts. On some level I understood them perfectly well. "It was bad here, bad everywhere. I was handling the nurse's motor pool, and every vehicle had to double as an ambulance, every driver as a corpsman, with or without medical training. Five straight days—never time to clean up the blood—they were handing out Benzedrine to keep us awake." I stared ahead for a minute or two, remembering things I'd rather forget. Maureen leaned close, so absorbed that she'd even stopped taking notes.

"Some of the things I saw there," I went on, "still keep me awake. Some of the things I had to do..." My knuckles clenched on the steering wheel, white under their tan. "And that was nothing to what the nurses went through."

A current of empathy flowed from Maureen. *A tremor in my voice, a catch in my breath, and she'll reach out to touch me, comfort me, put that half-raised hand on my shoulder...my thigh...*

I turned abruptly with a half-smile. "But yeah, if it had to happen, I wouldn't have missed it. And later, when we had our perimeters more or less under control, there were nights when we'd take a case of cold beer up on the roof of some old French villa and watch Puff the Magic Dragon blast away at VC island outposts in Cam Ranh Bay. Or we'd see our choppers hammering the hills with rockets and tracers. Better than any fireworks you ever saw, and we'd cheer for the good guys—until it was time to go try to put the broken ones back together. Or into body bags."

Maureen straightened and got her pen moving. "Um, 'Puff'?" she asked, eyebrows raised.

"C-130 heavy cargo plane fitted out with heavy-duty artillery. Don't know who came up with the name, but it sure works up a storm of fire and smoke."

"Okay. Puff. Good one. I won't ask whether beer was all you had up there on the roof."

"If you can't manage a laugh once in a while, one way or another, you get so brittle you crack," I said. "It's all about survival." Maureen nodded. I had the feeling again that she might reach out and touch me—and I knew for certain that my body's reaction would be far from anything resembling comfort. Disappointment battled with relief as I pulled into the WAC compound.

Our guard dog jumped up into the back as soon as I slowed. "Here's another fine dragon," I told Maureen, and ruffled his ears. "This is Spike."

"I see that this one's armed with heavy-duty teeth," she said, extending a fearless palm to be sniffed. Spike, putty in female hands, leaned his big ugly head on her arm, nudged against her breast, and sighed.

I nearly sighed too. It was no use pretending that she didn't set off a fizz under my fatigues. Good thing the ride was over, and Miss Maureen O'Malley/O'Hara would be somebody else's responsibility. My only hope of resisting temptation was to assign another driver from the motor pool to show her around if we were stuck with her for long.

The few girls off duty clustered around the jeep, either to get a look at the newcomer or to collect the packages I'd picked up for them. Lila Tunney cradled her shipment from Tokyo with care. "I'd be happy to share some of this make-up with you, Marjoe," she said slyly. "One of these days the captain might start enforcing regulations and make even you wear lipstick."

"Not so long as she needs her wheels kept in running condition." This was no time for Lila's teasing. After brief introductions I herded Maureen toward the admin building, resisting the urge to put a more-than-friendly arm around her.

What was the deal with this sudden, dangerous attraction? Yeah, sure, the stresses of wartime and all that. But I'd managed so far to keep a purely sisterly attitude—well, mostly pure—toward the women I worked with. Was it because Maureen wasn't "family" that my subconscious was allowing lust to break on through?

"Captain Ramsey will be right with you." The unit's cute little secretary surveyed Maureen with open curiosity. "Help yourselves to coffee."

"Thanks, Wilma." I was already at the hot-plate in the corner. "What do you take, Maureen?"

"Black is fine." She accepted a cup. "What was all that about regulations?"

"Just a holdover from the fifties." If Wilma wanted to listen, she might as well get her money's worth. She always got a kick out of bringing out the worst in me. "Now and then the military gets a bee up its butt about women soldiers being models of femininity. In the States some officers get tight-assed about it, but nobody enforces it in war zones."

"Sergeant Hodge!" The one voice that could make me jump sounded right behind me. I spun around so fast that hot coffee sloshed onto my shirt.

"I think it's time to make an exception in your case." Captain Ramsey's tone had taken on a don't-you-challenge-me edge. "I expect to see you wearing lipstick within the next week. Consider that an order."

Wilma snickered. The captain turned calmly to Maureen, who had just handed me a napkin. "Miss O'Malley, I hope Marjoe has been taking good care of you."

"Oh, yes," Maureen replied demurely, watching me dab at the wet splotch on my left breast. "Very helpful."

"I'm glad to hear it. Your congressman has asked that we give you every possible aid and protection."

"I'd appreciate that," Maureen said sincerely. "Just while I get my bearings."

"This next week could be difficult," Captain Ramsey said. "The Tet holiday is coming around again. Our intelligence indicates stepped-up activity, though not on the scale of last year. While you're here, under our protection, I'm going to have to insist that you go nowhere beyond the base perimeters without Sergeant Hodge. She'll be your designated driver." She looked at me with an entire lecture condensed into one stern glance.

"But Captain, I'll be too busy...I thought I'd assign..."

"I'm delighted to hear that you've been thinking, Marjoe," she said drily, "but no one else has sharpshooter rating on both .45s and M16s. It's a matter of security."

"Women don't get sharpshooter ratings," I protested. "We're not even technically allowed to carry weapons."

Wilma had kept quiet about as long as she could manage. "Just the same, it's in your 201 file," she said. "From Basic at Fort Benning, but you'll never see a badge for it."

"So that's settled," the captain said with finality. "Wilma will handle any further details. Show our guest around, Marjoe, take her over to the mess hall, and then finish whatever motor pool maintenance is scheduled. Wilma can be my driver for the next week."

She held out her hand to Maureen. "It's been nice meeting you, Miss O'Malley. Don't hesitate to let me know of any problems. I suggest you have Marjoe drive you into Saigon tomorrow for some orientation."

"A sharpshooter?" Maureen asked with interest when the

captain was gone. "How did you pick up that skill?"

Wilma was miming putting on lipstick, pursing her lips and working them together with gusto. I grabbed at Maureen's diversion. "Where I come from, in northern Wisconsin, the better you shoot, the better you eat. It's a family tradition."

"So what brought you all the way to Vietnam?"

I could sense that mental tape recorder flickering behind her green eyes. "Getting as far away from family tradition as possible," I said. "So, Wilma, where do I dump Miss O'Malley's gear?"

In her room, temporarily vacated by a lieutenant on leave, Maureen slumped onto the narrow cot. I retreated to the doorway. "Jet lag hitting hard?" I asked. Her short skirt was hitched so high that I could tell what color panties she wore. Pale pink. "How about you get some rest, and I'll save a sandwich for you."

She yawned and stretched. Both skirt and undies inched higher. For an instant I could also tell, no surprise, that she was a real brunette. Then she sat up.

"No, they say the best way to reset your internal clock is to eat meals on the local schedule. Just let me change into something that hasn't been sweated in for twenty-four hours, okay?" In one sudden motion she pulled her blouse off over her head. Her pale pink bra was very nicely filled indeed. She bent to rummage in her suitcase, breasts nearly spilling over, and I edged farther away.

"Marjoe?" Her voice was muffled by the knit shirt she was pulling on. "How come I'm not bunking with you? For security?" Her eyes emerged, gleaming with mischief. Her skirt slid down to be replaced very, very slowly by a pair of sleek black slacks. Every wriggle was deliberate. She knew exactly what she was doing to me. What I hadn't figured out was just why she was doing it.

"I sleep with the jeeps. Alone, except for Spike." *And he wouldn't be any protection for you.* I gave thanks as never before for my lean-to hooch built against the side of the motor pool's Quonset hut. I'd be in desperate need of some alone time tonight—if I could wait until then. She was building enough tension to have me punching holes through plywood if I couldn't get relief soon.

The WAC division didn't have its own mess hall, so we ate at the 24th Evac hospital with the nurses and the ambulatory patients. I didn't try to prepare Maureen for what she'd see, but after one quick clutch at my arm she handled herself like a real trooper. By the time I left she was circulating among nurses and amputees and men trailing IV trolleys like the best of the Red Cross Donut Dollies (a term I use with the greatest respect).

I looked back once and saw her kneeling beside a wheelchair, listening intently to a kid who could barely speak through his bandages. Her hand rested on his arm. I wondered cynically, or maybe jealously, whether it was compassion or journalistic skill that drove her.

She was still at the hospital at six, pale and strained behind her bright lipstick but managing to smile for the boys. I tracked her down in a ward of patients who couldn't make it to the mess hall. After forcing her to come along for some dinner, I half-carried her back to the barracks. Jet lag and sudden immersion in the realities of war had pretty much knocked her out.

"Get some sleep before you forget how." I eased her onto the cot and tried to get away. She held tight, her arms around my hips.

"Stay with me, Marjoe. Please." Her face was pressed against my crotch. She had to know, by my aroma, by my pulse, how much I wanted to stay.

"I can't." I pulled away. My butt burned where her fingers had dug in. "Maureen, I have a job to do over here. I need to keep my hands clean." Hands that shook with the urge to reach out to her, stroke her dark hair, pull her face hard into the ache between my legs...

"Always?" she asked.

"Except for motor grease and mud. And blood," I added, before I could stop myself. So much for keeping it light.

"You've never touched a woman over here?"

"Who's asking, the reporter?" I said nastily.

Those green eyes really were magnificent in anger. Relenting, I added, "I'm not absolutely sure. There was this head nurse—we both dived into the same bunker one night during a heavy bombing. She asked what I had in my canteen; when I told her it was water, she said, 'Good, mine's whiskey, we can mix and share.' Which we did. I can't remember clearly just how much mixing and sharing went on."

"Right," Maureen said sarcastically. "How much liquor does it take to get you in that state? And where can I buy it?"

"Forget it. The next time I touch a woman, I intend to remember it."

I stepped forward. She inhaled sharply, lips parting, breasts rising. I yanked the army blanket up to cover her. "Get some rest," I said. "You'll need it."

I shut the door behind me carefully. If those plywood walls hadn't been too flimsy to filter out even a whisper, Miss Bright-Eyes-and-Heaving-Bosom would've had more than jet lag and in-country shock to exhaust her.

Maureen seemed rested by morning, but I wasn't. Much

more of this, and Spike would go looking for a quieter hooch-mate. He sniffed my crotch with interest before I lit out for the showers extra early. I was reaching for my towel with dripping hands about the time Maureen stepped naked behind the canvas partition. I caught her checking out my ass. Fair enough. One brief glimpse had left her smooth curves printed indelibly on my memory.

The twenty miles to Saigon had their share of tension. I usually traveled with a Colt .45 tucked inconspicuously down beside the driver's seat, regulations be damned, and this time the captain had wangled an M16 rifle for me. I didn't ask how. No firepower would deflect a grenade or a mortar, but you did what you could and wore risk like an extra stripe on your uniform.

As we started out, Maureen said demurely, "My mother taught me never to distract the driver, so I'll try not to bother you."

"You'll distract me less once we get you outfitted to blend into the background," I told her. The tight black slacks and white tank top definitely stood out. The helmet I'd made her wear looked more jaunty than utilitarian. "Rumor says the North Vietnamese have offered twenty-five thousand dollars for an American woman, a 'round-eye.' I've never heard of anybody collecting, but there's no point offering one up gift-wrapped."

"Only twenty-five thousand?" She preened teasingly, hands running over chest and thighs.

"A journalist might bring in more." I reached out to give one breast a sharp pinch. No point now in letting her get away with much. "Especially one more generously upholstered than the typical Vietnamese girl. At least the NV value us more than the U.S. Army does, with the puny ten-thousand-dollar life in-surance policy we get."

I steered the subject into the universal griping-at-bureaucra-cy routine. Maureen was good company the rest of the way, asking intelligent questions, paying attention to the answers, and keeping teasing to a minimum.

In Saigon we drove down boulevards lined with elegant French Colonial architecture, crowded with trucks and old Re-naults and the pedal-driven rickshaws called cyclos. I pointed out the Caravelle Hotel where most war correspondents hung out.

"Writing 'frontline' dispatches at the bar behind a line of brandy-and-sodas," Maureen said dismissively. "Getting all their news from the Pentagon's 'five-o'-clock follies.' No thanks."

I looked at her with new respect. Maybe she knew this re-porter business better than I'd realized.

At the notorious Thieves' Market you could get anything that had ever passed through an American PX, and many items that never would. We got Maureen outfitted in tan and olive drab shirts and pants and the ubiquitous blue jeans.

"Wait a minute, we forgot something," Maureen said ur-gently over lunch at the California Bar and Grille on the liveli-est strip of Dong Khoi Street. She waved toward the honey-skinned working girls replenishing their makeup, preparing for a later influx of horny GIs.

"You want one all to yourself," I asked, "or can we share?"

"Not my type," she shot back. "I'll stick with round-eyes. But shouldn't we pick out some lipstick for you? Captain's or-ders?" She made kissy-lips at her compact mirror while fresh-ening her glossy lips. "How about my Burgundy Passion?"

I'd been working on forgetting that little incident. But the captain wouldn't. "Lila offered to share. Just once will get me off the hook."

"Cocky, aren't you," she said, with a look that made me consider some blacker-than-black-market shopping, but we needed to beat the rush hour, Saigon's most dangerous time.

Not that danger couldn't strike at any minute. Fifteen miles out we hit a military roadblock. Smoke billowed from around a curve. I detoured onto a longer, narrower riverside track, making sure my guns were accessible.

Maureen kept quiet for a while, but finally blurted out, "Did you ever shoot anyone?"

"Maybe," I said shortly. There was firing in the distance, either from the road ahead or the roughly parallel highway we'd left. The driver of a supply truck going the other way motioned us wildly to go back. I slowed, started to turn—and heard the unmistakable whoosh of a rocket launcher somewhere behind us. An explosion rocked the area where the supply truck, now out of sight, might have been.

"Hang on!" I veered off on a rutted cart track toward the river a hundred yards away. A fringe of trees would hide the jeep, I hoped, but just in case I made Maureen scramble out and lie with me farther along, behind a log where I could brace my M16. We waited, watching the road.

Maureen pressed against my side, her body shaking just slightly more than mine. "I don't know whether I've ever killed anybody," I said conversationally. "In Nha Trang they overwhelmed our perimeter, looking for medical supplies. It was dark, chaotic, but I think…well, I don't usually miss. And we beat them off."

I was wound tighter than Jimi Hendrix's guitar strings.

Maureen stroked gently up my spine to the nape of my neck and massaged away some of the tightness, but tension of a different kind radiated from her touch, ripples of heat licking all the way down my body. Even my toes twitched inside my heavy boots. I couldn't keep my hips from shifting. Maureen slid her hand down my back to my butt.

"We do what we have to," she said, her breath warm on my ear. Her dark hair tickled my cheek. "You'd be out there leading a platoon if they'd let you." The pressure of her hand increased, her fingers digging in just slightly.

"Maybe," I said, steeling myself not to react visibly, however damp my khaki briefs were getting.

Maureen's fingers dug deeper, then moved between my buttcheeks. "Am I distracting the driver too much?"

"Hell no! Good practice for capture and torture." Danger and lust pumped adrenaline through me, triggering a fight-or-fuck response. If I didn't fire a gun soon, something else was sure going to go off.

Maureen heard the approaching truck a fraction of a second before I did. I lifted my head, tightened my grip on the rifle— and she pulled me back down, cramming her helmet over my hair. "Don't wave your fucking red flag at them!"

"Thanks." I peered carefully over the log at an ancient flat-bed farm truck. The grim-faced young Vietnamese riding on the back didn't look like they'd been laboring in the fields.

We didn't breathe. I could feel Maureen's heart pounding in time with my own. The truck passed out of sight, and still we lay immobile.

"Will there be more?" Maureen asked at last.

"Maybe. We'd better wait…"

My words were cut off by her mouth covering mine. I'd

barely set the guns aside before we were in a rolling clinch, scrabbling to get through each other's clothes.

Maureen won. Her hands were inside my pants, one on my bare butt and the other working hard between my thighs, before I got through her shirt and clinging tank top. With my fingers finally inside her lacy bra, I hung on, pinching her swelling flesh. The feel of her nipples hardening to rigid engorgement intensified my clit's response to her demanding thrusts.

She worked me hard and fast, our mouths pressed furiously together with only a few moans and grunts escaping, until I had to get enough air for the noises she forced from me. With one wild glance to be sure the road was empty, I let go and shouted up into the quaking leaves of the trees.

By the time I could breathe, Maureen was naked with her shirt spread under her arching hips. I dove right into her luscious tenderness, feeding her need with tongue and hands until her yells made the leaves quake, too. And then, after a short rest in each other's arms, we started all over again. Frequent checks of the road for traffic only added a spice of danger to our frenzy.

As sunset approached I had to consider what to do next. We'd finally got dressed, and cleaned up at the edge of the muddy river, when we heard cars approaching slowly: two jeeps, one driven by an MP, one by Wilma.

"Company," I murmured. Maureen barely managed to brace before a furry, joyful Spike rocketed into us.

"Easy, boy!" I grabbed his collar and went to meet the captain.

"You're both all right?" she asked sharply, then saw Maureen emerging from the trees with hair quickly combed and burgundy lipstick freshened. "It's a good thing we brought the pooch. He alerted us that you were in there."

"We took cover for a while, Captain." I looked her straight in the eye. "There were indications of enemy activity ahead and behind." Whatever she might suspect, I could defend my reasons for leaving the road.

"You were right," she said. "But the area is secured for now, so let's get moving."

By the time I retrieved my jeep the MPs had gone and Wilma was chatting up Maureen. Her prattling ceased, and she began whistling a familiar tune. Everyone looked at my rumpled shirt. I'd scrubbed my face in river water, but...

"Marjoe has lipstick on her collar," Wilma said gleefully, in case anybody hadn't recognized the Connie Francis song. "That doesn't count, though. She's not off the hook yet, is she?"

Maureen stepped right up to the plate. "Of course it doesn't count. But this should." She put her arms around my neck and kissed me hard enough to weaken my knees. "Thank you, Sergeant," she said, pulling away, "for taking such good care of me."

The captain's face was impassive, except for a twitch at the corner of her mouth. She wiped a neatly folded handkerchief across my lips, gazed at the results thoughtfully, and said, simply, "That will do."

A week later Maureen wangled a ride with a chopper pilot heading toward Pleiku in the highlands. Two months later she sent a clipping of her first published article. Others followed. I kept them deep in my duffle bag, along with several intimate items imbued with her scent, mementos of a few more rushed, intense encounters scraped out of the quagmire of war. I have them still, wrapped in a rumpled, burgundy-stained shirt that will never be washed again.

DREAM DATE

Radclyffe

Kay wasn't really the diamond drop-earring kind of girl. She wouldn't even have *had* diamond earrings if her great-grandmother hadn't left them to her, and in the five years that she'd had them tucked away in her jewelry box, she'd never worn them. They weren't overly large or blatantly ostentatious, but they *were* bright and bold and…okay, a teeny bit showy. In short, they just weren't her. She wore small gold posts, unassuming and reserved: like her.

Well, she thought, *today was a day of firsts, so I guess for tonight at least, the diamonds are me.*

Brushing her thick curly blonde hair back from her shoulders, she shook her head and watched the diamonds sparkle in the mirror over the dresser. She had spent the afternoon in the salon, having a massage and a facial and getting her hair done. That wasn't something she ordinarily did, not just because it strained her teacher's salary, but because she didn't pamper herself. Tonight, for a few hours, that was going to change. Tonight, the last night of the cruise, she was going to finish off an unusual day with a night like none she'd ever known. Taking in her strapless red dress with the plunging neckline and cutaway hem that left most of one thigh bare, she laughed, knowing that none of her friends back home would recognize her. And that was part of the fun—she had come on the cruise alone so she could do what she wanted and not have to hear anyone say, "Oh, Kay, that's so unlike you!"

She was going to the formal dance, and she was going to look the way and dress the way and act the way she had always dreamed. The only other thing she needed to make the evening complete would be arriving any moment.

At precisely 7:30 p.m., a knock sounded on her cabin door. For one second Kay had a moment of sheer panic. What had she done? This was so absolutely not her!

"And that's the point," she whispered as she pulled open the door and smiled brightly. "Hi. I'm Kay."

Her dream date smiled back.

"Hi, Kay. I'm Ryan."

I don't care who you are, you're perfect. And of course, she was, because Kay had chosen her based upon her photograph and date profile on the escort web page: *5 feet 8 inches and 140 pounds of blue-eyed, black-haired sex on the prowl. A butch for all seasons—tops with ease, bottoms with expertise.* Tonight, she looked even more edgy and exciting than her picture or the glimpse Kay had caught of her, quite by accident, earlier in the week. Lean-hipped and lithe, her plain-fronted tuxedo shirt revealed the barest curve of small breasts beneath the starched fabric. Unable to resist, Kay glanced down and thought, but couldn't be sure, that she saw a slight swelling to the left of the fly in Ryan's silk tuxedo pants. Just thinking about what might be tucked away in there made her pussy clench.

"I'm sorry," Kay said somewhat breathlessly, "I'm staring, aren't I?"

"That's all right. So am I." Ryan grinned. "You look fantastic."

"Thank you." Kay stepped back. "Come in for a minute. Is that all right?"

Ryan stepped inside. "Anything you want is all right. Tonight, the only thing I want is to please you."

Kay wasn't sure how Ryan managed it, but she sounded sincere. Practice, she guessed. It didn't matter. She was getting wetter by the second.

"Would you like a glass of champagne? The dance doesn't start for at least an hour, and I'm a little nervous. Maybe if we—"

Ryan gently lifted aside Kay's hair and kissed her on the neck, just below the angle of her jaw. Her lips were warm and very soft.

"You have nothing to be nervous about." Ryan framed her face and kissed her lips, slowly and carefully. "Anything you want. Anything at all."

Weak-kneed, Kay steadied herself with both hands on Ryan's shoulders. Her breasts felt heavy and she knew her nipples were hard and pushing out against her dress. She didn't usually get so excited so quickly. Maybe knowing that whatever she did or said was all right, no matter how *unlike* her, had unleashed something in her she hadn't even known she wanted. "Can I ask you questions?"

"Of course." Ryan slid her arm around Kay's waist and directed her toward the sofa in the sitting area. A champagne bottle sat in a wine cooler on a small low table. "Sit down while I pour."

Kay studied Ryan again as she popped the champagne and filled two flutes. She was clear eyed and confident, moving with easy grace. Her hands were long-fingered and slender. And as she watched Ryan bend to pour the champagne, Kay saw she'd been right earlier. A sizable cock nestled against the inside of Ryan's left thigh.

"Isn't it uncomfortable like that…for hours?"

Ryan followed Kay's gaze. "Not with the right fit. It can get a little intense when I'm excited, but that's natural."

Kay took the glass Ryan held out, feeling her face flame. "I have absolutely no idea where that came from. I'm so sorry."

"There's no need to be." Ryan sat down next to her, leaving her champagne glass on the table. "If it's not what you want—"

"It is," Kay said quickly, not caring if she sounded a little desperate. She felt a little desperate. Desperate and breathless and terribly terribly terribly horny. She took a generous swallow of the champagne. "Sometime tonight I want to touch it."

Ryan drew a sharp breath and when she spoke, her voice was deeper. "I'd like that." She leaned closer and kissed Kay's neck again, then cupped Kay's face and kissed her mouth.

She was a wonderful kisser, softly teasing and stroking with her tongue as she caressed Kay's neck and shoulders with both hands. She let the diamonds at Kay's ears play across her fingertips as she kissed along her jaw, but she didn't touch Kay's breasts. And after a few minutes of Ryan's mouth on her skin, Kay ached to have her nipples massaged. She was getting too excited too fast and she finally pulled away. Ryan was breathing quickly, too. Realizing that Ryan enjoyed what they were doing made Kay even more excited.

"You're really not pretending, are you?" Kay whispered.

"You're very beautiful. Very sweet." Ryan traced a fingertip over Kay's chin, then down the center of her throat. "Feeling your excitement excites me. Thinking about you touching my cock makes me hard and wet."

"Are you? Now?"

"Yes."

"I don't think I'd better kiss you any more right now," Kay said, moving away but keeping her hand on Ryan's arm. "All I can think about is going to bed, and I spent all day getting ready for tonight."

"There are a lot of pleasurable things we can do outside of bed." Ryan retrieved her champagne glass and emptied it in several long swallows. Then she stood and held out her hand. "You look too beautiful not to show off. Let's go dancing."

For one second, Kay contemplated blowing off the dance. She wanted to kiss Ryan again. She wanted Ryan to play with her breasts. She wanted to caress the hardness in Ryan's pants and make Ryan's breathing get harsh again. "I don't know how long I can wait. I don't think I've ever been so unspeakably aroused in my life, and we've only kissed."

"Whatever you need," Ryan whispered, kissing her, "whatever you want."

"Oh, god. We'd better leave now."

Kay took Ryan's hand as they left the cabin and walked down the hall. They rode the elevators to the main deck and followed the sound of music and laughter. The night was dark but the ship was blazing with light, and Kay imagined it must look like a roaring inferno from a distance. She certainly felt like one.

"Did you want to ask me something else," Ryan said, releasing Kay's hand and putting her arm around Kay's shoulders.

Kay circled Ryan's waist and leaned against her. "It might be personal."

"Whatever you want, remember?"

"I saw you Sunday night in the theater. You were with a woman, a really beautiful blonde in a short leather skirt."

"Yes."

"Was she a date?"

Ryan guided Kay to a shadowed area along the railing. "You're my only date this week."

"I watched her come with your cock inside her."

Ryan's arm tightened around Kay. Her voice sounded tighter too. "Yes."

"It was very sexy. When I got back to my room I thought about it and masturbated. I came three times."

"Kay," Ryan groaned.

"Can I touch your cock now?"

"Yes."

When Ryan reached for her fly, Kay stopped her. "I want to take it out while you kiss me again."

Ryan leaned against the railing and pulled Kay close, kissing her more intently than before. Kay felt the hardness between Ryan's legs pressing against her belly and she rubbed herself against the prominence, clutching Ryan's hips. With her mouth against Ryan's, sucking her tongue and her lips, she slid Ryan's zipper down and worked her hand inside the opening. When her fingers closed around something full and firm, she gasped.

"Oh, my god. It's warm. It feels…so soft."

"It's cyberskin," Ryan murmured, her fingers sifting through Kay's hair. She nipped at Kay's earlobe and ran her tongue along the rim of Kay's ear. "Do you like it?"

"Yes," Kay said, tightening her fist and massaging the bulge. Ryan lurched against her and groaned. "You can feel that?"

"Oh, yeah," Ryan said shakily. "You're jerking off my clit too when you do that."

"I want to see it."

"Take it out."

Kay angled her body against Ryan's so they faced the ocean and no one could see what she was doing. She worked the cock out through the opening in Ryan's pants. It looked long and pale in the moonlight, and when she closed her fingers around it, just the head was exposed. She tried sliding her hand up and down its length, and when she did, Ryan's hips lifted and fell. "Does that feel nice?"

"Very nice."

Kay found a rhythm that made Ryan's breath hitch. "Will you come?"

"Is that what you want?" Ryan's chest heaved and she grabbed the rail. "Kay? You have to tell me what you want."

"Kiss me."

Ryan's mouth was insistent, her kisses urgent and harsh. The harder Kay pulled on Ryan's cock, the deeper Ryan plunged her tongue into Kay's mouth. She loved the grunting sound Ryan made deep in her chest each time she stroked her. She'd never felt so powerful.

"Tell me how to make you come," Kay demanded, watching Ryan's face.

"Faster." Ryan's eyes were beseeching. "Faster."

When Kay wrapped both hands around the cock and worked it rapidly up and down in Ryan's crotch, Ryan's knees buckled and she sagged.

"I'm going to come," Ryan said through gritted teeth. She grabbed Kay's waist for balance. "Do you want me to? Can I? Tell me what you want."

"I want to know how it feels," Kay whispered, "when I do this to your cock."

Ryan groaned and closed her eyes briefly. "Like there's a fireball in my belly...getting ready to...explode." Ryan stiffened and stared down at Kay hammering her cock. "Oh, fuck...I'm going to come. Right. Now."

"You're so sexy." Kay kept up the motion as Ryan thrust into Kay's hands, pumping her hips in short, hard jerks. Even when Ryan's fingers dug painfully into her waist, she didn't stop. Not until Ryan groaned and went limp against the railing. "So sexy when you come."

"Oh, baby," Ryan sighed. "You're good at that."

Kay smiled. "Really? I've never done it before." She leaned against the front of Ryan's body, bending Ryan's cock so it nestled against her stomach. "I wish I could put it inside me right now. I'm so wet from feeling you come I know I'd come in a second."

"We can go back to your room." Ryan cupped Kay's breast and thumbed her hard nipple. "I'd love to fuck you."

"Was that your girlfriend? The one who came in your lap in the theater?" Kay found Ryan's other hand and put it on her breast, catching her lip between her teeth as Ryan squeezed both nipples simultaneously.

"My mistress."

"Oh." Kay reached down between them and tucked Ryan's cock back into her pants. Then she carefully settled it against Ryan's thigh again. "Is that good there?"

"Perfect."

Kay zipped the fly and patted Ryan's cock gently, thinking about how the blonde had touched her own clit when Ryan was inside her. "She doesn't mind when women make you come? She doesn't get jealous when you fuck other women?"

"No."

"Will you tell her that I made you come standing out here where anyone could have seen us?" Kay swayed, rubbing her pussy back and forth against the prominence in Ryan's pants. Her clit jumped in time to the pull of Ryan's fingers on her nipples.

"Do you want me to tell her what you did?" Ryan rolled Kay's nipples harder. "That you played with my cock until my clit was so hard I came in your hands?"

"Uh-huh." Kate nodded and covered Ryan's hands on her breasts with hers. "Feels so good."

"If I tell her what you did, she'll get wet and she'll want to come."

"What will she do?" Kay felt almost drunk on sensation. Her pussy swelled and tightened.

"She'll make me kneel on the floor between her legs while she plays with her clit. When I tell her you jerked me off on deck, she'll order me to kiss her clit."

Kay shivered. "Will her clit be very hard?"

"Very big and very very hard." Ryan bit down gently on the side of Kay's neck. "When I tell her that I asked you for permission to come, she'll let me lick her cunt. Then she'll come in my mouth."

"She's beautiful when she comes." Kay's eyes slid closed as the sharp pleasure in her breasts spread to her belly and focused in her clit. "After I watched her with you that night, I kept seeing her face while I came and came."

"Would you like to watch again?" Ryan breathed the words into Kay's ear.

"Oh, yes." Kay dropped her head on Ryan's shoulder. "I want to come so hard right now."

"Anything you want."

"I want you to put your cock in me."

Ryan nuzzled Kay's neck. "Do you want to go back to your cabin?"

"I want to dance with you and feel your cock rubbing against me and know that I'm going to come on it later." She shuddered and pulled Ryan's hands off her breasts. "I'm going to need it so bad by then."

Ryan linked fingers with her. "Dance with me."

Kay followed her into the huge ballroom where a sea of women in tuxedos and gowns and leather and lace danced and caressed and celebrated. Ryan danced like she kissed, sensuously and totally in tune with Kay's body. Kay rested her cheek against Ryan's shoulder and floated, feeling her body ripen as the hours passed and Ryan continually caressed her shoulders, her back, her bare thigh. Her breasts ached against Ryan's chest. Ryan's hard cock brushed rhythmically against her mons, ever so lightly tapping her clitoris, taking her just to the edge of release and leaving her aching inside.

"I've never felt so wonderful in my life," Kay murmured as the last song finished. "Thank you."

"You don't need to thank me. I'm having a great time. You feel fantastic in my arms."

Kate tilted her head back, knowing her eyes must look heavy with sex. "I want you to have a good time, too. I know it's work—"

Ryan touched her finger to Kay's lips. "This is not work."

"Will you…will you make love to me now? I'm past needing you to make me come. I think I might die if you don't."

"I would love to." Ryan circled Kay's waist, held her close, and kissed her temple. "I want tonight to be even better than you dreamed."

Kay smoothed her hand down the center of Ryan's chest and over her abdomen. Fleetingly she touched the cock between her legs. "I want this."

Ryan tightened her hold but didn't hurry her pace as she led Kay through the crowd toward a staircase. "As many times as you want."

"Where are we going?" Kay asked as she realized they were headed to an unfamiliar part of the ship. She stifled a gasp of surprise as Ryan spun her against the wall and pinned her there with the force of her body.

"You know where."

Then Ryan was kissing her, and Kay forgot her next question. She clung to Ryan as Ryan's kisses went from gentle to fierce in a heartbeat. She dug her fingers into Ryan's shoulders and parted her legs, her dress riding up her thighs as Ryan's hips ground against her. The floating feeling was gone and in its place, she burned. Her clitoris pounded and her pussy contracted powerfully each time Ryan plunged her tongue into her mouth. She fumbled at Ryan's fly.

"I need you to fuck me."

Ryan caught her wrist and pressed Kay's hand to her cock. She skimmed her teeth up Kay's neck. "I need to fuck you. I've needed it for hours." She pulled Kay along the hall by the hand. "Hurry."

Kay followed. Tonight was her night to be bold.

Ryan slowed before a cabin door and pulled the key card from her pocket. She kissed Kay softly, as softly as she had been rough when she ravished her mouth just moments before. "Anything you want. And nothing that you don't. All right?"

"Open the door, Ryan." Kay tightened her grip on Ryan's hand and stepped inside.

A small blonde sat reading in a large upholstered chair on the far side of the room. She wore nothing except black bikini panties and a see-through black silk tank top. The outlines of her breasts and nipples were clear. She put her book carefully aside, her gaze shifting from Ryan to Kay. She smiled softly. "Hello."

"Allie," Ryan murmured softly in the dimly lit cabin, releasing Kay's hand. "I'd like you to meet Kay." She gently cupped the back of Kay's neck, stroking her lightly. "Kay, this is my mistress."

"Hello," Kay said, the crystal-clear image of Allie climaxing as she rode Ryan's cock flashing through her mind. Her stomach rolled with a wave of arousal and she knew from the way Allie's smile flickered on the edge of laughter that she saw it.

"Has Ryan been good to you?" Allie asked, fanning her fingertips, one after the other, over her right nipple.

"Yes, very," Kay said, her gaze fixed on Allie's breasts. "She's a magnificent dancer."

"She dances like she fucks." Allie shifted in the chair and

parted her thighs to expose the thin strip of black silk covering her sex. "Has she made you come yet?"

"Not yet," Kay said, aware of Ryan breathing rapidly beside her. Ryan's hand trembled against her neck. "I'm afraid I was a little eager and I made her come first."

Allie jerked infinitesimally and her fingers tightened on her nipple. "Did you?"

"Yes."

"What did you do?" Allie's voice was slow and deep. She cupped both breasts, thumbs brushing her nipples rhythmically.

Kay took a deep breath. "I'll tell you while Ryan licks you."

Allie's lips parted soundlessly and her eyelids fluttered before her gaze fixed on Ryan. "Come here."

To Kay's surprise, Ryan drew her along until she was close enough to see the wet sheen of excitement seeping beneath the silk onto Allie's legs. Then Ryan knelt and carefully skimmed Allie's panties down and off.

"I thought about her fucking me every day since I arranged for her to be my escort tonight," Kay said, watching Allie's face. "I wanted to masturbate tonight before she picked me up, but I made myself wait. When I saw her at my door, I was already wet."

"Ryan," Allie said softly without taking her eyes from Kay's face. She sighed when Ryan leaned forward and put her mouth against her cunt.

Kay slid a little closer and rested her fingertips against the back of Ryan's head. Her clit ached and she wanted to touch herself. "We kissed and I was so excited. I felt her cock against my leg." Allie moaned. "My pussy throbbed and I wanted her inside me so much."

Allie arched forward, her stomach contracting, and slid her hand behind Ryan's head, her fingers just touching Kay's. "Lick me harder, Ryan."

"I waited all this time so I would need it so much I'd come over and over and over when she was finally inside me." Kay twined her fingers through Allie's. Allie was gasping, her eyes shining brightly. Her thighs trembled against the outside of Ryan's shoulders.

"You're going to make me come in her mouth," Allie said breathlessly, staring at Kay. Her hips rose and fell against Ryan's face.

"I know," Kay said. "I made *her* come in my hands while I jerked her cock—"

"Oh, god." Allie made a choking sound as her shoulders lifted into the air and she curled forward.

Kay knelt quickly and circled Allie's shoulders, her fingers still joined with Allie's behind Ryan's head. She held Allie as she shuddered and climaxed in wrenching jolts. Kay was so excited she could barely breathe. She'd been on the edge of orgasm for so long she couldn't wait any longer. She pulled her dress up and pushed her panties aside.

"Wait," Allie said sharply and Kay stopped.

"Ryan, lie down and get your cock out." Allie opened a drawer in the small table next to the chair and pulled out a condom. She quickly knelt beside Ryan and rolled it down the cock that stood up from Ryan's open trousers. Then she grasped Kay's hand and pulled her forward. "Ride her."

Kay was already straddling Ryan's hips, her dress pulled up to her hips, one hand gripping Ryan's cock and the other holding herself open. She lowered herself until the cock pierced her lips. The first jolt of pleasure was so sweet she cried out. There was no way she could stop until she had it all, and she took it all in one long sweep, driving the cock head deep inside her. Her back arched and she screamed.

"Don't come yet," Allie ordered, taking Kay's face in her hands. She licked Kay's lips and slid her tongue inside her mouth.

Kay rocked on Ryan's cock, sliding up and down, working it in and out, while Allie fucked her mouth. Distantly she heard Ryan groaning, felt Ryan's hips thrusting to match her strokes. Her pussy clenched on the cock and her clit swelled against it.

"I'm coming on this cock," Kay exclaimed.

Allie swiveled sharply and straddled Ryan's shoulders, facing Kay. She lowered her cunt to Ryan's mouth and caressed Kay's face. "Wait for me, baby."

"Oh, god it's good," Kay whimpered. "She's so good." She grabbed Allie's shoulders, unable to support herself as her thighs went soft and her belly rolled. "You're beautiful. Oh, god, I really need to come."

"So do I," Allie said through clenched jaw. "Just one more minute...give me one...oh, yes...she's got me..."

"Oh," Kay wailed, exploding on Ryan's cock. "I'm coming."

Allie cried out and Kay crushed her mouth to Allie's, swallowing her pleasure. Kay came so hard she thought her pussy would never stop pumping. Allie finally slid off Ryan's chest and curled beside her, rubbing her palm in slow circles on Ryan's stomach. Kay leaned forward and braced her arms on either side of Ryan's shoulders with Ryan's cock still curled inside her. Ryan looked dazed, her face covered in sweat.

"Are you okay?" Kay kissed Ryan lightly.

"Perfect."

"You need to come?"

"Already did." Ryan grinned lazily. "With you."

Kay nibbled on Ryan's lip. "Good." She glanced at Allie, who rested with her cheek on Ryan's outstretched arm. "I can't think of anything better than watching you come while Ryan's cock is inside me."

Allie smiled. "I'm glad Ryan brought you by."

"Me too." Kay carefully rose, sighing as Ryan slipped out of her. "I guess I should go."

"Ryan," Allie said sharply, sitting up. "Get yourself together."

"Yes, Allie." Ryan tucked her cock back in her pants and disappeared into the bathroom. A minute later she returned and took Kay's hand. "I'm going with you."

At the door, Kay turned to Allie. "Thank you…" She glanced at Ryan. "This has been a wonderful cruise, but tonight was the very best part."

"The night's not over." Allie smiled and opened the door. "And neither is your date."

Kay wrapped her arm around Ryan's waist as they stepped into the hall and the door closed behind them. She skimmed her fingers over Ryan's cock, thought of Allie's face as she climaxed, and knew the rest of the night would be better than she'd dared dream.

ON SNOW-WHITE WINGS

Shanna Germain

The year I turned twenty, I read a poem about how true love flies in on angel wings. I didn't believe in angels, but I believed in poetry and I was desperate for love, so I took to watching out my kitchen window, listening for the whisper of feathers against the panes. June and July, I looked for girls who thought they could leap from rooftops, recited poems to every chick who was so pale I swore I could see through her, finger-fucked women until they hollered about God in heaven. I hadn't found anyone who resembled what I thought love should look like, and I figured I'd made my way through at least half the summer beach crowd and most of the regulars.

But, as it turned out, the poem was wrong. My love clomped in on snowshoes in the middle of the hottest, driest August my twenty years had ever known. She had a golden braid down her back and eyes that could have fought the sky for the title of True Blue and won. Her snowshoes were the old kind—wooden frames on the outside, and on the inside, ropes woven like giant spiderwebs that had caught her tiny bare feet.

That god-awful hot day in August, love sand-shoed her way over to the shade of my lifeguard chair and sat down on my bottom rung.

"Shit fuck," she said, breathing heavy. The air was so still I could smell her; tangy and lip-cutting as a blue ice-pop. "Where's the snow?"

"You can't sit there," is what I said, looking down on her from the height of my chair. After all, I didn't know she was love yet. All I knew was that she was blocking my path to the ocean. You never knew when somebody might get caught in a riptide trying to cool off.

She scooted over about a quarter-inch, then lifted one side of her buttcheek and pulled her red swimsuit out of it.

"Isn't this Snow-On Beach?" she asked. I figured I didn't really need to answer since the chair she was sitting in the shade of said just that in big white letters. And if she hadn't seen that, there were the life preservers against her shoulder that also said PROPERTY OF S.O.B. I figured if she thought that meant something other than Snow-On Beach, then she wouldn't be talking to me.

She picked up the other side of her butt and pulled at her suit again. I put my sunglasses on so I could watch her pink-painted fingers digging into the middle of her.

When she got herself comfortable, she tapped the life preserver. "So, where's all the snow then?"

I turned my attention back on the ocean. Sometimes, you can't tell what's a gull and what's a drowning kid's head unless you keep the whole roll of waves in your sights at all times. The poets don't say anything about that, but you lifeguard through high school and those years when you're supposed to be in college, and you learn that all by yourself.

"You can't sit there," I said again. And then, because she didn't seem about to move, "Besides, you ever seen snow on a beach?"

She seemed to consider this. Her sigh was the only breeze I'd heard all day. "I thought there'd be snow for sure."

"It's a hundred-two," I said, and just saying it made it so. My shoulders sizzled so hot I'd have been afraid to touch them if I wasn't already wearing them. I like the heat. As a kid, I'd wanted to be either a dharma bum or a beach bum, and when I realized how much time the former spent in dark bars, I'd picked the latter. But this weather was getting to be too much for even me. For the first time in my life, I wanted a breeze, an air conditioner, a place that didn't think ninety degrees was just a warm-up.

She pulled the back-end of her braid around and put it in her mouth. She chewed on it, sucking it in and out of her mouth until it looked like the point of an arrow, sharp enough to pierce her lips if she wasn't careful.

"Needs to be freezing for snow," she said around her hair.

I figured that kind of statement didn't even require me to say anything back. Some things you just don't have to comment on out loud.

She spit her hair out of her mouth and looked up at me again, not shading her eyes. I felt a moment of vertigo, like I was looking into the sky even as I was looking down.

"You want to get ice cream after this?" her pink lips said. "If there's no snow, then I want some ice cream."

Ice cream sounded good, although I didn't want to eat it. I wanted to rub it over my shoulders, over the red that my knees were turning despite being slathered in SPF 30. I wanted to melt it on her pink nose and suck it into my mouth like the tip of a leaking sugar cone. "Yeah, sure," I said.

After that, we looked out at the ocean for a while. Me looking for kids who looked like gulls or gulls who looked like kids. Her, I don't know what she was looking at. She was still in my way, but I couldn't tell if I cared anymore. I sat that way my whole shift, looking at the ocean and then down at her hair part, the way it got pinker and pinker and made her hair look more and more like gold. I wanted to give her my hat, but then I wouldn't have one. And like I said, I didn't know then that she was love. I just thought she was another whack job disguised as love come to torture me.

At the Snow Cone, I told her that's what I thought she was, another whack job.

"You get a lot of those?" she asked. She peeled bits of pink skin off her nose and dropped them on the table between us.

I raised my shoulders up a little, felt them burn. SPF 30, my ass. I fished an ice cube out of my coke and ran it over the tender skin at the edge of my strap line. "It's a vacation town," I said. "Girls see a strong girl in a swimsuit, and it's all over." I figured I didn't need to tell her I'd been inviting my fair share of those whack jobs into my life.

We'd trekked from the beach to the Snow Cone—me in my flip-flops and her with her feet still webbed in the snowshoes— to get ice cream, but then she ordered cokes and grilled cheese and bacon sandwiches for us both. A hot sandwich was about the last thing I wanted, but stopping her seemed about like stopping the weather, and I sure didn't have the energy or the know-how to do that.

Despite the greasy fans that tick-ticked overhead, I swore it was hotter in the shop than it was outside. The heat off the grill made my legs stick to the vinyl seat. I peeled one leg up, then the other.

She scooted sideways and put her feet up on the seat beside her. As she undid the bindings on the snowshoes, I could see the way her feet were crisscrossed with red skin and white, like a temporary tribal tattoo made from sun instead of ink.

"Don't you wear sunscreen?" I asked.

"Sunscreen?" she said, like she'd never heard of it.

As she undid her other snowshoe, I sucked on my coke and checked out the rest of her. This close, I could see her better. Her pink lips curled down just a little at the edges, and a tiny round mole sat on the corner of one blue eye like a chocolate sprinkle.

She rubbed her hands across her feet and then turned back toward me. She slid her feet into the hot space between my thighs. A shiver of cool air brushed the inside of my legs and crept up my belly.

"Who are you?" I asked.

She'd gone back to peeling the skin off her nose, and now she stopped long enough to hold out her hand across the table. "Shit fuck," she said. "I thought I told you. I'm Dakota."

An ice cube wedged itself into my throat. My heart thump-thumped around the ice, shaking it so I had two heartbeats. I coughed once, and the sharp edges of ice turned, but didn't move. I breathed through my nose, as the ice melted in trickles down my throat. Finally, the cube slid down to a place where I could swallow it.

I took her hand, her cool and rough and hot hand, and that's when it all kicked in. That's when I realized that whatever answer she'd given to my question, I knew who she was. She was love.

"Shit fuck yourself," I said, just as the waitress came by with our plates. When we let go of hands, the waitress put the plates down on the table, setting Dakota's right down on the pile of pink skin peelings that she'd collected.

Even with Dakota's cool feet between my thighs, I couldn't bear to touch the sandwich. She ate hers and, after pointing at my plate in question, mine too. With her mouth half-open around the steaming bread, I decided she didn't look much like love, after all. She looked like lust, and I'd had about enough of that. Still, I sat in that heat and watched her mouth move, my teeth crunching the near-melted ice out of the bottom of my glass, and my insides tingling every time her feet wiggled against me.

"Where are you staying?" I asked.

"Staying?" Dakota said. "Oh, I'm not staying."

It was time for me to go. I didn't know if I could handle another L-word in my bed that didn't have any of the other letters I was looking for. I stood up to pay the bill, and Dakota held out her snowshoes. "Want to try them?" she asked.

I did, just like I wanted to try her, but I shook my head. Dakota stood, barefoot, and padded after me to the register. I was digging cash out of my bag when she handed over a credit card. "I got it," she said, and I let her pay, but I hoped it didn't mean I owed her.

Outside, the sand was hot under my feet, even through my

flip-flops, and I almost wished I'd said yes to her and her snow-shoes. But then I wouldn't be able to hold out my hand to hers, to shake it and say good-bye and leave her standing at the edge of Snow-On-Beach, with her snowshoes and her choco-late mole and her sun-striped feet.

Of course, I didn't leave her, or that would have been the end of the story. I tried to leave her, but when I held out my hand, she gave me her snowshoes. And then she said, "'You remember how she disappeared in winter, obscured by snow that fell blind-ly on the heart, on the house, on a world of possibilities.'"

"What?" It was the longest thing either of us had said to each other, and I had no idea what it meant.

" 'You remember how she disappeared in winter—'"

"I heard you." For some reason, I felt angry. Making me stand there with her stupid snowshoes in my hand, the sun beating down on my already sore shoulders. "I just don't know what the hell you're talking about."

"It's from J. D. McClatchy," she said, and sighed and looked at the sky. "I love that poem."

I didn't know that poem. I knew a lot of poems. Her snow-shoes weighed nothing in my hand. In my other hand, her fin-gers captured mine.

"Should we go to your place?" she said.

And I said we should.

Walking into my place, I didn't dare look out the kitchen win-dow. If my love was out there right now, whispering her wings in my lawn, I didn't want to know it. I put Dakota's snowshoes by the door and kicked my flip-flops off next to them.

The living room was cooler than my upstairs bedroom, and I

led Dakota there. It was okay while she walked around, touching stuff, blowing dust off the piles of books, but once she sat on the edge of the futon, I wasn't sure what I was supposed to do with her. I was having second, third, and fourth thoughts. My heart was saying one thing, my body another. I couldn't tell which was which.

I thought we might talk, maybe about poetry, so I sat on the chair opposite her and pulled a book up from its dusty pile.

"Fucking hot," she said. "Wish it would snow." She pulled her tank top over her head, exposing her flat, pale belly and then the small snowdrifts of her breasts. Her nipples stood out, deep red berries.

"Uh," I said. I've never been much of a talker, but that day, it was like when you go out in the cold and your lips get so frozen you can't form the round vowels. Frozen, in a hundred-two heat. I tell you what.

Dakota lay down on my futon and slid her suit down over her small curves. Her braids lay like shiny gold chains across her body.

"Get undressed with me," she said.

All the women I'd fucked in the naked light of summer heat, and I was shy in front of her sky eyes.

"Roll the other way," I asked.

She didn't laugh or try to reassure me.

"No," she said. "Make it equal." She put her hands over her eyes, keeping her fingers far enough apart that I knew she could see me through them.

I didn't know what the hell she was talking about, but I must have been getting used to that, because I slid the straps of my guard suit over my sun-tinged shoulders. I let the suit fall down to my ankles while Dakota watched through the spaces in her fingers. My skin was goose-pimpled, but it couldn't be from cold. Still, I wrapped my arms around myself and shivered.

"Now we can be even," Dakota said, and she rolled away from me, to face the wall.

I took her in, from the bottom up—her feet, so white on the bottom, her long legs, the curves of her pale ass and hips, her small back—and I understood what she meant about being even.

There, on the skin over and between her shoulder blades, a dozen snowflakes tattooed in white ink, each one different, each one as small as my pinkie nail. I got down on my knees before her small back and put my finger over each one. When I touched them, I thought they would feel cold, but they didn't; they just felt like skin. I ran my tongue over them, each one, and thought they tasted like snow, clean and pure, the kind that you catch coming down from the sky.

"More," Dakota said, when I stopped. Her voice came from over her shoulder, far away.

I tasted her back until my mouth felt like I'd been sucking icicles, until she shivered and took my hand round the front of her. Even then, I tasted her skin with my fingers, letting them lick the warm-cool skin that was her belly and below her belly. Her hair was shaved short. My fingers played at the folds of her and she pushed the curves of her ass against my body. Her snowflaked back met my chest.

Her breathing was as heavy as it had been on the beach, when she'd first sat down on my chair. Other than that, she was quiet until she said, "What's your name?"

My fingers played at the folds of her. "What?"

"I have to moan something," she said. Was it the first time I'd heard her laugh? It must have been, but somehow it was as though I'd heard it a million times. "I can't just say, 'Oh, oh, oh.'"

I'd never wished for a great name before, but I did now. "Joan."

"Touch me again, Joan," she said.

I did, inserting two fingers inside her to find her wet and cool. And then I pulled my fingers out and found her clit. I made it wet with her own fluid and started circling the hard point of it.

"Joan," she said. But it didn't sound like my name ever had before. The way she breathed it, the way she moaned it, it sounded like *join* and then *poem* and then *own*. The fifth time or maybe the sixth, it sounded like *joy*.

She rolled over slow, so my fingers stayed on her, until she was facing me. Her tongue across my lips was a child licking her first Popsicle. Just the tip, then, pressed between my lips until they opened and let her in. She brushed her knuckles across each of my nipples in turn, until my back arched and I was trying to make words in her mouth. I wanted to say her name back, to make it into something else, but I couldn't with her tongue on mine, all spongy and sweet.

Dakota's still-cool fingers tucked into the space between my legs, spread my thighs. She touched so light at first that it was nothing, snowflakes that melted instantly on my skin, and I pushed my hips forward until she entered me. Her fingers brought their coolness inside, but it didn't last. It was too hot—I was too hot—and I rode her hard, until I was so wet that I swore her fingers had melted in me. She pulled her fingers out and I was surprised that they were still there, still fingers after all. But then she dipped them inside the melted core of me again, and I couldn't be sure of what I'd seen.

I pushed two fingers back inside her and swept her clit with my thumb. We were making each other arch and moan and buck, and yet our mouths never came apart. Even the heat, the way it made the sweat catch in the curves of us, wasn't enough to break us apart.

"Coming…" Dakota sighed, and the word was mine too, until I couldn't tell who'd said it.

It felt like forever until we were two again. Once we had our own mouths back, our heavy breaths startled us, made us laugh into the heat of the room. Dakota pulled her fingers out of me in a long slow slide that left me jellyfished. My own fingers were salt-soaked and pruned from being inside her.

We lay facing each other, our breaths going in and out. The room smelled of salt and sweat.

Dakota made her fingers into legs and walked them across the hill of my hip. "Do you have any? Tats, I mean."

"No." It seemed an odd question; she'd just seen my whole body.

She pointed to the front of my hip, just inside the tan line my swimsuit made. "You should get one here. A sun, I think."

Her sky blues turned toward my lips. "Hungry?" she asked.

I was surprised to find that I was.

"Got any ice cream?" she asked. "I'm fucking hot as hell."

We ate naked in the kitchen, with the freezer door wide open. Plain vanilla was all I had, but Dakota said it was perfect for smearing. She dolloped it on my nose and licked it off, like I'd wanted to do to her what seemed like days ago. We didn't talk while we ate, but as soon as it got dark, Dakota said, "Let's walk on the beach."

We got dressed, and Dakota pulled on her snowshoes. I wanted to ask about them, but I didn't. She talked the whole way down my clamshelled driveway and down to the beach, half of it shit I didn't understand, about snow and moving on, so I just held her hand and listened. The night breeze was coming off the ocean, making me shiver, but her skin was warm enough that I could just lean close to her and it was like being near one of those space heaters.

The moon came out and we followed its light to my lifeguard chair, ghost white and empty against the darkness of the surf. The waves were high and white coming up on the shoreline. A storm was coming. You could hear it in the crash and tumble, see it in the high fast curls of white.

The only thing I said was, "Stay."

The only thing I understood was, "Snow." Or maybe it was "No."

I pushed Dakota down on one of the tubes, her snowshoes sticking up in the sand in a way that made us laugh. Then I slid my fingers under her shorts, fucked her hard. I wanted her to remember me in the morning, to touch herself there and feel fresh pain. Like leaving my own tattoo without ink, one that said my name the same way she'd moaned it earlier. Sand and salt stuck to my skin, scraped my knuckles, and still I fucked her, until her voice was louder than the voice of the waves.

Dakota stayed with me that night, slept with her back to me, and her head in the crook of my elbow. Her hair, loose of its braids, took up what seemed like half the bed. She took up the other half, and still there was room for me. I traced the snowflakes on her skin until I fell asleep.

In the morning, she was gone. I'd known she would be.

There was no trace of her. The room had risen back to its usual heat, the books had regathered their dust, even her snowshoes were gone from their home beside the kitchen door. I made coffee and sipped it at the kitchen table, thinking about poetry and how it was just words that somebody else made up. How it sounded pretty but maybe didn't mean so much.

I didn't have to work, but I was craving the sun and the sand. I was craving the company of waves, the way they hushed the shore, but never said snow or shit fuck or breathed a line from a poem. I could hear the wind outside, the way it whipped against the house. A storm was coming; that's why the big waves last night were so loud. Today, I knew they'd be even larger, white and angry, grabbing pieces of the shore to take home until it was gone.

I stood and looked out my kitchen window, toward the ocean. The wind was picking up sand and carrying it everywhere. Sand swept across the clamshell driveway, swirled in miniature tornados, snowed down on the mailbox.

In the middle of it all, Dakota stood barefoot. She had a snowshoe in each hand. Sand settled in her hair and in the crevices of her clothes.

When she looked up and saw me in the window, she waved with her snowshoe hands.

From that far away, through the shimmer and bend of the kitchen window, the curves of wood and twine looked like wings. And Dakota looked just a little like love, flying her way back to me.

TOUGH ENOUGH
TO WEAR A DRESS

Teresa Noelle Roberts

The boutique owner approached me as I entered. "May I help you?"

For a moment, my surroundings didn't register very much, because all I could see was her. She was built like a goddess—tall and extra-curvy—and dressed like a '40s movie star, in a nipped-waisted suit that accented all those tasty curves and made everything else look sleek and airbrushed because it fit so perfectly. Her hair looked like auburn silk, and my fingertips burned to touch it.

I was so dazed that she had to repeat her question.

"I hear you might be able to make me something..." My voice trailed off as I looked away from the gorgeous creature and around her shop.

I was a bulldyke in a china shop, a jeans-and-

Docs-clad intruder in femme heaven. Amazing evening gowns hung everywhere, interspersed with more vintage-inspired outfits like the one the auburn-haired goddess wore.

Clearly I'd come to the wrong place.

I backed toward the door like Wile E. Coyote trying to backpedal through a wall.

Ridiculous what a sense of panic welled up in me just from being surrounded by all the feminine accoutrements. I loved seeing other women wearing pretty, girly clothes, but for me? No way. I'd faced down a mugger once with no weapon other than bravado, and that had set my heart racing less than the mere idea of wearing a dress.

She laughed, a throaty, erotic chuckle that seemed as film noir as her outfit. "Don't worry. I can see you're not the evening-gown type, although I have to say you have the figure for it, with that cleavage and that tiny waist and that round..."

"Okay, I *know* I have a big butt. Don't rub it in!"

"It's not big. It's delicious. You're built like Jessica Rabbit."

"Body of Jessica Rabbit, heart of a butch. It makes it hard to buy clothes off the rack." She was obviously flirting with me—and I was more than happy to flirt back—so why deny what she'd clearly already figured out?

"I'm Kate, the owner of Kate's Creations." She extended her hand to me.

I didn't quite kiss it, but the way I bowed over it let her know I was thinking of it. Not something I'd always do, but it seemed to go with her retro look.

"Andie Pace. I'm a fundraiser at the hospital—and I'm tired of renting tuxedos that never fit me for our black-tie events. One of my volunteers recommended you for custom tailoring."

Kate closed her eyes for a moment, and when she opened

them again, I could tell she'd seen a vision. "Not a tuxedo, exactly," she said. "A man's vintage suit, but one custom-made for your body. Very Marlene Dietrich."

What I knew about contemporary fashion could fit on a penny, with room left over for something actually interesting, like a hot woman's phone number in very tiny type—but I know my old movies. I nodded eagerly. Marlene in a suit, looking all hot and gender-bending, was my idea of the perfect evening look.

"There's just one condition," she said in a conspiratorial whisper. "The suit's got to make its first appearance on a date with me. It just seems a shame to waste it on a crowd that won't fully appreciate it—or the butch wearing it."

That had been four months ago, and since then, my Marlene suit and I had enjoyed ourselves thoroughly, escorting delicious Kate to dinner, to the theater in New York City and Boston, to a holiday drag show in P-town—and to play parties in all sorts of places.

Both Kate and I were pure sensation players, not into roleplay or power exchange, just pleasurable pain and edgy pleasure. She was more a top and I more a bottom, but we weren't hidebound about that. We both, as it turned out, had a bit of an exhibitionist streak. And when we showed up at a play party, me in the Marlene suit and her in whatever one of her femmelicious creations she was wearing that particular night, women's heads turned, assuring we'd get a good audience.

And then the time came for the New England Fetish Festival.

We'd each attended it before on our own, but the idea of going with Kate made my pulse race and my pussy throb: three days at a hotel with the sexiest and sweetest woman I'd ever dated, surrounded by a bunch of fun, kinky people. There'd be lots of play parties, lots of new toys to check out (I love toys), and, since Kate loves any opportunity to play dress-up, and I love any opportunity to appear in public with her on my arm, lots of chances to parade around in our best fetishwear. For Kate, the highlight of the Fetish Festival was the Saturday masquerade ball. For the past month, she'd been working late nights at the shop, finishing up a vinyl version of Edwardian evening wear, and I was dying to see her in it—I knew it would be killer with her curvy, girly figure. My fetish wardrobe was much more limited than hers, but the way I saw it, as the butch my job was to look tough yet cute and not upstage her. I planned to throw all my variations on the theme of black leather into my suitcase, along with the Marlene suit, and have her help me put together outfits that wouldn't embarrass her in public.

By the time the Saturday evening of the event rolled around, our hotel room was a chaos pit of clothes, shopping bags, and toys of various sorts, and it smelled like a busy day at the bordello. First, we'd gotten a new flogger and clover nipple clips and had to test them out on me. Then we'd found a new dildo for my strap-on rig and had to test that on Kate. (All of these purchases worked scream-inducingly well.) Then we ran into some friends who'd just bought their first cane and wanted pointers on how to use it. Kate was happy to demonstrate, using me as a stunt butt. (In my opinion, the only thing more fun than a good caning is a good caning with an attractive and appreciative audience.)

I floated on the endorphins from that scene all the way through dinner, getting a fresh hit every time I squirmed in my seat—and trust me, I was squirming in my seat deliberately, feeling that lovely, painful afterglow and anticipating more action later.

Especially when Kate whispered something about wanting me to wear the strap-on to the party.

I don't usually pack. For me, the fun of packing would be all about sexual opportunism, but the squishy packing dildos that look like actual relaxed boy-bits are no good for fucking and bit of an exhibitionist or not, I'm not about to go most places in the everyday world with a silicone stiffy at my crotch. In this setting, though, it could be entertaining, if it amused Kate, and apparently it did.

Had she gotten invites to a private play party? Did she want to sneak off and have a quickie in a dark corner of the ballroom? (The masquerade was supposedly a no-genital-sex zone, but late enough in the evening, no one really cared.) Or would we just be teasing each other all evening long, her body pressing against my artificial dick until we were both insane with need?

The possibilities had me wet and thrumming with lust by the time we went up to change.

We knew we'd never leave the room if we got into the shower together—a tempting thought, but Kate had worked so hard on her dress that I wanted her to have a chance to show it off— so I claimed the bathroom first, knowing I'd be out quickly and could dress and read a couple of chapters of the latest Stephanie Plum mystery while Kate put together an outfit for me.

When I got out of the bathroom, though, there was something very wrong spread out on the bed for me to put on.

A dress, or to be more specific, an evening gown.

A damn gorgeous gown, all burgundy velvet and slink and swagger. I could easily imagine the cleavage-enhancing, waist-flattering, butt-cupping, torso-lengthening magic it would work on some other woman.

But I knew it wasn't for some other woman.

Not when my new dildo and my jaunty cowgirl-model leather harness were laid out on top of it, and my knee-high Docs, polished to a mirror shine, were at the foot of the bed.

At least she wasn't trying to get me into girly shoes, I thought as the panic rose in my throat, threatening to bring dinner with it. "No," I managed to choke out, and the word took on three or four syllables as nerves made me stutter.

Kate, naked and ready for the shower by this time, folded her arms around me. "Andie, sweetie, it's just fabric. A costume for the masquerade. It doesn't change who you are. I'd love to see you in it, but you don't have to."

I burrowed into the warmth between her breasts, breathing in her exotic spicy perfume, the smell of sex, the smell of comfort. Face safely pressed against Kate, I couldn't see the dress taunting me anymore, couldn't see the memories that went with it.

She was right, of course. But logic had very little to do with what I was feeling, with the wave of memories threatening to drown me.

"Did you know," I said, talking to my lady's beautiful breasts because I was afraid to meet the nonexistent eyes of a formal gown, "that I was one of the candidates for prom queen back in high school?"

"You? My tomboy Andie?"

Despite the weird way I was feeling, I could only laugh at the incredulity in her voice. "I was actually one of the popular girls back then. The other girls liked me because I was funny and because I'd attract boys' attention and then let my friends flirt with them. Like a bait and switch to get customers in the door, you know. They got extra boys and I got to hang out with the cheerleaders in their little short skirts, and go into dressing rooms at the mall with the hottest girls in school. Stuff like that. So, anyway, it's prom night 1988 in a small town in New Hampshire. Picture me with big hair."

"And lots of ruffles, I bet."

"Bright turquoise ones. But the ruffles were all on the bottom, and the dress showed off my cleavage, and I guess I looked pretty good. Good enough that one of the other candidates decided to tell everyone I was a lesbian so people wouldn't vote for me."

I took a deep breath, remembering a night I thought I'd blocked out pretty thoroughly, as if it were yesterday. "Which I could have dealt with. Hell, I could have batted my eyes at a couple of boys and everyone would have been like 'Oh, Mary Ellen's just jealous; Andrea's so not a lezbo,' but my mom was one of the chaperones that night, and someone was dumb enough to do her rumor-mongering in the bathroom—where my mom was at the time. I could lie to the entire high school but not to my mom."

"So after semipublic humiliation you got to have one of those awful talks with your family?"

"Make it a huge fight with my family, the kind where my father didn't speak to me for about a month except to say 'pass the ketchup.' They've come around okay since, but then it hit them completely out of left field. I'd tried to fit in, done all the standard girl things—they kept saying a pretty girl like me, a girl with a closet full of nice clothes and shoes, couldn't be a lesbian."

"Guess they'd never heard of femmes," Kate said dryly, then

kissed the top of my head, ruffling my short-cropped hair in the process. "I'm sorry about surprising you with the dress, sweetie. I just thought it might be a fun thing to do for the masquerade."

"I've never really talked about it to anyone. It was too painful and too stupid at the same time. All that public drama and I hadn't even kissed a girl yet! But once everyone including my parents knew..." I took a deep breath. "Well, I just stopped trying to fit in, put my head down, graduated, and headed to college for the summer session instead of waiting until fall. And once I got to school, I decided no one was going to be able to blackmail me about being queer again because I was going to make it obvious. First I got my hair cut. Then I went to a consignment shop and traded in all my girl clothes for a leather biker jacket and some boots. And then I went looking for the lesbian and bi women's group on campus."

Kate didn't say anything, just lifted my chin and pulled me into a dizzying kiss, a kiss into which she seemed to pour her whole heart and all her feelings.

Her hands snaked their way down my back, awakening the skin behind them, to cup my asscheeks. Knowing how I liked mixed-up sensations—a little pain with my pleasure, a little edge with my tenderness—she pinched at the fiery little welts left behind from the afternoon's adventures.

Yeah, she knew me all right, knew the best way to distract me from difficult memories (or from just about anything else that might be bothering me) was with sensation, with sex. I fell into the kiss, opened my legs to give her hands access to my sudden wetness, let my hands roam over her silken skin.

She didn't give me a chance to do much to her but backed me up to the other bed, the one that didn't have our dresses spread out, the one that was already pretty much destroyed by sex, and pushed me down onto it.

Then came kisses and bites, caresses alternating with sharp slaps on my thighs and already tender nipples, just hard enough to be punctuation. She didn't use any toys, although we had a room full of them, just her lips, her teeth, her clever hands. My brain shut off, focused only on the pleasure and the pain, on the fire and need building between my legs, on the feel and smell and miracle that was Kate.

I can't take her whole hand without lube and a lot of time, and we didn't have a lot of time, but three fingers ground into me easily, and then she moved her mouth down to work in concert and I screamed loudly enough that they probably heard me back in my old hometown, let alone in the next room, and bucked and convulsed around her hand.

And as my head cleared, it really cleared. I figured something out that I probably should have figured out about twenty years before. "Stupid to blame the clothes, isn't it? I was hiding behind them, but they're just clothes. If I wear a dress with the right attitude, everyone will know..."

Kate kissed me with lips that tasted of me. "That you're a dyke in a costume," she finished for me. "A fabulous, flattering costume—but one that enhances who you are, instead of hiding it."

I glanced over gingerly at the other bed—at the dress, the Docs, the strap-on. "Especially if I have a huge silicone cock making a tent in the front of it," I said, laughing. "Sure, I'll give it a try. But you're going to have to help me into it—and out of it later."

"I will," she promised. "Besides—look." She pulled out her garment bag and took out her outfit. "We'll both be in drag."

It was a vinyl Edwardian outfit all right. A vinyl Edwardian men's outfit, tailcoat and pants with the black-on-black stripes, like a Merchant-Ivory film gone wildly askew.

I admit I followed her into the shower and tried to distract her. I even succeeded for a few minutes, but we still made it to the masquerade, Kate in her vinyl Edwardian splendor, me as Jessica Rabbit.

If you imagine Jessica Rabbit with short-cropped hair, big stompy boots, and a plunging neckline that drew all eyes to her dick.

As we entered the room, someone whistled. Heads turned.

And while I still felt weird, I knew we looked good; knew that with our roles reversed so strikingly, in fact, we might look better, or at least more head-turning, than ever.

Yeah, I thought, *I'd pick me up if I were single.* I'd have picked Kate up if she hadn't already picked me up.

At first, though, I hid on the sidelines, enjoying the heated, curious glances we were getting, but not sure how to dance in a long gown.

Then a slow, sultry song came on. Kate dragged me onto the dance floor, and I discovered I could dance no matter what I was wearing as long as I was dancing with her.

And when we made our way back to our room, I pulled my skirt up, and then pulled Kate's trousers down, and I fucked her hard and deep, fucked her thoroughly, fucked her with velvet and vinyl caressing my skin and hers until we both saw stars.

A real butch, I decided as we curled up together, spent, in a heap of costumes that would need dry-cleaning and repair, is tough enough to put on a dress to please her lady.

At least if there's a strap-on involved.

A NIGHT AT THE OPERA

Evan Mora

I'm waiting for you.

I'm seated facing the entrance to the restaurant, at a choice and intimate table of
your liking. I slowly swirl the contents of my
glass—something subtle and red, uncorked and
awaiting my arrival; a vintage of your choos-
ing. It changes with each sampling—elegant,
mysterious, and complex, with a subtle but unmistakable intensity. I am reminded of you.

I sit with an air of casual disinterest in my
surroundings, outwardly poised and relaxed.
Nothing in my demeanor betrays the nervousness I feel as I await your arrival, save for a
slight tremor in my hand as I raise my glass to
my lips. I am dressed as you asked, in a simple
sleeveless black dress, a favorite of yours.

The door opens and you cross the threshold,

your gaze immediately and unerringly finding mine. My heart skips a beat, then resumes at an erratic, accelerated pace. One corner of your sensuous mouth curls slightly upward—I am revealed. I set down my glass and fold my hands in my lap, lowering my gaze. Your effect on me is profound, even at a distance. My body tightens with awareness and anticipation, as though awakened by your presence.

I raise my eyes to meet yours again—they've not left my face; I had not expected that they would. I drink in your appearance—your perfectly tailored gray suit with only the top button casually fastened, your black dress shirt accentuating your short dark hair and brilliant blue eyes. The hostess has engaged you in conversation, your body is inclined slightly toward her, and you answer her inquiries in your calm self-assured way, your gaze still firmly holding my own. And then you move, slowly crossing the distance that separates us with lithe, confident strides. I am held captive by the strength in your frame; your body moves with the fluid grace and power of a jaguar stalking its prey.

You sit opposite me, and though my body yearns for your touch—your lips pressed to my cheek, a casual hand on my shoulder, a simple stroke of your finger on the inside of my wrist—you do not touch me, and my body struggles in desire and disappointment. My discomfiture pleases you, and you do nothing to alleviate it. Instead, you skillfully guide the conversation through appetizers, dinner, and the bottle of wine, coaxing detailed and thoughtful responses from me despite the simmering arousal in my body that refuses to abate. You are fiercely intelligent and demand no less than my complete engagement in this as in all areas. You challenge me—and I am as seduced by the intensity of our debate as I am by the heat of your gaze and the promise of what is to come.

I am distracted by the sensual movement of your thumb stroking the curve of your wineglass. I can't look away, watching the pad of your thumb move in small lazy circles on the smooth surface of the glass. You ask me a question, but I'm rendered incapable of speech, transfixed by the hypnotic movement of your hand. My body swells and responds as though it is me you are caressing, as though it is my flesh you are exploring and not some inanimate vessel. I close my eyes for a heartbeat as a wave of intense longing floods through me. I am helpless, trembling at the mere suggestion of your touch. When I meet your eyes, I see the knowledge of your power over me reflected in their depths, and I am stripped, as surely as if I were standing naked before you.

We are headed to the theater, so I excuse myself to the restroom for a moment, in hopes of regaining a measure of control over my arousal. I brace my hands on the edge of the sink, head lowered, drawing deep calming breaths. But my respite is short-lived. I hear the barely perceptible sound of the door swinging open and look up into the mirror to find you slowly advancing toward me. I move as though to turn toward you— but you stop me with a shake of your head. My back is to you, our gazes locked in the mirror, and you halt your advance only when your body is a hairsbreadth away from my own, your heat mingling with mine.

Still, you don't touch me.

You lean forward, placing one hand immediately in front of my own on the edge of the sink, your mouth—your beautiful sensuous mouth—next to my ear. You tell me to take off my panties, and I gasp at the intimacy of your command. I hesitate for only a fraction of a second, but I know it's too long, and your hand moves with decisiveness from the sink to the back of my neck, and I am slowly bent forward at your insistence, moaning now from the combined pleasure of your touch and the vulnerability of my position. With your other hand, you reach beneath my dress, fingers splayed, palm sliding up the inside of my thigh until you reach my wetness. I am drenched with my desire, and whisper only "Please..." but I am denied even now, and your knuckles only glance over my flesh as your fingers wrap around the fabric of my thong and tear it off with a firm jerk of your hand.

My body trembles in the wake of your controlled aggression. You relinquish your hold on my neck, your hand slowly descending, tracing the curve of my spine, moving outward until it rests lightly against my hip. I feel you then—for one brief, almost imagined moment, I feel you—feel the reflexive tightening of your grip in the same instant that I feel your hips rock forward, the thick length of your cock unmistakable against my ass. I close my eyes, drowning in the sensation of you pressed so tightly against me...but just as quickly, you're gone. My eyes snap open and I cry out at the loss of your touch, but you are already moving to the door, holding it open and waiting for me to precede you out of the restroom, tucking my ripped panties into your suit jacket. I search your face for evidence of your desire, for some small sign that lets me know you are as affected by this exchange as I am, but your composure is intact, your face a mask that gives no emotion away.

We leave the restaurant, walking the short distance to the theater in silence, yours contemplative, mine tormented. I am awash with arousal, miserable with desire for you, and my body is proclaiming its need of you with wet, aching clarity. I am acutely aware that my sex is exposed beneath the thin veneer of my dress; the cool evening breeze kisses the moisture that has accumulated there and my cheeks flood with shame. I feel your knowing stare, and struggle to regain my composure, but I can't. I know that if you were to lead me down any of the shadowed alleys we are passing and push me to my knees, your hand knotted in my hair, pressing my face to the front of your suit pants, I would eagerly use lips and teeth and tongue to free your cock and greedily swallow the length of it. I would work your cock until I gagged, until every inch of you was wet with my saliva, until your breathing grew ragged and your hips jerked convulsively and you threw your head back with the force of the orgasm tearing through your body. I would beg you to let me touch myself; I'd stroke my clit for you right there—on my knees, on the pavement in that shadowed alley until my cunt clenched and my clit exploded and I cried out my pleasure for you.

But you don't lead me down any alleys...you remain collected, smooth, and utterly in control.

Tosca is superb, but right now I hate Puccini. I hate the seconds and minutes and hours that stretch between this dark theater and lying naked beneath you. I hate that I think these thoughts, squirming quietly in my seat, when you are so clearly enjoying the performance. I feel like I am somehow letting you down because I can't rise above this driving need pulsing through my body. I worry my hands distractedly in my lap, unable to keep them folded demurely as I should.

I gasp with surprise at the feel of your hand on my thigh, and am immediately stilled by its solid pressure. Though I can't make out the nuances of your expression, I feel your gaze locked on mine and feel a moment of quiet comfort—there is a measure of ease to be found in knowing that the play of emotions and wants coursing through my body are directed by you, like the maestro with his orchestra below.

With aching slowness your hand traces invisible patterns across the top of my thigh. I scarcely breathe for fear that you will stop, and am rewarded for my stillness when your hand dips lower, to the sensitive flesh of my inner thigh. The sound of the opera recedes, and my world narrows to the feel of you stroking me, inching closer to my wetness. Still, you keep me off balance, refusing to settle into a predictable rhythm; you stroke me and then pause, and I can do naught but tremble and hold my breath until you resume. Your fingers linger teasingly at the edge of my skirt until I bite my lip to keep from moaning aloud in supplication. Then with a sinfully slow slide they ease beneath the material and continue ever higher, until you are stroking my cunt, spreading my folds and taking possession of the wetness that meets you. My thighs spread farther apart of their own accord; this is my offering to you, this hot flood of arousal. Here in this confined space where I am stripped of words and actions to show you how I feel, it is all I have to offer. It is yours—it belongs to you, as surely as I do.

I know you approve because the heel of your hand clamps down on my pubic bone and your fingers penetrate my cunt so that you're gripping me firmly, my slick sex held tightly in your palm. You lean into me and whisper that I'm going to come for you, right here in the middle of the theater, sitting perfectly still, and without making a sound. Your voice is like sex to me; I feel each word you breathe into my ear across my clit, so wet for you that it drools off your knuckles and trickles between the cheeks of my ass. I nearly come from your words alone and nod my head, though really, it's not a question of agreeing. You slide your fingers out of my cunt and up to my clit, all teasing gone, demanding my orgasm with hard strokes, and then I'm coming in waves, cunt heaving as pleasure wracks my body. A second rush begins to coil in my belly, but you stop your movement and say, "*Enough,*" and I gasp—halted immediately on the edge of that precipice and robbed of breath, the pain it produces as acute and intense as the pleasure that hammered through me moments ago.

You wait until the sensation subsides, then remove your hand, wiping it clean with a handkerchief produced from your pocket. I feel dizzy and disoriented, and the final moments of the opera pass in a blur of music and applause, bright lights, and the buzz of conversation sliding past me. I am aware of only the firm pressure of your hand in the small of my back, guiding me through the noise and into the quiet of your car, and of the constant thrum of my arousal as you guide us skilfully through the night, your beautiful square jaw thrown into profile by the passing headlights of oncoming traffic.

You don't touch me again until the door of your penthouse clicks shut behind us and you push me to the ground, one hand opening your fly even as your other reaches in to free your dick. I scramble to my knees as you grab the back of my head and then your cock is filling my mouth. I grab on to your legs to steady myself as hard silicone buries itself in my throat with a rough thrust and I feel myself choke on its thick length, tears filling my eyes. I am filled with bliss, so wet I'm running down my thigh, thrilled at last to be able to touch you; to be used by you; to please you. You fuck my mouth and I struggle to take you in with some measure of grace but I cannot, and feel myself sinking into sensation: the feel of your suit pants beneath my fingertips, the wet slide of your cock over my lips, the feel of your hands knotted in my hair, pulling my head toward you in time with the rhythm you drive out with your hips; your smell, a heady combination of cologne and arousal assaulting my senses. The silence is broken only by the shallow erratic sound of my breathing.

I want you to come. I want to feel you unravel and lose control. I want to feel the tremor in your thighs, feel your hands tightening in my hair. I want to show you how good I am for you. But you have other ideas. You relinquish your hold on me and take a step back, robbing me of your warmth and support and I falter, kneeling awkwardly before you, eyes downcast.

"Look at me," you say, and I do. I watch you release the button on your jacket and shrug it off, then toss it to a chair by the door. You remove your cufflinks, then your watch, placing them on the console table. You roll your sleeves up to mid-forearm, then unbutton your black oxford and leave it hanging open, lying in contrast to the white tank top revealed beneath. I drink in your appearance hungrily: your dark hair falling casually across your forehead; the slight flush staining your cheeks; your small firm breasts and taut stomach outlined by your tight white tank. I watch as one hand descends, wraps around your cock. I watch you stroke yourself, your cock still wet with my saliva. You are wildly beautiful, and I want you more than my next breath.

You tell me to get up, and with slow deliberation close the gap separating us until I can feel your hot breath on my cheek and I need to look up to meet your eyes. You keep inching forward until I have no choice but to take a step back, and then another, until I'm up against the door with nowhere left to go. You ask me if I enjoyed dinner. I tell you I did. You ask me if I enjoyed the opera. I say yes. You shake your head, eyes glittering dangerously—I know better than to lie to you, you say. You pull my dress up until it's bunched around my hips, and your fingers find me again, thrusting deep into my slick hole, your eyes never leaving mine as I gasp with pleasure. You press your body against mine, still inside me, fucking me with a hard even rhythm, telling me how you watched me squirm in my seat, how you smelled my arousal, like some bitch in heat. *"Isn't that right,"* you say, and I nod my agreement—I am whatever you tell me I am.

"You want my cock, hungry bitch?" you growl in my ear. I whimper and close my eyes, drunk on the heady combination of your words and the feel of your fingers pumping my cunt. But then you slap my face and I cry out, jolted back to the moment, mind racing, trying to figure out what I've done to displease you. *"I asked you a question,"* you say, *"don't make me repeat myself."* And I trip over myself in my eagerness to be redeemed, nodding my head, mewing my assent, telling you in a halting breathy voice I barely recognize as my own how much I want to feel your cock inside me, how starved I am for it. I beg you to fuck me, and feel my cheeks flood with heat. I am the greedy whore you name me, my hungry cunt aching for release, and all the while you finger-fuck me, grinding into me up against the door.

I am rewarded for my answer with a kiss, and for the first time tonight I feel the sublime touch of your lips against mine, your tongue teasing the corners of my mouth then aggressively demanding entry. I moan and eagerly yield to the pressure of your kiss, hands snaking up your chest to delve into the soft hair at the nape of your neck, revelling in the feel of your tongue stroking wetly against my own. You kiss me hungrily, dominating my mouth with ruthless intensity, the heat between us rising white hot.

You grip me by the waist, never breaking the kiss, and lift me up, my back still pressed against the door. I wrap my legs around your waist and you lean into me hard, moving one hand beneath me to bring yourself into position, and then I feel the thick head of your cock probing the mouth of my cunt, finding no resistance, and then filling me, inch by agonizing inch. Hands beneath my thighs, your hips thrust slowly forward as you lower me more fully onto you, until I am filled to overflowing with you, breaking the kiss with a gasp as my body stretches to take you in. You smile then, the corner of your mouth moving upward with that same slow seductive curve you flashed in the restaurant. *"Is that what you want?"* you ask me, rocking forward again. *"Yes!"* I hiss, and I feel you deep inside of me, feel you fucking me at last, feel your hips grinding into me, driving out the rhythm my body's been craving all night.

There is no teasing in this now. You are strength and force and raw sex, giving me all that I can take, fucking me hard and fast, hips pistoning into me, growling that you want my orgasm, you want to feel my slobbering cunt clench around your dick, you want to feel my nails digging into you, hear me grunting, taste the sweat on my skin. I feel the tension rising in my body, feel it coiling tighter in my belly with every brutal thrust and moist word you breathe. My thighs clamp around your waist even tighter, wanting more of you, ravenous for you even as you fuck me with a roughness that borders on violence. I know I'll hurt tomorrow—feel that sweet ache in my cunt that reminds me of this, of you. I moan with pleasure at the thought, and grab on to you all the harder, working my cunt feverishly on your cock in time with your raw thrusts until orgasm tears through my body and I cry out my release.

You keep fucking me, never slowing your rhythm as spasms of pleasure rock through my cunt, and one wave of pleasure spills into the next until I think I can't possibly take any more.

Only then do you stop, lowering me spent and exhausted to the ground. I want nothing more than to curl into you and rest, but there's no respite for the wicked. You turn me over so that I'm on my knees in front of you, shoulders on the ground. You kneel behind me, one hand on my ass, the other guiding your slick cock into my aching cunt until I am impaled on your thick length. I can't help but moan at the feel of you filling me, and again as you start to move, slow thrusts pulling back until only the head of your cock is in me, then forward again, feeding me your cock a bit at a time. You tell me to stroke my clit for you and I whimper a little, my flesh overly sensitive to the touch, but I obey you, circling the engorged tissue with light strokes. You tell me you want me to stroke myself for you like that until I come again, and I know a moment's misery because I don't honestly think I can. You slap my ass hard and I cry out—"*Do it,*" you say, punctuating your words with hard thrusts.

It's easier somehow like that—with your cock driving into me aggressively, your hands gripping my hips tightly. I'll have bruises there too, evidence of your possession. I like your marks on me; I feel less naked in my nakedness with them. You moan then, and your fingers tighten reflexively on my hips, the speed of your thrusts increasing. Some primal feeling breathes new life into my sex, and I press my fingers more firmly into my clit, feeling it pulse, feeling that delicious tension start to rise again in time with your arousal. I hear your breathing, shallow and erratic, feel the tremor in your hands as your pleasure mounts, and stroke my clit harder, feeling my own pleasure rising in turn. I am undone by the feel of you coming apart, losing control as you pump your cock into me as hard and fast as you can, until I hear you cry out your own release, and my orgasm hits me like a freight train.

We collapse in a heap of tangled limbs and rumpled clothes and lie quietly until our hearts slow and our breathing calms and the cool air chills the sweat on our heated skin. You stand, offering me your hand, and lead me to your bed without a word. With gentle fingers and soft kisses you remove my clothes, and then your own, pulling back the coverlet and sliding in beside me, urging my head onto your shoulder, and covering us in a warm cocoon of blankets. You kiss my forehead tenderly and whisper that I am a good girl. That I am your girl. My heart soars. I belong to you.

PLEASE (ACT III)

Linda Suzuki

After we watched the sun set, I surprised Sloane
with the news that we were going out to the
women's bar. She looked hurt, and I knew she
was wondering if I was bored with her. Still,
she dressed without complaint to my specifica-
tions, in a white tank top and jeans with nothing on underneath. As we drove toward the
city, she was pensive, staring out the window.

There were nearly as many women on the
sidewalk outside the club as there were inside.
The women outside smoked, or waited for
friends, or had dramatic confrontations with
their exes. I parked around the corner where
no one from the club could see us.

"Wait ten minutes before you come in," I
said. "When you get inside, get a drink and finish it, then come find me."

I walked around the corner, but instead of going into the bar, I crossed the street and stood in the shadow of a doorway, watching. Exactly ten minutes later, Sloane turned the corner and I watched her walk through the crowd outside the bar. Every woman there followed Sloane with her eyes. A few of the braver butches even spoke to her, attempting a seductive, "Hey," or "How's it going?" Sloane returned their greetings with a shy smile, but hurried into the club.

When I got inside, I saw that Sloane was ordering a drink from the bartender, so I walked to the bar at the far end of the club and ordered my own. From there, I found a bar stool in a shadowed corner and sat watching Sloane. As soon as she had taken a sip from her bottle of beer, the woman standing next to her was offering to buy her another. She and Sloane chatted for a moment, but then Sloane went and stood at the edge of the dance floor. Several women asked her to dance. I couldn't hear her over the throbbing music, but she seemed to have told them that she was waiting for someone. I guessed that because the women continued to watch her, as though wanting to see who that someone was.

Sloane finished her beer quickly, set it down on an empty table, and crossed the room directly to me. I was impressed—I hadn't even seen her searching the room with her eyes, but there was no doubt she knew exactly where I was.

"I was scared you wouldn't be here," she whispered in my ear. She stood between my legs, pressing against me.

"Look up," I told her. She raised her eyes to the small balcony above the dance floor. Legend had it that the bar had once been a bank and the balcony was for an armed guard who kept watch from there over everything happening on the floor. Now, the balcony was used only for storage, littered with broken chairs and empty kegs. The balcony was high enough that it was above the steel grid holding the dance floor lights, so the only light was the reflection from the mirrors on the walls below.

I drew her tight against me so she could feel through my jeans the strap-on I was wearing. "I'm going to take you up there and fuck you in front of all these people." Her hand, which had been resting on my thigh, moved up higher so it was hidden from view in front of her. She ran her fingers over my crotch, tracing the outline of the dildo.

I could see she was surprised to feel that it wasn't the four-teen-incher I had strapped on to fuck her with before. I turned her around to face the dance floor, and pressed the dildo against her ass so she understood. She leaned back and began subtly rubbing herself against my crotch.

"But first," I whispered in her ear, "you're going to let me watch you make some other woman cum."

She tensed but said nothing.

"The next woman who walks through the door alone," I told her. "Dance with her and when you're sure she's wet, make up some excuse to come back over here alone."

Sloane walked back across the dance floor to the door, just in time to meet a woman dressed in full cowboy regalia, with black boots, tight black jeans, a silver belt buckle, a black shirt with silver collar tips, and a black hat. The woman's cowboy nonchalance disappeared completely the moment Sloane asked her to dance. I'd never seen Sloane dance before, but it didn't surprise me that she moved seductively, suggestively, her hips keeping time with the music, and all the while keeping close contact with the two-stepping dyke. They danced until they were both sweating under the lights, then sat out a song at the bar over beers. The woman could not keep her hands off Sloane, and could not keep her eyes from darting around the room, ready to challenge anyone she caught looking at Sloane. When their beers were gone, the woman led Sloane back to the dance floor and they danced even closer than before, the woman's hand low on Sloane's ass, drawing them together.

Midway through the song, the woman leaned in close and whispered in Sloane's ear. Sloane pulled away from her with a smile, then whispered something back, turned and walked across the room to where I sat.

Sloane's eyes were bright with anticipation as I pressed a tiny tube of lube into her hand. "Go to the bathroom," I said. "Get your ass nice and wet for me."

I felt more than heard the moan that escaped Sloane's lips, as she turned to go. I caught her hand and drew her down close so that my lips were against her ear.

"Take her with you, let her do whatever she wants—except make you cum."

I watched Sloane cross the dance floor and saw her catch the eye of the woman who by then had returned to the bar to nurse her bruised ego. The woman glanced in my direction, but didn't appear able to see my eyes in the shadows. Then she hurried after Sloane.

Sloane chose the stall farthest from the door. The woman entered a moment later, pushing against each of the stall doors, finding the doors locked or the stalls empty. When she reached the last stall, she pushed open the door and found Sloane leaning against the wall, waiting. The woman kissed her at once, forcing her hands up under Sloane's shirt, and fondling her nipples roughly.

"My mistress wants you to watch while she fucks me up the ass," Sloane whispered.

The woman stopped and looked around.

"Not here," Sloane smiled, "Out there. But first," she held up the small tube, "she wants you to get me nice and wet for her." Sloane turned, facing the wall and bracing herself against the cool tiles. The woman reached around and opened the fly on Sloane's jeans, then pushed the jeans down around her ankles. She grabbed the lube from Sloane and squirted it onto her fingers. Sloane bent down lower, giving the woman easy entry into her asshole. The woman began moaning the minute her first finger slipped inside. Sloane told her how good it felt. The woman slipped another finger inside, and Sloane said, "God, yes." The woman began driving her fingers deep into Sloane's ass, and Sloane could tell the woman was instantly on the verge of cumming. Sloane talked dirty to her, begged her to fuck her ass harder, until the woman let out a long sigh and bent her body over Sloane's, cumming with a force that left her trembling. Sloane stood up straight, pulled her jeans back on, and pressed her whole body against the woman's. "Now you get to watch her fuck me," she whispered and walked out.

The entrance to the balcony stairs was down a short hallway that also led to the loading dock out back. Sloane took her time climbing the stairs, enjoying the sensation of her dripping pussy and asshole with every step. On the balcony, I was leaning against the wall just above the dance floor, and I smiled as I watched her make her way to me. When she stood in front of me, she returned my smile, then without a word, undid her jeans, pushed them down, and stepped out of them. She paused for the briefest of moments, then also lifted the tank top up over her head so that she stood completely naked in a room full of a hundred women, none of whom would have believed what they were seeing if they'd looked up at the balcony.

Sloane bent over, bracing her hands against the balcony rail and spreading her legs wide apart. The lube ran in shiny rivulets down her crack. I unzipped my jeans, reached in and pulled out the dildo, and rammed it into Sloane's asshole, not stopping until my cunt was pressed against her ass.

She yelped in pain, but the sound was drowned in the music. I stroked in and out of her asshole until Sloane's pain gave way to ecstasy and she arched her neck in pleasure, begging me to fuck her. It was then that I spotted the woman Sloane had danced with. She was standing against the bar at the far end of the room, gazing up at us, her mouth slightly open, her eyes glassy as though she'd been hypnotized. I dug my fingers into Sloane's hips to pull her toward me each time I thrust forward, and when she came, I was buried deep inside her. Sloane's eyes were closed, but I got to watch the woman below as she came too.

HARD TO GET

Rachel Kramer Bussel

With some girls, you know the minute you
meet them you're going to wind up between
their thighs, your tongue coasting along their
lower lips, diving deep inside, lapping up their
sweet sex juices until they're almost gone, then
making more. You can tell from the way they
say your name, a certain lilt that makes you
picture them calling it out, hoarse and breathless, during sex. You know from the sparkle
that bursts from their eyes, from the shiver you
get as their fingers oh-so-gently stroke your
arm. Gay, straight, bi—it doesn't really matter what these girls call themselves, they give
away their fuckability instantly. Once you feel
that spark, that surge of heat that plummets
deep inside, dropping from the catch in your
throat to the pounding of your heart to the

somersaults in your stomach before giving way to the heat
blasting through your pussy, they're all yours—and vice versa.
Any obstacles in your way, be they a boyfriend or the fact that
you've never even met, are nothing compared to the insistent,
urgent way your whole body tingles, propelling you forward,
and you know that the minute you make contact, she'll feel that
magic dance like you're two magnets drawn together as natu-
rally as the sun shines every day. Getting those girls to succumb
to your charms is fun, hot even, but it's hardly a challenge.

With other girls, though, it takes longer for the magic message to work its way between you. It's like you can see it, hear
it, taste it, and touch it, but they're tuned to a different frequency, and your task is to make sure they hear yours so loudly
it fills their heads with nothing else. For me, Nikki was the
second type of girl. I think I made my way through all her
friends before she so much as deigned to call me by name. It
was never "Angie" or even "Angela" or "A," as some of the
girls called me. It was just "Hi" or "Hey" or even a nod, her
eyes glassy, seeming to look anywhere but at me. She was never
rude, but I got the sense that Nikki wanted to get away from
me, was just waiting for me to leave so she could cut loose. I
hadn't done anything to offend her, except date her friends,
and run my eyes up and down her luscious curves. But beneath
her hostility I knew there was a heat I had to touch, to conquer,
to stroke until she exploded against my touch, melting in my
arms. More than once, I called out her name as I touched myself, wishing her fingers were inside me, mine inside her, both
of us wet, wailing, willing. But Nikki's the kind of girl who's
worth waiting for.

One night I sat on a chair at the bar, with Tracy on my lap,
her petite body fitting easily against my sturdier one, making me

feel powerful beneath my men's button-down shirt and brand-new jeans, my hair shorn so only the lightest layer graced my head. I was every inch the powerful butch to her femme, one of the few black couples at the club who clung so tightly to roles many thought were over and done with. When her ass pressed backward against my crotch, I almost felt like I had a real cock between my legs, not just the one I'd put on for the night. But even as intoxicating as Tracy was, and Cara, Janet, and Nina before her, something about Nikki made her stay on my mind. Later that night, when Tracy got on her knees before me, wearing only a hot-pink push-up bra and tiny Day-Glo pink thong panties that seemed to light up against her deep brown skin while she smoothly took the silver silicone dick between her lips, I almost called out "Nikki," catching myself just in time. "Nice, that's nice, baby," I said.

When Tracy crawled on top of me and sank her sweet body down along the toy, pressing her curves firmly against me and giving me access to those big hard nipples right in front of my face, I gorged on them, stuffing them both into my mouth, flicking my tongue as she moaned loudly, but still wishing it were Nikki in bed with me. I wound up breaking it off with Tracy and moping around at the various gay bars, familiar haunts and newer ones on the edges of town where I could drown my sorrow in whatever the bartenders wanted to throw my way. I felt off my game, my crisp shirts losing some of their sparkle, my sharp haircut morphing into scattered, haphazard fuzz; my neat, shiny black shoes becoming scuffed. When I got home one night, I looked in the mirror. My eyes were bloodshot and a little sad, my clothes ragged. I was no longer the butch stud I aspired to be. "Forget about her," I told myself, but I couldn't. Nikki haunted my dreams, all the more alluring for her elusiveness, for the fact that I knew almost nothing about her save that she worked for a local fashion designer, liked to dance her ass off...and wouldn't give me the time of day.

But one morning, after waking up with my pussy throbbing so badly I needed a solid thirty minutes of my most powerful vibrator pressed flush against my clit while I fucked myself with my favorite dildo, until my body shattered and shuddered and surrendered to the vibrations, I knew I had to do something. Over the past few weeks, I'd wound up confessing to the other girls what was wrong, how much I just wanted to talk to her. Okay, I wanted to do more than talk, but it was a start. They weren't any wiser than I as to what her problem was, but insisted that I just try one more time to make conversation.

With their encouragement, I felt a renewed sense of energy. I didn't just want to get Nikki into my bed for a one-shot deal that would make things more painful if we hit it off between the sheets, never to see each other again. I was in this for the long haul, I realized as I perked myself up, determined to show her just how suave and sexy I could be. My friends told me to head over to Glitter, the hot new dyke dance night—and to dress the part. I went all out, buying a whole new wardrobe, including a black hat that I tipped across my head, newly shined shoes, and tight black jeans that accentuated my curvy ass and pressed against my sex just so, turning me on with every step. For contrast, I slashed some bright red lipstick across my lips, the only sign of femininity save for my breasts, and even those were more solid than curve. I like my size, the way I can stomp around with the guys, and not having to worry when I gain an ounce; the way being a butch allows me to appreciate the femmes I see around me. I can be like a guy, but not one, part boy, part girl, all me. But sometimes I like to mess with the all-macho look, toss in something unexpected like a diamond earring or a splash of pink or a slash of lipstick, to make sure that those who pass me on the street or check me out at a bar can't be sure what to make of me. I like to keep them guessing—and was hoping maybe Nikki did too.

I didn't see Nikki there when I arrived, but I acted like I didn't mind, and soon, I didn't. You'd be amazed at what a little lipstick on a butch can do for her sex appeal. I sat at the bar and ordered a Bud, and no sooner had I laid down the bills than some sweet young thing (and I do mean young—she had to just be pushing twenty-one) sidled up to me. "Haven't seen you around here before," she observed, puckering her lips and giving me the once-over.

"Maybe you haven't been looking hard enough, sweetheart," I said, laughing the first genuine laugh I'd let myself experience in months.

I was just letting myself take in the way her caramel-colored breasts pressed together temptingly, her black lace bra resting just against her nipples, giving the illusion that they might pop forth at any moment, when I saw Nikki across the room. She'd gone all out, too, wearing a bright red sparkly top that ran from her left shoulder in a diagonal across her breasts, and a black latex miniskirt that gleamed from across the room. My first thought after licking my lips, longing for a taste of those tits, was whether Nikki was wearing panties or not. I had to find out.

"Excuse me," I said before I became a cradle robber, and left the girl checking out my ass. It was time to get what I'd come for. The more I'd lusted after Nikki, the more I'd realized that if I was going to get her, I had to take her. Well, not truly take her; if she didn't want me, I would make my peace with that. But as I went over every cold aside, every time she'd checked me out then skittered away, and her dangerous combination of a genuine smile mixed with a "stay away" vibe, I knew what I had to do.

I marched over to her, getting right up in her business. She'd been grinding against another equally hot, equally scantily-clad girl in tall platforms and a skirt so mini I could almost see her panties. "Nikki, I think you've had enough dancing for the night," I said, putting my hand on her sleek, latex-covered hip. She tried to squirm away but I wouldn't let her, instead staring at the gold nameplate resting against her sweaty neck.

"And who are you to tell me what I've had enough of?" she snarled back, pushing me. I moved my hand lower, so it rested on her bare thigh, threatening to creep upward.

"Nobody. Except the woman who's gonna give you the fuck of a lifetime. Several lifetimes, actually," I said nonchalantly, as if my heart weren't pounding defiantly in my chest, roaring in my ears and trying to warn me away. "You're going to get off this dance floor and get in my car and come home with me, or else I'm going to lift you up, carry you over to that corner over there, lift that little skirt of yours, and spank your ass nice and hard until it stings so good you see stars." That got her attention. She stopped struggling and looked up at me, her glossy lips parted, as if trying to figure out what to say. Her eyes darted to the corner I'd mentioned, and I tried to keep the smile off my face as I realized Nikki was pondering which would be more pleasurable, getting fucked hard in my apartment, or spanked hard in public. I had no intention of getting us kicked out of the club for some kinky PDA, but she didn't need to know that. I stepped closer, closing the gap between us, then reached my hand around to cup one asscheek in my palm.

She shuddered, and this time didn't try to get away. I squeezed her flesh, watching this ultratough chick melt before me. Her surrender bolstered my confidence. I played with the edge of her panties, my fingers darting underneath, teasing the elastic as the rest of the dance floor ceased to exist. Then just when she thought I was going to plunge inside, I pulled my hand out, resting my warm fingers on her arm. "Ready?"

"Damn you," she uttered under her breath, unable to keep the hint of a smile from edging her lips upward. "I've been trying to stay away from you, Angie. I don't want to be just another girl in your stable, someone you hook up with then discard and move on to the next pretty chick to cross your path. You're too good for all that but you don't even see it, like you need to be some big bad black butch stud to prove yourself." She spit the words out defiantly, her wrist shaking and moving my arm with it, but she wasn't really trying to get away. Her face lit up as she talked, and I wondered again about her panties.

"Nikki, Nikki, Nikki...what is wrong with you, girl? I've been dreaming about you since day one."

"No, you haven't," she said, her words bratty and sharp, her face pausing to consider whether I might, just might, be right. I didn't want to argue with her, especially since all this time, it seemed our differences had been imaginary ones.

I leaned close to her. "Okay, have it your way. But I'm ready to make up for lost time, even though I still insist you were the one playing hard to get."

She moved closer still, so her breasts were pressed right up against mine, her chest pounding as she looked directly into my face before snaking her hand down between our bodies to fondle my cock. "We'll see about hard," she said, her voice lilting, a foreign but welcome sound.

She toyed with the dildo until I couldn't stand it anymore, and grabbed both her wrists, grateful for the daily workouts I'd logged in the last year. She whimpered as soon as my fingers closed around her skin, trapping her. "Turn around, Nikki, and show me that cute little bottom of yours, the one I'm going to take across my lap and spank very soon." Her shudder was visible, her body undulating like a belly dancer's for just a moment before she started marching. The stiff, shiny latex sheathed her ass, hinting at what lay beneath, but still leaving a little to my imagination. I followed, my mouth going dry as I realized I was finally going to have the object of my affection in my bed.

In the back of my mind, as confident as I'd tried to be, part of me had thought Nikki was a lost cause, and that whatever I'd done, real or imagined, I couldn't undo. So to have her slip so easily into place before me was hard to believe, yet so right. She stopped outside the club door, unsure where to turn, and I tucked my hand under the waistband of her skirt, my knuckles pressing against the small of her back. "I'll guide you," I said, and felt her melt against me. That moment, when a woman lets her body sink just so into my arms, lets me lead her, lets me control the dance we're about to do, is the one I live for. It puffs me up more than any cock or shirt or "sir" will ever do. It lets me know she trusts me enough to take care of her, to turn her pleasure into our pleasure.

I steered Nikki toward my car, but as I fumbled for the key, I realized I couldn't wait. Not now, not after so long. I reached around her, unlocked the passenger door—then did the same for the backseat. "Get in," I said, pushing her in that direction.

"You'll be fine," I told her, reading the question in her eyes. I wasn't about to let anyone catch us. I got in behind her and shut the door, knowing we were far enough away not to draw the bouncer's attention, and if any club-goers should see us, well, we'd probably make their night.

I settled into the middle of the seat, then spread my precious prize across my lap. Nikki wiggled against me, pressing against the dick and making my nipples hard. "Lift up your skirt for me, Nikki, and ask me to spank you," I told her, trying to keep the trembling out of my voice. It must have worked, because she reached behind her and pulled up her skirt, the act infinitely more erotic than if I'd done so myself. I needed to see and feel Nikki give herself to me, freely offer her body as smoothly as she'd withheld it.

"Please, Angie, I want you to spank me. I *need* you to spank my ass for being such a brat all this time." I wasn't expecting that last bit, and when Nikki buried her face in my knee, smearing her lipstick against the denim, breathing hot and hard through the fabric, I let loose. My hand crashed down upon the perfect apple curve of her bare brown cheek. Oh, yes, I'd been right—the girl had gone out without any panties to protect her pussy, or her ass. Now, both were exposed to me and I savored the view, raining blow after blow against her sweet curves.

"You like that, don't you, Nikki?" I asked, bringing my voice deep and low for the ending as I punctuated my words with solid smacks and her breath hissed, then stuttered, then seemed to stop altogether. I gave her a pinch, already feeling the urgent throbbing of her sex. "You're not going to answer me, Nikki?"

"Yes, yes, I like it," she said, then shuddered as my fingers dove into her sex without preamble. I plunged in as deep as I could, feeling a corresponding spasm from her cunt. "Oh, yeah," she mumbled softly as I teased her tender wetness, feeling her walls give against my touch.

My own private parts were starting to ache, and I eased myself off of her to kneel between her legs. I was pretending we weren't in a car in a fairly crowded parking lot; that's how bad I had it for her, I literally couldn't wait. "I'm going to fuck you now, Nikki, so hard you'll forget about every other girl who's come before me. I'm gonna fuck you until you forget everything except my name." The words just flowed from my mouth, with none of the practiced toughness I'd sometimes had to muster with other girls. No, she brought out that side of me that's pure animal, raw and needy and hoarse with want. The part where words don't matter, just actions. I ripped open the buttons of my jeans and out came my secret weapon, the extra-large dick that I only pack when I plan to fuck a girl until the earth really does move, until I feel like all of me is inside her, until I feel like she is inside me too, our bodies merging so well we trade souls, even if just for a moment. I rubbed the head of the cock against her sex, lubing it with her juices, and she bucked against me. "Wait for me," I admonished softly as I pushed my way in, and then we didn't speak. We didn't need to. Nikki and I had said all we'd need to say, and now we were in some other world, where it was just my cock, her pussy, and our hot breath steaming the windows.

I pushed deep into her, resting my weight on her body, my hands slipping beneath her to pinch her hard nipples. I kissed her back, nudging the shirt up with my nose to rest against her bare, sweaty skin, as the toy plunged in and out, seeking out her secrets, offering some of its own. My cock told her how to reach me, how to find that spot where I surrender as well, where it hits my clit and the thrill boomerangs back into me. We seesawed like that, shifting the pleasure, the ache, the bolts of desire as she arched her ass upward, giving and taking equally. "Oh, Angie," she cried out when I twisted her sweet pebbles fiercely, tuning her nipples to my favorite frequency, harder and harder as I slammed in and out, my motions so fast I barely knew where she ended and I began. Hearing her say my name catapulted me out of the car, doing a freefall as I came, bucking in and out of her all the while. I bit her back gently, needing to hold on to her in every way I could, as Nikki too succumbed to her climax, blubbering gibberish as she shook.

We couldn't get up for a while, and when we finally did, it felt surreal to pull my clothes back on, to see the dazed look on her face, like we'd both just awoken from a dream. "Did that really happen?" she asked, her fingertips tracing my swollen lips, then my cheek.

"I think so. But let's go back to my place and try it again just to be sure."

WAITING

Dylynn DeSaint

Anticipation is the most reliable form of plea-sure.—Gustave Flaubert

I'm standing in a line to check in at a hotel when my senses are jolted by the unmistakable scent of a perfume that I instantly recognize. It's *hers,* my illicit lover of the past several con-ferences.

The invisible tendrils of her perfume swirl around my face, caressing my skin ever so lightly, whispering and beckoning to me like a siren with the promise of all-consuming pas-sion and otherworldly pleasures of the flesh.

Almost involuntarily, I close my eyes and breathe it in again, this time more deeply. It only takes a few seconds for the fragrance and the steamy imagery associated with it to blaze right through my brain at lightning speed, triggering a series of searing impulses that go straight to my clit. I'm standing but my knees are threatening to buckle beneath me, and my body trembles. Goose bumps rise everywhere on my skin and my nipples become instantly taut. An audible sigh slips out of my lips, and I try desperately to shake my mind back to reality.

I hear a woman clear her throat quietly behind me from somewhere and without turning around, I bite the corner of my lip to prevent any hint of desire from appearing on my face.

It's *her.*

As calmly as possible, I step up to the registration desk, give the girl my credit card, and wait for her to give me a room key. Once she hands it to me, I repeat my number and ask how to find it. I reach down, grab the handle of my luggage, and turn around. As nonchalantly as possible, I scan the faces of the people behind me.

As soon as I see *her* another jolt careens throughout my body. I'm already soaked and my cunt is throbbing.

We make eye contact but neither of us allows our gaze to linger. We don't acknowledge each other but I can see the glint in her eye, and I know she can see mine.

I make my way through the lobby and sit on a soft leather couch where I can still see the registration desk. Under the pretense of looking for something in one of my bags, I watch discreetly as she stands at the counter, getting her room key. Once the girl hands it to her, I get up and walk toward the elevator. She heads in the same direction.

We both wait quietly in front of the elevator, not saying a thing but stealing furtive glances at each other.

I stare ahead and reflect quietly on how *we* came to be.

Both librarians, we are required by our respective libraries to attend professional conferences a few times a year. I met her at one about seven years ago. The instant our eyes met, I felt my body overheat with sensual longing. I had no idea at the time if she was even a lesbian or not. It didn't seem to matter; I just wanted her very badly.

I snooped and found out what workshops she'd be in and did everything in my power to be in the same space as her. After several planned "run-ins," I finally had myself in the position to talk with her. I casually asked her if she'd join me for a drink one night to talk over library stuff. A few drinks later, I discovered she wouldn't prove too difficult to seduce. Luckily for me she was just as attracted to me as I was to her.

Since then we've met about four times each year at conferences throughout the United States. Our private lives are kept separate from our adulterous rendevous. She has her own lover and so do I. We have a pact that neither shall call the other nor make contact of any kind. The only communication we have is when we meet each other at the conferences. I haven't seen her in four months now, and my body aches for her like no other.

When we are away from each other, thoughts of her relentlessly occupy my mind both during the day and in my dreams. I've tried like hell to suppress my cravings for her but to no avail. I knew I was addicted and could not live without my time with her. Her heartbeat kept mine pulsing with life that only she knew how to sustain. Each day that we spent apart increased an immense emotional and physical longing. At times, the distance felt unbearable. Not only was she a satisfying sexual partner, but through our strong emotional connection, she had grown to be the ethereal extension of my soul. Contained within the both of us was an insatiable carnal appetite.

I willingly and happily accepted the fact that she held the key that unlocked and fueled the aggressive and indulgent beast that lay deceptively and silently beneath the thin veneer of my otherwise benign exterior.

For the few short days that we would be together, hours and hours would be filled with wild and reckless pleasure. By the time I would reunite with her again months later, my appetite and longing for her would be voracious. I'd ravage her body unmercifully until we both were sexually sated.

"Giselle! Giselle!" someone yells in our direction.

My thoughts are abruptly interrupted. I turn and see a colleague from another library running with her baggage in tow, quickly trying to get to where we are so that she can ride in the same elevator.

I feign delight.

"Lori! It's so nice to see you again!" I exclaim, giving her a hug before we all walk into the elevator together.

"Giselle, I'm so glad I caught you. I don't know a soul at this conference and well, I was hoping that I could tag along with you; that is, if you don't mind?" she asks eagerly.

Before I can answer her question, she shoots off what feels like a dozen more questions throughout the ride up. I'm thankful when we reach her floor and she steps out. I wave to her as the door closes.

"You know she's going to be a problem," I say as I turn to Leila, using my body to pin hers up against the railing in the elevator.

Brushing my lips against hers, I kiss her lightly while I slip my hand underneath her skirt. I murmur my approval when I discover she is pantyless and stroke the smooth flesh of her inner thighs and the soft lips of her cunt. As I do this I'm thinking that some horny security guard is probably getting his rocks off while watching us on the security camera in the elevator. I look up and see a lens in the corner and smile in its direction.

Just as I'm about to dip my fingers inside of her, the soft chime of the elevator signals it's time to get off.

"Are you wearing it?" I ask her, my eyes searching her neck and stepping away as the doors open up.

With her eyes cast downward, a demure smile forms on her beautiful pouty lips and she murmurs, "Yes, Mistress."

Tugging at the fabric, she lowers the neckline of her turtleneck blouse, so that I can see the leather collar—with the shiny metal letters forming the words *HER SLAVE*—wrapped snuggly around the smooth skin of her neck. The darkness contrasts beautifully with her tawny brown skin and beautiful black hair. The big metal ring in the front looks lost without its leash. I can fix *that* problem later on.

As soon as I see it, I walk off the elevator with her trailing behind me. We search for our separate rooms. I find mine, open the door, and push my luggage inside, letting the door close behind me. I listen for hers to close too. I wait. Soon I hear the door handle to the room adjacent to mine turning. She opens it. I grab her by the wrist, pull her roughly inside my room, and shove her up against the wall. She cries out as I grab a fistful of hair, yank her head back and kiss her hard, bruising the soft lips that I've craved with mine. Shoving my hand under her blouse I maul her breasts roughly with my free hand, pinching her nipples between my fingers until she whimpers against my lips.

"Miss me?" I taunt her.

"God, I did...so damn much!" she gasps breathlessly, biting my lips like a bitch in full heat and wrapping her legs around my thigh. I can feel the heat and moisture from her cunt searing into my leg.

"Show me how happy you are to see me then," I say as I release her from my grip.

She takes me by the hand and leads me to the edge of the bed.

"Mistress, will you please sit?" she asks carefully.

I plop down on the mattress and stare at her. She is playing a dangerous game, but I understand her and know that she has a tendency toward misbehavior after long absences from each other. She's going to push the envelope. I just know it.

Fully expecting her to ask for permission to open my trousers, I'm surprised when she instead stands closely in front of me, her knees almost touching mine. She lifts her blouse and pulls off her bra. Slowly unzipping her skirt, she lets it fall to the ground. My eyes follow the soft curve of her hips, accentuated by the lacy black garters that she is wearing, down to her shaved mound and pouty cunt. I subconsciously run my tongue over my lips while my gaze continues down her long stocking covered legs and ends up at the black high heels.

I look back up at her. The sight of the black leather collar around her neck combined with her naked body makes my clit stir with excitement.

She eyes me seductively and turns around, her bare ass only about a foot away from my face and close enough for her to feel my hot breath on her skin. Slowly, she bends over so that her ass is exposed to me in its succulent and fleshy glory. I see something shiny, black, and rubber protruding from her hole. It's a small butt plug.

I shift my hips slightly, feeling my groin begin to heat up.

Pleased with my reaction, she reaches back and strokes her

ass lightly with her fingertips, kneading her flesh, and sighing softly.

Grasping the butt plug, she pulls it out slightly and pushes it back in slowly, arching her back and moaning quietly. She continues to fuck herself, shifting the weight of her body on each stroke so that she is moving in a tantalizingly sensuous way. I watch as her petite fingers continue to pull its stiff length out farther and farther, the black toy glistening with lube, then push the whole thing back inside her ass again.

I am stoic and emotionally unyielding but internally fight the temptation to grasp on to it and fuck her with it myself. *Patience you.* I decide to wait.

"I wore it for you, Mistress," she purrs. "Every time I moved or sat down, it reminded me of how sinfully you fuck me."

She was right of course. Leila adored being fucked up the ass more than anyone I'd ever been with. Every time I delivered that particular pleasure to her, I completely lost myself in the act. I'd ride that fine derriere until she was absolutely spent and could not take it anymore.

Each sigh, moan, or gasp that left her lips during our lovemaking I breathed in and possessed as if it were my own. Even now, as she taunts me by fucking herself in my presence, I feel my mind slipping into a sensual state that only she can put me in.

She moans quietly and begins to fuck herself in earnest with one hand, the other rubbing her clit. Her knees buckle slightly.

"Stop!" I growl at her.

"Yes, Mistress!" comes her stunned reply. Immediately she stops and turns around, but avoids eye contact with me.

"You were about to come weren't you?" I ask her as I stand up. My face is so close to hers that my lips brush against her ear as I speak, "And were you planning on asking for permission?"

Silence.

"They say the eyes don't lie," I stare at her, piercing her eyes with mine.

She attempts to look at me but can't hold my gaze.

"I expected as such." I say, sneering at her.

Despite the sternness in my voice, I indulge the tenderness that I feel for her by allowing my eyes to wander over her face, silently stroking her soft skin with invisible featherlike caresses over her cheek and then resting on her lips.

Those luscious lips. They've explored every inch of my body, leaving their hot imprint in the most intimate of places.

She shudders when I push away a lock of hair from her shoulders and run a lone finger lightly across her neck, then downward to a pert nipple adorned with a stainless steel ring. Circling it with my fingertip, I grasp it and tug it slightly, watching the expression on her face.

"I was going to stop...." She groans at first but the sensation from her nipple ring being tugged stops her in midsentence.

"You're lying," I state matter-of-factly and release the ring.

She winces but I catch the bratty look in her eyes for a split second before she lowers them again. Without being told, she hurriedly crawls onto the edge of the bed with her ass up in the air and her face down on the covers.

"I'm sorry for being so bold, Mistress," she whimpers. "I only wanted to show you my new toy and how much I missed you."

Whack! The sound of my raised hand making contact with the bare flesh of her ass fills the emptiness of the room.

"Oh, my god!" she yelps.

I spank her bottom repeatedly until pink welts rise everywhere and my hand becomes warm. She squirms and flinches but gloriously revels in the illicit pleasure. Her cunt begins to convulse with each strike. Soon I see small glistening drops of moisture emerge from her slit. I watch the sweet honey make its way down her leg. The air around us is filled with the heady and musky scent of her excitement, and it drives my desire to take her body and senses to new heights.

"Please don't stop!" she begs, her voice cracking; it is husky and heavily intoxicated with desire. I watch as the muscles in her body both tense and release with each stroke of my hand.

"You're a naughty little whore," I say, not letting on that she has ignited a fire now burning so wickedly hot in my cunt that I can barely stand it.

I continue to deliver the pleasure and pain that she wants until my hand burns and I can't continue any longer. *Next time I won't forget the leather flogger.*

I stop abruptly and she groans miserably, almost crying.

"Patience, woman," I warn her as I tear off my shirt and un-button my trousers, causing the huge dildo I've got strapped on to spring free. I catch a glimpse of us in a large mirror on the wall and smile wickedly. The narcissist in me enjoys the sight of our naked bodies; she adorned in black stockings and high heels and me with my love weapon.

Positioning myself behind her, I gently thrust my knee be-tween her legs to get her to open up. I reach between her burn-ing globes of soft flesh, grasp the plug and gently but slowly give it a tug, testing it to see how tightly it's embedded in her body. She lets out a soft moan but it slides out easily enough. I quickly toss the plug onto the bed in front of her.

She's well lubed and ready for something bigger and there's no time to waste. I want her *now*.

I place the dildo against the delicate pucker of her ass. She's hot for it and moves her rear back against my hips. It takes no effort on my part to bury it completely and deeply inside. Like a warm knife through butter, the big boi glides smoothly into her.

I grasp her by the shoulders and work it in and out slowly in case she needs to adjust to its girth and length but almost immediately she begins to slam back against me *hard*. Her fierce need releases the beast inside of me and I lose control of any sensitivity and civility. I pound the dildo so roughly into her that my hips jar her body forward. I dig my nails into her skin and hold on to her tightly to keep her from slipping away from me. She howls loudly, unable to contain her passion, and wraps her ankles around the back of my thighs. When I lunge forward with the strongest thrust yet, she cries out as a blistering climax careens through her body.

Before we can catch our breath a loud rapping on the door startles us both.

"Giselle? It's me, Lori," the voice through the door chirps happily.

Leila shoots me a look and panics. I point to the closet and she quickly scurries in, throwing out one of the hotel's terrycloth robes in my direction before slamming the door shut.

"Lori? Hang on a sec."

I put on my best professional face, wipe the sweat on my sleeve, and open the door.

"I was taking a nap."

"Oh, dear, I'm so sorry," she says apologetically, "I just wanted to see if you would be interested in having dinner with me tonight."

Wondering why the hell she didn't call, I reluctantly agree to her invitation. She smiles and apologizes once more and waves good-bye as she walks away.

I close the door and Leila peers cautiously out of the closet.

"Who on earth does she think she is?" she asks incredulously.

I pull her out and plant a quick kiss on her lips, effectively hushing her inquiry.

"Guess who you're having dinner with tonight?" I chuckle, smacking her butt playfully.

"Her? Me? Why?" she stutters.

"If I don't do something with her soon she's going to hound me for the rest of the conference."

"But why me too?" she looks at me, confused.

"I don't want to get stuck with Lori by myself and besides she doesn't know anything about *us* and as far as she's concerned you're another colleague. Don't worry, everything will be all right, baby." I pull her into me and kiss her gently this time.

She murmurs into my lips and grins mischievously. "Mistress, did you notice when you went to the door, that you had a woody under your robe?"

"What?" I look down and see the big bulge peeking out. "Oh, shit!"

"Do you think she noticed?" I look at her horror-stricken.

"Well, I certainly did," she giggles playfully, grabbing at my crotch and refusing to give in to worry. "Let's go out onto the balcony."

"I'll be out in a second," I say and slip away into the bathroom. No telling what she's got up her sleeve. I want to be prepared so I pull off the dildo and wash it in the sink then strap it back on.

I join her outside. High up in our room on the ninth floor, we look out at the gorgeous view of the Pacific Ocean and the throngs of swimsuit-clad men and women milling about on the boardwalk and beach below us. Some are on roller skates, dancing in rhythm to the loud music blaring below.

We're standing side by side taking in the view when a gust of cool ocean breeze catches her long hair and blows it off of her shoulders, exposing her silky skin. She leans forward with her elbows against the railing. Closing her eyes, she slowly runs her tongue over her lips, making them glisten in the warm California sun.

She opens them and looks directly at me, giving me a smoldering hot and sexy look, a clear signal that she wants me to fuck her.

"How thoughtless of me, baby, I've completely ignored your poor little cunt." I smirk.

She straightens up and I stand closely behind her, confidently holding her by the waist with one hand and then lifting the back of her robe with the other. I slip my fingertips toward the fuzzy lips of her cunt and am greeted with a pool of sweet nectar. I immerse my fingers in the wetness and push them up inside of her easily. She's so wet I could shove my whole hand in if I like. I know she'd enjoy that immensely but now is not the right time.

"Hold on tight to the railing," I instruct her.

I withdraw my fingers and holding on to the thick silicone appendage, position it so that it sits right at the entrance of her cunt. Not quite in but just resting there.

She shivers.

I take my time and ease it into her at an excruciatingly slow pace.

Provoking her even further, I trace my tongue along the edge of her ear and whisper, "Baby, I want to fuck that tight slut hole of yours so thoroughly that you'll carry our secret with you long after we've left this place."

Unable to stand the teasing, she sucks in her breath and pushes her hips into me, effectively lodging the whole thing inside of her body.

Since I don't want to make it completely obvious what we're doing with so many people out and about, I begin to sway side to side, moving her along with me, giving the appearance that we're dancing in rhythm to the music below us. I stagger our movement slightly so that she'll feel the dildo slide out and then move back inside her when our bodies sync up again. Each time it moves in her, she groans softly and pushes back against me to get it still deeper.

"Please..." she utters in a barely audible voice and then gasps when I shove my hips upward, effectively impaling her against the railing.

I feel her lose her balance momentarily. She clutches at the rail with all her might.

Since there's only so much I can do in public, she begins to move her hips in a tantalizingly sensual way that would barely be noticeable to anyone below. I lean into her so that she gets the full length of the dildo.

Soon I can feel my own cunt beginning to twitch just watching her do her magic.

"Fuck," I groan. She's moving her hips in such a way that I'm feeling the friction of the dildo moving against my clit. I sink my teeth into my lower lip in an attempt to maintain some sense of control over an orgasm that is threatening to drop me to my knees.

My legs start to tremble and she senses that I'm teetering on the edge and ready to come at any moment. Every movement she now makes brings me closer and closer to exploding. My breath quickens and I clutch tightly at her robe.

I hear her begin to moan and soon our voices merge in an explosive set of orgasms that shake the both of us.

Holding on to her body for support, I struggle to catch my breath.

"You're going to be the death of me," I halfheartedly chuckle as I look at her through hazy eyes. My mind is still struggling to recover from the sex-induced stupor.

Stumbling, I make my way back into the room and collapse onto the bed. She slips in next to me.

"C'mere you." I pull her close, nuzzling her neck and taking in the warmth of her body.

She sighs contentedly and we both fall asleep in each other's arms.

We're stirred awake by the sound of a telephone ringing. I reach over Leila and grab the receiver.

"Hi again, it's Lori!" the annoying voice sings.

"Hey, Lori," I blink in disbelief. *Does this woman ever stop?*

"I forgot to ask you what time we should meet for dinner. It's five o' clock right now, do you want to meet at six in the restaurant downstairs?"

"Sure," I say. "Oh, Lori, I hope you don't mind, but another colleague of mine would like to join us for dinner. I'm not sure if you know her. Her name is Leila Rousseau."

"No," her voice sounds pensive, almost hesitant, then finally she says, "That'll be fine, Giselle. I'll meet you both in an hour."

"Will she ever leave us alone?" Leila yawns, resting her head under my chin and snuggling into me.

"It doesn't appear that she will, does it? I wonder why she's being such a pest."

I kiss Leila gently, lingering on her soft lips, and then feel her grind her body against mine.

"Hey, now. I'll have none of that, you insatiable vixen! We have to meet her in an hour. Off you go, let's shower."

We arrive at the outdoor patio and spot Lori. She's sitting at a table by a fire pit. It looks cozy and away from the crowd. I'm pleased with her choice.

I note that she sits primly with her legs crossed and is dressed in typical librarian garb: a neutral-colored skirt, conservative blouse, scarf, and a cat pin. *What is it with librarians and cat pins?* She's a pretty enough lady though and could definitely pull it off if she wore something sexier. At least she's got great taste in shoes; gorgeous designer four-inch-heeled ones at that. *Hmm...not bad; not bad at all, nice legs too.* I wave to her when she sees us.

Once we get ourselves seated, I introduce Leila to Lori. We order our meals and after a few drinks, we've all loosened up a bit. Before I know it, we're all laughing and joking around like old friends.

I'm relieved because I had thought this was going to be an extremely long night.

While they talk, I quietly observe them both. I'd seen Lori at conferences before but never spent this much time with her. She seems nice enough.

I'm starting to get buzzed from the wine that we've been drinking and decide to smoke a cigarette. As I reach down to collect my purse from under the table, I look Lori's way and à la Sharon Stone, she uncrosses her legs and exposes a beautifully trimmed slice of heaven. My jaw drops.

I compose myself once I sit up and light the cigarette. Lori looks directly at me and smiles seductively. Leila notices this and shoots a questioning glance my way. I look at the both of them and then I'm not quite sure what to do. I look away and blow the smoke into the night air while trying to make sense of things.

I'm buzzed but I know what she did and what I saw. *What the hell?* Confused and thinking that maybe I've had too much to drink, I silently signal to Leila that we should go.

Not letting us abandon her, Lori asks to join us on our walk back to our rooms.

"I think you two lushes are in need of an escort and since I'm the only half-sober one of the bunch, I guess that makes me the one in charge."

They're both obviously drunk and laugh raucously while I'm still stuck in my head on why Lori behaved that way at the table.

I get between them and put my arms around both of their shoulders, attempting to guide them in the right direction, when Lori trips on some loose carpeting. She nearly falls but I quickly reach out and catch her by the waist and pull her safely into my body.

"Are you okay, Lori?" I ask, genuinely concerned.

"Yes, Mistress," she gasps breathlessly, unnerved.

For a stunning moment of silence, we three look at each other and say nothing.

Lori looks pale, obviously embarrassed, and I can tell she has no idea what to do or say.

I'm the first to speak.

"Lori, join us for a nightcap." It's not a question but more of a command.

"Yes, Ma'am," she quietly replies, releasing the scarf around her neck and revealing a jewel-studded collar.

I look at Leila, then Lori, and grin wickedly. *And people think librarians are boring. Little do they know there's more tied up than those buns on their heads!*

"Library conferences," I chuckle, "they're just getting more and more interesting every year."

I gather them both by the arm.

"Okay, ladies, let's go."

The two commence to giggling like schoolgirls. With a glint in my eye, I smile at my good fortune.

THE PLACEMENT OF MODIFIERS

Jean Roberta

I'm standing behind three dykes in leather jackets, two well-groomed young men in matching
burnt-orange sweaters, and a queen whose big
hair must be seven feet above her platform
soles. "Doctor Chalkdust," chirps Alison the
bartender. "What will you have?"

"These customers were here before me, Alison," I tell her. "You should serve them first."
Catching sight of my reflection in the chrome
coffeemaker, I see that I have not grown any
taller than my usual five feet and three inches.
I am still a woman in middle age, with large
brown eyes, luminously pale skin, a girlish
nose, and full coral lips. My simple black T-
shirt shows a hint of cleavage and the two
points of my nipples. I am braless in Gaza,
so to speak, because my breasts still stand as

proudly as they did in my youth (if somewhat lower), and they still like to breathe freely.

It seems that I not only have tenure in the university where I've taught English for fifteen years. None of the regulars in this bar ever touches me without my permission.

One of the dykes, who must be uncomfortably warm in her black leather jacket, turns to look at me. She is clearly older than the other two, and a certain bitterness shows in the set of her jaw. "Hey, we were here first." She speaks in a classic bar-dyke monotone.

"As I said," I say calmly.

One of her companions digs her in the ribs, and that seems to make her more determined to grab and hold my attention. I am always amused to notice how much the behavior of an apparent opponent resembles that of a graceless admirer.

"You want to take it outside, Susie Sunshine?" snarls Ms. Willing-to-Die-in-Leather. She undoubtedly cherishes an image of herself as a maverick because she has worn out her welcome in several other watering holes.

"No," I answer. "I see no need for that. I think we should get our drinks, then take them to a table where we can talk without creating a disturbance." I glance at the two younger dykes who look like sidekicks or apprentices. "I'll pay for this round," I tell them. They look at the floor.

"Bernie," mutters one of the sidekicks to their leader. "We don't want any trouble."

Bernie has to choose between ordering a drink or losing face and losing her place in line. She orders a pitcher of draft beer, then jerks her head toward a dark corner. The two sidekicks push their way through the crowd to claim a table and four chairs.

Bernie and her retinue watch me order a gin-and-tonic and make my way to their table. As I pass under a black light, my drink glows as eerily as a witch's potion. I know that the light must be picking up the silver streaks in my long chestnut hair, held back by a tortoiseshell clip.

The heat of Bernie's stare is such that several bystanders follow the line of her gaze. "Doctor Chalkdust, it's good to see you here," says a slim young man with a very expressive face. He is an actor who fell in love with Shakespeare in my class, and he still seems to think of me as the Dark Lady of the Sonnets. He looks at Bernie. "Let me know if you need my help with anything."

"I'll do that, Reginald."

Bernie wastes no time on pleasantries. "You think you can buy anything or anyone, don't you, Miz Professor?" She doesn't wait for a response. "You don't own this fuckin' bar."

"Not completely," I agree. "I only own shares worth a quarter-interest."

The look of distress on the face of one of the sidekicks seems strangely familiar, and then I remember her from one of my first-year classes of last year. She looks from Bernie to me and back again as though trying to decide which of us makes a better role model. I hope she will make a sensible choice.

I break the silence. "Would you like to dance with me, Bernie?"

She stands up without answering. I am pleased to watch her removing her leather jacket. For a moment, I see a look of pained longing on her face, like that of an unwanted child in a large, poor family in an obscure country who has just been told that most Western children are given toys for Christmas.

We walk to the dance floor together and encounter a new dilemma: one song just ended and the next one is slow, requiring physical contact. Neither of us wants to give up and leave the public arena.

Bernie is at least four inches taller than I and solidly built, but she moves with surprising grace. She gently holds me by the waist and shoulder, and we begin moving together. She has such a sense of rhythm and a courtly manner that I let her lead.

The bra under her shirt feels like armor, and my nipples harden like bullets from the constant contact. I can smell Bernie's tangy sweat mixing with some cologne which is marketed to young men who want to score with chicks. I note the subtle heat that comes from the crotch of her jeans, and her refusal to simply push herself into me. Our movements are slow enough to allow for conversation.

"You feel good," she snickers into my hair. "I know your type, honey. You like to go slumming with dykes because we're the only ones who can get you off. Then you go back to your safe middle-class neighborhood and pretend you don't know us if you see us on the street."

She doesn't miss a beat, and neither do I. "Bernie," I coo back. "You still don't even know my first name. And you won't unless you learn a few other things first." The song ends, and I pull her by the hand to a relatively private corner.

"Were you planning to invite me to go somewhere with you?" I am still grinning.

"My truck's in the parking lot, babe," she grins back. "It's really comfortable. Some of the whores who work the truck stops don't mind going with women like me, and they like what I do for them. I bet you wouldn't give them the time of day, but a bitch in heat is a bitch in heat." She pinches one of my nipples, running her other hand down my back.

I laugh and step out of her reach. "Ah. No one could dispute it. But there's a question of trust here, Bernie. I'm sure your paid companions never exaggerate your value to them because they need your money. And I do enjoy your company, although you really don't seem to know why. Unfortunately, I'm not tempted by your hospitality. Your rudeness is neither sexy nor admirable, and it makes you seem untrustworthy, not a quality you want to flaunt if you're trying to pick up a bitch like me."

I sigh. "I'm not going to leave this building with you. But there is a room upstairs where we can be alone. After we take our leave of your friends and mine, of course. Would you like me to give you a tour of the place?"

Bernie tries so hard to affect boredom that she is amusing to watch. "Sure, why not? It's a bar, babe, not the fuckin' museum, but if you want me to go upstairs with you, let's go."

I slide an arm around her waist to guide her back to the table where her two dykes-in-training have been joined by Reginald and the director to whom he is currently loyal. All are watching us with interest.

"Bernie agreed to let me give her a private tour of the premises. She hasn't seen the upper floor yet, and she's something of a bar connoisseur." I imagine her literally seeing the floor from a prone position. "I hope you won't feel bereft if I take her away from you for some time. We'll return in due course."

Bernie's two sidekicks look confused for a moment, then one gallantly pipes up. "Oh, we're okay, Doctor Chalkdust. Take as much time as you need. We'll keep each other company." Reginald seems to be smiling from ear to ear, and his date or patron archly raises one eyebrow at me. I wonder how long it took him to perfect this expression in front of a mirror.

The whole bar feels as drenched in lust as the worn carpet is drenched in beer and the ashes of cigarettes which are now excitingly illegal if smoked indoors. For the sake of her self-image as a gift for bitches in heat, Bernie seems determined to regain some control of the situation. She probably imagines my cunt as a lonely pit of yearning for her psychic dick or something more tangible. I am almost moved to compassion when I think about the surprises in store for her.

We are at the foot of the creaky wooden stairs that lead to the dimly lit second floor, the setting of many titillating rumors. "Go ahead, honey," Bernie tells me, seizing both my lower cheeks and giving them a slight push.

"Of course," I tell her over my shoulder. "I have surer footing on these stairs." I exaggerate the sway of my hips as I climb the steps ahead of her, giving her the show she obviously wants.

I unlock the door of a large room with soundproofed walls. I have abandoned the pretense that I am going to show her every corner of this venerable building, which is allegedly haunted by an older generation of deceased gay men and a few legendary dykes who were the founding parents of the organized queer community in this town. I'm sure that Bernie's vibes would offend some of the spirits here.

Peace, I tell the ancestors in my mind, suspecting that they can hear my thoughts. *Respect can be learned.*

The room is only lit by the lights from outside. Bernie grabs me in a crude bear hug, reaching for my mouth with hers, while I struggle to squirm out of her grip so that I can turn on the lights. "Light," I tell her, hoping that a one-word command will penetrate the mental static of her rising hunger.

"We don't need it, honey." She holds me to her armored chest. She tries to grab one of my asscheeks with one hand while holding me with the other, and this weakens her hold on me enough to enable me to raise one foot, clad in a narrow-heeled shoe, and stomp her toes through her thread-bare running shoe.

"Aw, shit!" she gasps. "That hurt, bitch. You really wanta play rough?"

I turn on the wall-lights, a stately set of Victorian sconces holding yellow lightbulbs. "Bernie, would you like me to fetch the bouncer up here? If I do, our little tryst will be over."

"Well, don't step on me with your stupid heels anymore."

I decide to grant her that; after all, my heels have a steel core which can punch holes in hardwood when I'm not minding my step. And there are so many other simple but effective devices that I can use to make an impression on her.

"I'll show you something, Bernie. Before we do anything else, I want you to see the view from the window. There's something out there that you can only see from close up."

In front of the window is a large oak desk. The chair that matches it has been pushed to the side. She walks uncertainly up to the desk, apparently not noticing the padded cuffs that are permanently attached to the back of it. Or else she assumes they are not meant for her.

"You can lean right over the desk," I encourage her, "then look down." I am cheered by her obedience as I enjoy the sight of her fleshy butt in tight denim, projecting toward me as she almost lies on the desk, peering into the darkness. I quickly grab her right wrist and fasten a cuff around it before she can pull it away.

"Oh, ha-ha," she sneers. "You want to tie me down and make me yours?"

"Yes." I am pleased by her understanding. "I'll release you if you want, but in that case, we'll be returning downstairs and you won't get any relief. Unless you get it from someone else."

Bernie tugs at the cuff and seems shaken when it doesn't budge. In her current position, she can't get a firm foothold on the floor. I can see her awareness of her vulnerability gradually spreading through her mind like the light of dawn chasing away the darkness. To be safe, I stand well away from her feet.

"Uh, you're not really into this bondage stuff are you, Professor?" She racks her brain for a way to persuade me to let her go. "This is kinda stupid when you think about it. What do you think I can do for ya if I'm stuck here?"

"Quite a bit, my dear. I'm waiting for your answer. Are you willing to take what I'm more than willing to give you, or would you like to call it off?"

"Jesus fuck," she grunts, squirming against the edge of the desk in a way that clearly heats up the center seam of her jeans. "I hope you didn't think I was treating you like a—I mean, I don't mean any harm, Doctor Chalkdust."

"You were unforgivably rude," I explain. "The strength of a butch can be a fine quality, but your crude imitation wouldn't attract a woman who has been stranded on a desert island for twenty years. I'd like to give you some polishing if you'll let me."

And then Bernie moans in a way I have come to recognize. The sound seems to come from deep in her cunt as she shamelessly rubs her sweaty, restricted breasts and her itchy crotch against the desk, realizing that she has nothing left to lose. "Oh, honey," she begs. "I mean Mistress, whatever you want me to call you. I guess I've been asking for it, but I don't have much experience as a slave or whatever. No experience, really. I hope—um, are you planning to hurt me?"

I stand close to her and run a leisurely hand down her back, feeling her shiver. Then I reach under her to unbutton her shirt as she respectfully cooperates by raising herself as much as possible. "That depends on how you define 'hurt.'"

She is subtly trembling all over under my hands, and the feeling is delicious. I wordlessly coax her to pull her free arm out of its sleeve, and I gather up her shirt near her cuffed wrist. I unhook her sports bra, tug it off her full, hanging breasts, and push her down so that they are mashed against the cool, grainy surface of shellacked oak. I see sweat shimmering on her back.

"Give me your left wrist, baby." She does, although she knows what I'm planning to do. I secure it with a cuff, and now she is evenly pulled over the desk, her eyes facing the night sky and the lights from the apartment building adjoining the bar. "You can be seen from Elmview Terrace," I tell her, working my fingers under the low waist of her jeans. I reach the crack of her ass. "Some of the inhabitants are very interested in this place. I've seen them watching this window with binoculars."

"Oh, man," she groans under her breath. Beneath her bravado, I realize, this woman is shockingly innocent. What she really thinks of as her knowledge of the world is partial knowledge of a small corner of it.

Beneath her jeans, Bernie wears sensible panties. I manage to pull everything down over asscheeks which look appealingly pale, like paper waiting to be written on. I can feel her tense muscles under a layer of fat. My own cunt feels hot and moist.

I've left her legs free so that I can pull her clothing completely off them. I let her watch me, head turned, as I wad up her musky-smelling pants and underwear and throw them into a corner as though aiming for a wastebasket. I can see from her red face that my implied value judgment does not escape her.

"Hold still," I tell her. She tries to lower both her heels to the floor, but they don't quite reach. "Don't worry," I assure her, removing her shoes and (phew!) pungent socks and sending them to join her clothes. "Your feet will be secured, but these cuffs are different from the ones on the desk." I guide one of her ankles toward a hinged cuff, handmade from a tin can, which is connected by a chain to a bolt in the floor. Like the resourceful dyke who made them, the ankle-cuffs show creativity with a lack of finesse.

These cuffs are spaced far enough apart to keep a victim spread open slightly beyond her comfort level. Once both of Bernie's ankles are held fast by the tin-can bands with a little lock on each, I explain what she can't see. "You look delectable, Bernie." I imagine her ass growing as flushed as her face, as it soon will. "Try not to move your feet at all because those cuffs have sharp edges. You could get cut if you struggle."

She moans as though she can hardly believe how easy it is to sink into bottom space. I reach between her legs to check her soft cunt-folds, and find that she is already wetting the desk. Her clit is probably as large as it ever gets. "Good," I tell her. "Your attitude seems much improved already."

She twitches almost imperceptibly as I stroll to the small fridge, open it, and remove the long plug of ginger that I peeled yesterday, hoping I would get a chance to use it. It feels cool, damp, and slippery, even on the broader end that is designed as a handle.

She tenses immediately when I gently spread open her anus and push the plug into her, inch by inch. At first, I can sense her relief that the thing feels cool and harmless. As the heat of her body warms up the plug and brings out the natural qualities of ginger, she gasps. "It burns."

"So it does," I agree. "It's ginger, a very old remedy for listless horses and naughty schoolchildren in an era of corporal punishment. Let it focus your attention, Bernie." I let her consider her dilemma for a few minutes as she squirms, trying to find a comfortable position.

I walk to the closet, open it, and find what I'm looking for. I bring back a variety of implements, which I handle casually, just at the edge of her field of vision.

"Bernie," I muse. "Is that short for Bernadette?"

"Yep. When are you going to take that thing out of my ass?"

"In a while," I assure her. "It needs to do its work. Ginger is wonderfully effective in curing arrogance. Bernadette, you seem to have been named for a saint. Did you attend separate school?"

"Yeah," she groans. "Damn nuns on my case all the time."

"And now I'm on your case." I put a smile into my voice. "I'm not a Catholic, but I'm not much different from them. Teaching is a sacred calling in itself, and I'm honored to serve the Goddess after whom I was named. You wouldn't have the right to call me by my first name, of course, even if you knew it."

I walk to the side of the desk, and dangle a flogger before her eyes. "And now to the business at hand. Your ass needs some attention on the outside too. I always let my students make choices, so you can choose the thing I'm going to use on you. This is a flogger." I lay it on the desk beside her. "This is a rattan cane, and it carries more of a sting." I lay it beside the flogger. "This is a paddle. The wood is nicely finished, don't you think? It could make your bottom glow all over." I put it down beside the other things.

I can see tears in Bernie's eyes as she turns her head away. Her wimpiness disappoints me.

I stroke her hair, which is softer than it looks. "Bernie, you've been punished before, haven't you? Not by your choice."

"Shit," she mutters. "Damn drunks in my family. And the nuns. They all thought I was guilty of everything unless I could prove I wasn't."

I run my fingernails lightly over her pale, freckled back. "I believe in your innocence, Bernadette. Really. And I'm not willing to punish you for anything you haven't done. I'll give you a safeword. If you really can't stand what I'm doing, you can say "purple" and I'll stop. Now I know you're tempted to safeword the plug out of your restless butt, but you'd be letting yourself down. You have courage, don't you?"

I am pleased to see that she isn't willing to brag. "I'm no jam-tart," she says as modestly as possible.

"That's what I thought. You can stand a certain amount of pain, especially when it's for a good cause. There is a grammar of physical experience just as there is a grammar of language, Bernie. Giving and accepting the right sensation at the right time is as fine an art as the effective placement of a modifier beside the word it serves. There are connections among all things. If you take your discipline well, you'll love the reward. Now choose."

"Paddle." She avoids my eyes.

"It's the devil you know, isn't it? Wise choice."

I stand behind her, practicing my swing as I study her inviting ass. *Whack!* She jerks.

"Aw!" she yelps. "My ankle."

"If you've cut yourself, I'll clean it later. Meanwhile, be careful. We're not finished." *Whack!* I love the sound of solid wood connecting with less-solid flesh. *Whack!*

I watch her striving mightily to lie still as each impact sends echoes through her flesh and jiggles the ginger against her delicate membranes. *Whack!*

"Oh!" The diphthong has a beautifully rich sound, suggesting shock, surprise, discovery, shame, surrender, and deep pleasure all at once. She reminds me of Archimedes exclaiming "Eureka!"

I speed up. *Whack! Whack!* Her bottom is red all over, as I promised. She still hasn't used her safeword. "Can you take two more, Bernie?"

"Yeah. For you, Doctor Chalkdust." She wants me to know that she is capable of chivalrous sacrifice. She wants herself to know that she is capable of responding with dignity to pain and humiliation. I feel inspired.

I focus more energy on the next swing, which connects solidly with her butt. Her cheeks are still quivering as I give her the last one. "Aw-oh-ooh!" That sound again.

"Good girl," I tell her. "I might gag you in the future, but this time, I like to hear you." I pull the plug out of her anus with teasing slowness and throw it onto her clothes.

I can easily fit three of my slim fingers into her gaping, overflowing cunt. I know that a few strokes would send her crashing into an orgasm almost strong enough to knock her out, but I want to prolong the suspense for both of us.

"Now you get a reward, honey," I tell her. "Gentle fingering to get you off, or a hard, deep fuck with a strap-on. Which would you prefer?"

"Oh," she moans as though my words alone have brought her close to the edge. "Please, please fuck me, Doctor Chalkdust."

I am quite heated myself, and my clothes feel excessive. I pull off my T-shirt in one motion, fold it neatly, and lay it on the oak chair. I quickly pull down my burgundy raw-silk pants and my black satin panties, and lay them atop the shirt. My shoes have a place beneath the chair, and I stand on the Persian area rug for a moment, enjoying the sensations of fiber under my feet and air on my skin.

I let Bernie stew in her own juice as I replace the flogger, the cane, and the paddle in the closet, where I gird my loins with the leather harness that holds my prized smoked-glass dildo. I will need to stand on a stool, so I pick up the one that waits in a corner of the room, and set it down between Bernie's spread legs.

The sight and the heat of Bernie's red buttcheeks are directly below me as I guide my hard, cool instrument deeply into her eager cunt. I reach under her to find and torment her swollen clit with cruel squeezes, pinches, and pulls. She almost screams with each thrust of my hips.

I coordinate my breathing with my rhythm. When I know I have enough air in my lungs for speech, I query her. "Will you ever make assumptions"—thrust—"about women you've just met"—thrust—"again, Bernie?"

"No-ohh!" She doesn't try to modify her answer. She is coming uncontrollably. I'm not far behind her in any sense, but I need more direct stimulation.

She has limited ability to control her movements, and I am afraid that all the cuffs will damage her more than I intended. I withdraw from her and undo the wrist-cuffs. I step down from the stool and watch as she cautiously raises her head and back, stretching like a cat as she lowers her arms.

I notice that standing bondage has its own esthetic appeal as she stands upright, legs still spread. "Hold still," I tell her as I kneel behind her to insert a little key into each little lock and open each ankle-cuff. She no longer seems to be feeling the sting from the cut on her ankle, so I decide to treat it with antiseptic and a Band-Aid once my own needs have been met.

"You're free," I point out.

This moment always gives me a certain frisson. Like most of the others, she is still bigger and stronger than I am, and far from being a committed and disciplined student. I know very well that her transformation has only begun. "Would you like to taste me, Bernie?"

She faces me with an amazed grin and reaches forward with outstretched arms as though to lift me off the floor. She stops short of touching me. "If you'd like me to, Mistress Doctor Chalkdust. You're so beautiful." She closes her eyes, apparently expecting me to kiss her. "Taste" to her seems to mean a French kiss.

"We can kiss as much as you like, honey," I tell her, "but first I need your hot tongue on my clit and as far inside me as you can reach. Fingers would be welcome too." I pull the stool away from the desk, sit on it, pull the clip from my hair and shake it over my shoulders. Then I spread my legs.

Bernie kneels before me, carefully keeping her butt away from her heels. She presses her mouth to my cunt as though my nectar actually had the power to heal her. I steady myself with my hands on her shoulders.

She is clearly a dyke who takes pride in her work. She daringly grazes my clit with her teeth as her tongue slides along my wet folds to find my dark, hidden core. She reaches in with one finger, then two, as she patiently rubs various spots on my inner walls to find the most sensitive place. This is one area of skill in which she definitely has experience.

She finds the right spot and presses her advantage. "Ah! Baby, that's—it," I moan, spasming against her mouth. As I hoped, she keeps going until my orgasm dwindles to a last little squeeze.

She grins proudly up at me, slowly licking her wet lips. "D'you like what I do, honey, Professor?"

"What's my name?"

"Doctor Chalkdust, Ma'am. Sorry about that. Sometimes I get carried away."

I can't help laughing. "So do we all, Bernie. It's all right this time, but make an effort to remember correct forms of address." I ruffle her hair. "You gave an outstanding performance," I assure her. "You have great potential. Did you know that?"

I am moved to see tears in her eyes. "No, Doctor Chalkdust. I didn't really know that."

I move the stool aside so that we can lie in each other's arms on the patterned carpet, momentarily feeling as innocent as children or puppies. Now it's time to kiss, hug, and tickle each other in gratitude and relief. As I expected, she loves playing with my long hair and hardening my nipples with her talented mouth.

"I hope your friends will forgive us," I tease her.

"I don't care," she swears with the fervency of her kind. "I don't care. Doctor Chalkdust, I'm so glad I met you."

"I'm glad too," I laugh, "you uncouth lump." I am grateful to Athena, Goddess of knowledge, for continually sending me what I need as She sends me the ones who need me. My life feels like an endless work-in-progress in which all the modifiers turn out to be perfectly placed.

VELVET

Lisabet Sarai

I must really be horny, to be sitting here fanta-
sizing about the keynote speaker. I squirm in
my chair and worry that I'm making a damp
spot. The geek next to me appears to be equally
captivated by the woman at the podium; there's
a big bulge in his lap. I wonder if he's catching
my telltale scent. Marta Hauser, founder and
CEO of VideoPlayHaus.com, takes control of
the stage. I can't take my eyes off her. She's the
only woman on the SoftCon opening panel,
addressing the ostensibly earthshaking topic:
"The New Net: Convergence or Confusion?"

In contrast to the casual beige of her fellow
Silicon Valley visionaries, Marta wears an emerald green pantsuit of rich velvet that molds
perfectly to her body. The businesslike cut only
makes her curves more obvious. She takes the

mic and struts around like the star that she is. The velvet gleams in the spotlight that follows her.

Her jet black hair is short, parted along one side with spiky sideburns that accentuate her cheekbones. Her eyes are dark, too. Even from the middle of the auditorium, I can see that her ripe lips are painted crimson. I imagine those lips claiming mine, firm, no nonsense, and then I imagine them lower, smearing my belly with scarlet, marking the insides of my thighs with lipstick brands before fastening on my aching clit. I can feel the soft nap of her trousers caressing my flesh as she parts my thighs with her own.

I'm so horny that it hurts. I consider slinking off to the ladies room, but I don't want to miss an instant of Marta's performance. I try to focus on what's she's saying. I'm sure that it must be intelligent if not enlightening. I keep getting distracted by the *V* of tanned skin above the closure of her jacket.

Finally she concludes, to rowdy applause, and reseats herself as the moderator calls the next speaker. I skim her bio in the program: American mother, German father; degrees from the University of Heidelberg and Stanford; stints at IIP and Oracle before she left to start VideoPlayHaus.com, her phenomenally popular site for collaborative video editing. When VPH went public last year, she became one of the few women among the ranks of Valley millionaires.

Another technology mogul, a pudgy guy in a denim jacket, drones on about ubiquitous computing and the personalization revolution. Marta scans the audience, looking bored. For a moment, I have this bizarre notion that she's staring at me. I hold my breath, my heart slamming against my ribs. I swear that I can see lust in her eyes.

Dream on, girl. What interest would a hotshot like Marta

Hauser have in you? You don't even know if she's into women.

It's just frustration. Since Rhys moved out nearly a month ago, I've been a veritable nun. I've been spending even more time at work than usual, trying to keep my mind occupied, trying not to miss her.

Rhys claimed that she left because she couldn't compete with my job. But that wasn't the real reason for the breakup.

Thinking about those days makes my pussy ache. I close my eyes and see Rhys's bronzed, compact body, her modest breasts with their purple-grape nipples, her bare pubes and downy thighs. It's so easy to picture her bold eyes and crooked smile, her buzz cut and her tattoos.

I told Rhys that my long hair didn't make me any less a lesbian. She'd nod, but then she'd start to give me grief about the traces of makeup I wear to work, or the fact that I occasionally splurge on a manicure.

Then there was the strap-on. I tried to make her understand, but she tended to take the whole thing personally.

I miss Rhys now. If she were to show up with her harness and that pink, veined dildo, I'd very likely spread my legs and beg her to take me.

But she's undoubtedly at work over at the Sisterhood Bookstore on University Avenue, and I'm here at Moscone, flogging my company's products. And it's time to get back to the booth.

Jim looks up from his laptop and grins. "How was the keynote session? Did you get startling new insights into the awesome future of technology?" Venkatesh, who's adjusting the LCD projector, just waves hello.

"Nah, same old, same old." I consider telling them about Marta Hausman; the guys love it when I talk to them about hot women. Somehow, though, that doesn't feel appropriate, especially when we're trying to be professional. "Anything exciting happening here?"

"It's been pretty slow. Probably because of the keynote. After coffee break, it'll pick up." Jim gestures at the fishbowl labeled WIN A FREE THUMBDRIVE FROM FACEQUEST. "All the morning's cards are in there."

I grab a handful of cards and start leafing through them, looking for any likely prospects. As team leader, I'm nominally in charge of the booth. But I hate the business side of my job.

"Tell me about your company. What does FaceQuest do?" The question is soft but clear, carefully articulated, with the faintest hint of an accent. I nearly jump out of my trousers. Scrutinizing the business cards, I hadn't noticed her approach.

She's here, in the flesh, standing in front of me in that outrageous velvet suit and waiting for my answer.

She's not as tall as she seemed onstage. That doesn't diminish her attitude of command. Her nose and chin are perhaps too sharp, but they're offset by the plumpness of her painted lips. She's not smiling at the moment. She's serious, wants to know about our products, is curious to discover whether there's some potential benefit there for her own company.

That's all she is interested in. Whereas I find myself craning to catch a glimpse of her tanned cleavage, desperate to brush my fingers over her velvet-clad forearm.

"Um, good morning, Dr. Hauser." She smiles, pleased to be recognized. I swallow hard and struggle for coherence. It's difficult with pussy juice dripping down the inside of my thigh.

"Um—well—FaceQuest is a startup with a unique solution to the problem of finding people on the Web. We offer an image-search engine, specialized for matching faces in digital

images. Our algorithms are based on the notion of caricature."
Venkatesh, realizing that I'm into my pitch, starts the Power-
Point, and I gesture at the slides projected on the screen at the
back of the booth.

"We can take a target face and reduce it to a simple sketch,
a set of vectors that offers an economical representation of its
essential features while still being recognizable to a human. We
do the same for faces that we find in the search set. Our matching strategy is more effective than the competition's, because
the vector features of the target and search candidate can be
geometrically transformed into the same frame of reference.
We can recognize search candidates in a much wider range of
head positions—as much as forty-five degrees from face-on."

"Interesting. Very interesting." Marta licks her ruby lips. I
swallow hard and work on controlling my breathing. "You
mentioned web-searching. Can this technology be used for biometric ID as well?"

"Definitely. We're actually in the process of discussion with
several government agencies regarding custom biometric applications."

"And what's your role in the company—Loretta?" When
she leans forward to read my badge, I catch a faint hint of her
perfume. It's sharp rather than sweet, and reminds me of new-
mown grass.

I hardly recognize that name. Everyone calls me Lori.

"I'm the leader of the development team." I pull myself up
to my full five-foot-three inches. "I designed many of the algorithms, as well as handling a lot of the coding. My senior
thesis at Berkeley involved computer graphics and image pro-
cessing."

"Oh?" She gives me a frank once-over. Like Jim and Venk,

I'm wearing a yellow polo with the company logo and navy linen pants. I suddenly wish I were more glamorous. "We should talk some more. Come on."

Marta beckons me to follow her over to the exhibitor lounge area. I watch her thighs flex under the emerald nap as she sits down across from me. I hope that I'm not salivating.

"How would you like a job?"

"I have a job, Dr. Hausman."

"I mean a real job, one where you get the recognition that you deserve." She licks her lips again. "I could use a bright young woman like you."

We're close enough now that I can see the gold studs in her earlobes and her lack of a wedding ring. Her eyes are so dark, they're practically black. She holds my gaze, challenging me to accept her offer. I have the sudden conviction that this would be the first of many challenges.

I can't take her stare for long. My gaze drops to my lap. I'm horrified to see a darker patch at my crotch. Hastily, I fold my hands over the small area of dampness, praying that she doesn't notice.

Her patrician nostrils flare. Her lips bow into a half-smile. "Loretta, can you honestly tell me that your current company appreciates you?"

I consider the twelve-hour days and the fact that I haven't gotten a raise in two years. I think about the cramped cubicle and the overflowing bookcase I have to share with Jim. I dare to wonder, for a moment, what it would be like to have Marta Hausman as my boss.

"Well, Dr. Hausman, FaceQuest was my first job out of college. I've been with them nearly three years..."

"Exactly, and it's time for you to move on. And drop the

'Doctor,' please. Call me Marta." She's watching my reactions. I can't help noticing how her breasts swell under her tight jacket. I am suddenly certain that she's not wearing a bra. Just the thought makes my pussy spasm with excitement.

"I'd like to consider making you chief architect of our video analysis products group. Your company is focusing on still images; we're trying to tackle the much more difficult problem of searching video clips. You'd have complete technical control, subject only to my review. Your own office. Gym and swimming pool on the company campus. All the coffee and soda that you can drink. Plus, of course, a substantial boost in your salary. What do you think?"

It's all so tempting. She is so tempting. I've always been a visual person and now I can't shut off the scene that's running through my mind. I'm on my knees between Marta's spread thighs. Naked. Unbuttoning the tiny, velvet-covered buttons that hold her jacket shut, one by one...

"Loretta?" I force my wandering mind back to the present moment.

"Sorry, Dr. Hauser—I mean, Marta. I have to get back to our booth."

"Think about my offer. Will you?" Her hand is on my bare arm; her skin is oddly cool, or perhaps I have a fever.

Her cell phone beeps. She whips it out and consults the screen, then turns back to me. "I've got a meeting now. But let's get together after the show and talk some more. I'll pick you up outside the convention center at five-thirty."

"Um..." She strides away into the crowd without waiting for my agreement. I rejoin my curious teammates back in the booth, slightly dazed, knowing that it's going to be a very long afternoon.

The exhibits close at five. I spend the next twenty-five minutes in the restroom, touching up my makeup, brushing my teeth, rebraiding my hair, and trying to make my pants more presentable using the hand dryer. Rhys would be so annoyed with me.

I consider bringing myself off. Maybe that would help me to stay rational and in control, to make an objective decision about my future. I don't, though. I have this weird notion that Marta wouldn't want me to.

When Marta pulls up to the curb in a vintage Eldorado convertible, my surprise almost wipes out my nervousness. I had imagined her driving a fancy pickup, or maybe a hybrid. She laughs when she sees my astonishment. "I like things with a history. Perhaps because I grew up in Europe, where everything is antique." She leans over to unlatch the door for me, and I get a quick but clear look down her neckline. It appears that I was correct in my guess. In an instant, I'm sopping again.

"Hungry?" She peels away while I'm still fumbling with the seat belt.

"No, not really." I sit back and try to relax. The leather upholstery embraces me in fragrant luxury.

"Me neither. Let's just go to my place."

She doesn't really mean that, I tell myself. Not the way I'm thinking.

"To talk some more about the job?"

I can barely hear her laugh above the roar of the huge V8. "Right. To talk." My whole body hums with excitement; the vibrations of the engine just intensify the sensation.

I expect her to get onto 101 and head down the peninsula, but she surprises me once again, weaving through city streets and up and down hills until she turns into the drive of a two-story Victorian in Pacific Heights. The house is beautifully detailed in green and gold. I realize that it more or less matches her suit.

Marta comes around to open the passenger side door and extends her hand to help me out of the monster vehicle. The skin-to-skin contact sends a bolt of electricity up my spine. Her grip is firm and lasts several seconds longer than strictly necessary. I'm so nervous I'm practically shaking.

"Are you all right, Loretta?" She searches my face, sensing my anxiety.

"Please. Everyone calls me Lori."

"I prefer Loretta—much more feminine. It has an aura of the past, the glamour and power of a forties film queen. Don't you agree?"

I don't, but I'm certainly not going to argue with her. I suspect that there aren't too many people willing to disagree with Marta Hauser.

The house is cool and dark and smells of lavender. Twilight filters through lace curtains, showing me rooms furnished in the lavishly ornamented style of Victoria's reign. I marvel that Marta Hauser, queen of high tech, would surround herself with these relics of a long-past era. I feel like Alice, as if I've stepped through a looking glass and I'm now lost in a world of strange marvels.

"Upstairs and left to the end of the hall. I want to show you the Turkish Room."

Marta climbs behind me. I have the distinct impression that she's admiring my butt. I'm wetter than ever, and hope against hope that she can't tell.

Then I realize it doesn't matter. If she didn't want me, I

wouldn't be here, in her elegant retro sanctuary. I don't know if she was serious about the job, or just trying to lure me into her clutches, but right now, I don't care. I swing my hips a bit, taunting her. I hear her intake of breath, and half expect her to slap me across my impudent ass, but for now she doesn't touch me.

The Turkish Room is somebody's lurid harem fantasy come true. The windows are draped in heavy, fringed layers of garnet velvet. Oriental carpets cushion the floor, with striped silk pillows piled in the corners. There's a chaise in one corner, upholstered in gold brocade. A brass filigree lamp hanging from the ceiling sheds rosy light over the scene.

Wonderland, indeed.

"Make yourself comfortable," Marta purrs. "I'll be right back." She disappears through a curtained aperture in the right wall.

I perch on the edge of the chaise, not wanting to stain the covering with my juices. My heart beats wild and fast. My nipples are puckered into aching knots that press painfully against my bra. I start to get nervous again.

I must be insane to be here. Marta is so out of my league. Plus getting it on with a potential future boss, no matter how hot she is, definitely doesn't sound like a good career move.

On the other, I'm always so practical, and where has it gotten me? I'm overworked, lonely, and horny. Maybe I can use a bit of insanity.

It's probably no more than five minutes, but my wait seems endless. I'm startled when Marta finally parts the draperies. One look at her and I know I know I've entered the asylum.

She's a vision of elegance and perversity. In lieu of her suit, she's wearing a man's robe of paisley quilted silk. She's carrying an article that I recognize as a riding crop. And she's smoking a cigar.

The fragrant smoke weaves through the air. I am suddenly light-headed.

"I told you to make yourself comfortable. Do I have to discipline you to get you to obey me?" She gestures at me with the crop. I'm simultaneously terrified and terribly aroused.

"No—no, Ma'am."

"Get those clothes off, then. Now."

I strip as quickly as I can, acutely aware of her dark eyes on me. In thirty seconds or less, my clothes are in a tangled pile on the cushions. I stand naked in front of her, suddenly embarrassed by the dark fuzz on my legs and in my armpits.

Marta inhales, deep and slow, then releases the smoke through pursed scarlet lips. She is silent as she circles my body, judging me. She's achingly close, but she does not touch me. I tremble every time I sense her moving.

She pauses behind my back, and brushes the riding crop lightly over my buttocks. I freeze. Will she beat me, mark me, make me hers? I brace for the pain, fearful yet strangely eager for the new sensation. Instead she places the crop where I can see it on the lounge.

"Not today, little one; not this time. Not as long as you are a good girl." I feel her heat, smell her musk mixed with the fruity cigar scent. My legs are rubbery, unstable. She massages my buttocks, molding them in her palms. All at once I feel her finger sliding from behind into my soaking cunt. I clench my muscles around the slender digit, trying to keep her inside me, but she slips free and holds her finger in front of my face. I breathe in my own damp, ripe aroma.

Her voice next to my ear is soft and smooth as velvet. "You

certainly are a wet little girl, Loretta. A deliciously wet little slut." She pulls my plait out of the way and kisses me just below the earlobe. Her lips send shivers racing through me, electric arcs that spark across my nipples and converge on my clit.

I'm dying for more, but she pulls back after that brief caress. Her fingers ghost down to the small of my back, where she pulls off the elastic that secures the braid. "When you're with me, I want your hair loose, free. I want to see it flowing over your shoulders." She arranges it that way as she speaks, then circles back around to evaluate the effect.

"Much better." She flicks a lock away from my breast, almost but not quite touching me. "But I certainly don't want to hide those adorable tits." Seating herself on the chaise, she beckons me to her. My nipples are just at the level of her lips. She warms one with her breath, and it tightens visibly. I want to scream, to beg her to touch me. She's running this show, though. We both know that.

She fastens her mouth on that needy nipple. I close my eyes as pleasure and relief overwhelm me. She sucks steadily. My clit twitches and dances as if her mouth were down there instead. I moan and try to rub my hungry pussy against her robe. She bites down hard on the swollen bud of flesh between her lips.

"Ow!"

"Naughty little slut! Maybe I need to use my crop after all!" Her actions don't match her words, however. I imagine her seizing her instrument of punishment and throwing me over her lap so that she can chastise me. Instead, she sinks to one knee in front of my pussy and opens me with her mouth and fingers.

I've been horny all day. The first broad strokes of her tongue are nearly enough to push me over the edge. Sensing this, she backs off, teasing me with licks and nibbles that build the tension without satisfying me. Her fingers probe my slippery depths, but she is expert in avoiding my clit. I grind myself against her mouth, unable to resist trying to take control. She reacts, once again, by pulling away.

Her cheeks are shiny with my moisture. Her lipstick is smeared. I glance down and see that my bare mons is streaked with crimson, just as I fantasized.

The sight alone almost makes me come. Marta crushes me to her body, kissing me fiercely. I taste my oceany juices and Marta's cigar. Her tongue probes my mouth as her fingers return to my cunt.

I'm close, so close, but she keeps me hanging. We're nearly strangers, yet somehow she has this diabolical knowledge of my body and its limits.

When she releases me, I'm breathless and ready to beg.

"Please...Marta..."

"What is it, Loretta? What do you want?" She pulls herself back to her feet and gives me an arch smile. Of course she knows what I want, what I desperately need. She shrugs off her robe, and I gasp at my first glimpse of her nakedness.

She's tanned all over. Her skin has a golden sheen that cries out to be touched. She's muscular and curvy, the swell of her luscious breasts contrasting with her sculpted biceps and quads.

She's so gorgeous that she's scary. Especially with the jet black dildo that juts out from the harness strapped around her hips.

She gestures toward the chaise. She doesn't need to say a word. Awkward, unable to look away from her, I shuffle backward until I feel the chaise edge against the back of my knees and sink down onto the brocade. The shiny fabric feels smooth and cool against my bare thighs and steaming pussy.

Marta steps closer. I can't help shrinking away from her. Before I know it, I'm on my back, settled in the cushions. She towers over me. The dildo bobs in front of my face. Her eyes drill into my soul.

I know what she wants. I want to satisfy her, to obey her, but I can't make myself do it. She grabs the pseudo-cock and shakes it. "Suck me. Make my cock nice and wet, Loretta. That will make it feel so much better when I push it into you."

"I—I don't—you…"

Her dark brows knit together, in annoyance or in confusion, I can't tell which.

"Don't you want to please me, girl? Don't you want me to pleasure you?"

"Yes, but…I'm a dyke. I like women. I don't like cocks."

"Not even mine? I think I can change your mind." Like lightning she's on me, spreading my thighs with hers, positioning the tip of that enormous phallus at the entrance to my cunt. She grips it in one hand and rubs the polished knob over my clit. The sensation drives away any thoughts of resistance. As my hips buck and jerk helplessly, she thrusts the fingers of her other hand into my soaking folds and swirls them around.

"You don't need any lubrication, girl. You just need to be fucked."

With a practiced thrust of her hips, she embeds the dildo deep in my cunt. The invasion shatters something inside me, some pitiful, silly resistance that I was clinging to. I scream and arch against her, wanting more, wanting whatever she can give me.

She moves like a dancer, sweeping the dildo in and out of me with the same confidence she exuded on the conference stage. First she pumps into my depths. Then she retreats to the fringes of my labia, teasing me with the most delicate strokes. Her breasts bounce deliciously with each thrust. I long to run my tongue over their perfect roundness, to suck on the crinkled nipples until she moans, but I'm helpless, pinned to the chaise by her force. I'm filled, shattered, torn, and tottering on the edge of total ecstasy.

It's nothing like those clumsy, fumbling men. She smells divine, the musk of her own excitement mingling with her foresty perfume. She is completely in charge as her own climax beckons. She slams her cock into me, again and again, as rough as any man could be and yet totally feminine. I'm bewildered and delighted and finally, at last, I stop thinking altogether.

My body is swirling electricity, sparks and waves of energy, a thousand nuances of pleasure. My mind is unfocused, roiling colors and textures, even the lustful images purged away. I open my eyes for an instant and see her amazing face hovering over me, full of joy and triumph. Her gaze locks on mine. Then she throws her head back, grinding her artificial penis into my pussy, overwhelmed, overwhelming me.

After all her force, the climax is intense but not violent. It swells up and spills smoothly through me, exquisite, soft and yet irresistible. Then as the velvet whispers of the first orgasm are fading, I come again, sharp and powerful as a grenade exploding in my cunt.

We lie together for a while, her plastic penis sticky and hard against my thigh. I finally get the chance to fondle her breasts, to lick the tanned hollow at the base of her throat.

All at once she's up again, brisk and businesslike, donning her robe and tossing me a purple silk kimono.

"Go clean up, if you like, then meet me in the roof garden.

Just follow the stairs up one floor." Just like that, and she's gone.

In the bathroom, I wash my face in the pedestal sink and try to run my fingers through my hopelessly tangled hair. The kimono looks odd on me. I'd never pick such a fragile thing, in such an extravagant color. Still, I'm not displeased with the girl looking back at me from the mirror, even if she is to some extent Marta's creation.

Marta is already on the roof when I arrive, seated in a wrought iron loveseat gazing out at the city. I sit beside her, thigh pressed against her warm flesh. She hands me a glass of white wine without asking if I want it. We sit in silence, sipping chilled chardonnay and watching the lights twinkle on the Golden Gate. After a while, she leans over and kisses me, a gentle kiss that is still rich with passion.

"So, what do you think?" We have been quiet so long that her voice startles me.

"About what?" She seems to expect me to understand her, but I don't. "About the job?"

"Well, that too. But I meant, about me. About us."

Us? I had assumed that Marta Hauser was just looking for a bit of entertainment. Some stimulation. But her eyes tell me that she seriously wants an answer.

"Well...you're fabulous. Amazing. I've never met a woman like you. You're—I don't know—outside all the categories. Above them all. You're unique."

"So are you, Loretta. You just need to adjust your perspective. To start making your own rules. I can teach you a lot about that."

She kisses me again, with more force, thrusting her hand underneath the gossamer silk to cup my breast. Amazed at my own bravery, I slip my fingers between her thighs and stroke the soft nap covering her pubis. She shivers with pleasure.

"And what about the job?" I finally get up the courage to ask.

"Well, you're clearly extremely bright. I know you'd make a significant contribution to the company. To be honest, though, I normally have a policy of not hiring my lovers."

Lovers. She is pushing the kimono off my shoulders, kneading my breasts, licking the salt off the sensitive skin at the crook of my armpit, then moving lower, but it's the word that sends the biggest thrill through me. Lovers.

After a while, she lets me catch my breath. "On the other hand," she laughs, "rules were made to be broken."

STUCK AT WORK
AND LATE FOR A DATE

Chelsea G. Summers

The secretary was bent over the desk with her skirt bunched up over her back and her panties pooled by her feet. Her breathing was strained and she tried to look at the wall clock by her left side, praying that her lateness wouldn't be noticed. Her cheap rayon H&M blouse was pushed carelessly up her chest, exposing her breasts, which had been pulled out and over the top of her beige bra.

Binder clips were cruelly pinching her nipples.

"Keep facing forward," she heard from behind her, and then the soft whoosh of the rolling chair's wheels on the industrial carpet. She flinched in blind preparation; she knew something painful was going to happen, but she wasn't sure what.

There was the clank and rustle of something to the right and behind her: the metal cup and rack that held her office tools. She knew the sound well.

The scratch of the open stapler. The bite of the staple remover. The relentless nip of the binder clips. The smack of the ruler. The poke and scrape of the letter opener. The smooth hardness of the RECEIVED stamp in her asshole. She knew them all, knew them well, wore the memory of the perverted use of these quotidian implements on her flesh like shameful, naughty undergarments.

"Lift your ass toward me," said the voice behind her. Not angry, not passionate. Not anything. Its tone could be requesting her to pass the salt.

Swack! She jumped involuntarily when the ruler hit the back of her thigh. A purple stripe of pain illuminated her head for a moment and faded, though her right thigh still rang with the hurt.

"What do you say?" the voice intoned.

"Yes, Sir," she intoned, and felt her face flush a bit pink. She had forgotten the complex linguistic rules. When she heard "ass," she had to respond "Sir." When she heard "pussy," she had to respond "Master." When she heard "whore," she had to respond "Boss." When she heard "slut," she had to respond "Daddy." And when she heard none of these words, she had to keep quiet.

It was hard to remember, sometimes. It was meant to be hard. It was made to trick her and trick her it did. It had been created to make her err, and err she did. She often needed correction.

The secretary lifted her ass, tilted it up and back, just a little bit, for that was all she could move. Her panty hose had been cut from stem to stern; they now hung in tatters around her thighs. Her ankles had been bound to the legs of the desk with packing tape and her long legs spread in a wide *V* on the acrylic desk mat, her hands leaned far forward on the desk's laminate surface. She had been placed so that she could only move a little bit.

She felt the desk's center drawer open against her thighs, a cool sliver of metal. She wished she could turn and press her burning thigh against its smooth, chilly surface. She knew she couldn't, and froze her body, uncomfortably spread and tilted, and felt warm breath on her thigh and the metallic rustle of hands rifling through the drawer's contents.

"You know," the voice said, hot breath on her thigh, "your pussy is very wet."

"Yes, Master," she said, gulping a bit on "Master" as she felt cold air blowing on her slit. The breath continued, a sibilant stream up and down the length of her pussy, its coldness illuminating exactly how excited she was. The blood in her nipples beat a slow tattoo of pain that seemed to pool, collect, and transform to pleasure in her clit.

"Such a dirty little whore." The drawer clanged shut underneath her.

"Yes, Boss," she said, her voice faltering just a tiny bit. She felt something hard pressed against her pudendum, just at the crux of her slit; something hard and cool pressing there, waiting. She didn't recognize it, exactly.

It could be the letter opener, she thought, but then she remembered that she hadn't put it back in the desk after opening the day's mail—she remembered seeing it on the desk's surface as she was getting ready to leave, packing her magazine and her empty lunch containers in her tote bag, preparing to switch into her drive-home sneakers, looking forward to an evening of television and takeout with the boyfriend, a date for which, if her internal clock was at all correct, she was now horribly late.

She felt the metal implement slowly inch its way down her pussy, pressing with an excruciatingly pleasurable precision. Slowly down her slit it moved, down, down, down the center of her cunt, pausing deliciously over her clit, passing it, descending to her cunt's opening, slipping in for a moment, drifting out, sliding with her wetness across her perineum to her asshole, and back up again. Over and over. The gliding smoothness of the unknown instrument told her how wet she was. The secretary could feel her pleasure burgeon and swell; she could almost smell her orgasm.

She knew from experience that orgasm would be delayed, possibly denied, depending on the capricious malice of her Dominator. Almost without her awareness, the secretary arched yet a bit more to meet the touch of the metal, now grown warm with her body heat; she willed it to linger on her clit just a moment more, just a moment, just there, just now.

"You're not going to come," the voice said, low and casual.

She knew that she wouldn't be allowed to come, she knew it with every memory of these little experiences, and yet she had hoped, perhaps, that this time it would be different. They had been meeting like this for several months now. It had started when, as a punishment for the secretary's habitual lateness, she had been summoned into her Boss's office and told that she would be kept late, two minutes for every minute that she had been tardy, and that perhaps this lesson would teach her the meaning and the value of time.

It had begun with her sitting at her desk, not working, just sitting, under the Boss's watchful eye. A week later, she was late again, and again the punishment and again the sitting, this time with the Boss behind her, standing, and this time the Boss made her sit especially upright. When the secretary's head dipped, a ruler rang *thwack!* loudly on the laminate beside her hand.

The next time, she had to stand, bent over on the desk. After serving her twenty-four minutes exactly, she went to the ladies' room to relieve herself; to her surprise, her panties were delicately glossed with her own egg-white wetness, the soft sea pungency of her desire wafting up to her from between her parted thighs.

And so it had progressed, slowly. From sitting to standing, from standing bent over to this same bent position, ever more exposed, ever more open, supplicant and willing, a slow and slippery slope of submission that inexorably led her to this moment, the close of a day when she had been not-quite-but-almost willfully late, and her present position: kowtowing on the desk, nipples exposed and tortured, panties down, hose torn, her pussy drippy wet from the touch of an unknown office tool, and riding the knife's edge between fear and desire for what would happen next.

"Put your face on the desk, and turn your eyes to the window." She did as she was told, feeling the cool laminate under her flushed cheek and seeing that outside the large plate glass windows it was dark and the city was lit up like a starlet's mirror.

"Stay there, slut," said the voice, behind her and farther away, moving perhaps into the office, perhaps down the corridor of the reception area for her Boss and into the open area of the lesser, general office assistants.

"Yes, Daddy," she said.

She heard footsteps approaching her, coming around her side to the front of the desk; she felt a hand slide through her hair, then soft breath on her ear and the whispered words, "So lovely," and the feel of lips on her ear. A hand snaked under her chest, pulling gently on the painful clip and then removing it, first one and then the other.

"Your nipples are sore, aren't they?"

She said nothing.

"You'd like me to kiss them, wouldn't you, whore?"

"Yes, Boss." She gulped. Fingers tenderly rubbed her nipples, and an exquisite mix of pain and relief coursed through them, down her solar plexus and directly into her clit.

"I'm not going to." Her nipples were dropped. Footsteps again, stopping with the Boss behind her. She heard it before she felt it: a swooping cut through the air that ended in a flash of pain on her ass, then a relentlessly gentle tapping of blows covering her behind with the dull brutal kisses. There was the punctuation of a thwaking blow, a pause, and a delicious scrape of the letter opener's blade. The ruler rained down on her ass and thighs, and she could feel them glow and heat, the blows causing her to inhale sharply. And then they stopped.

"Take your hands and spread your asscheeks," she heard.

"Yes, Sir," she said, slightly unsure how to respond and fearing retribution, and she did as she was told, taking her round ass in her manicured fingers and spreading it wide, aware that she was exposing the dusky rose of her anus and both shamed and excited that she was doing so.

"Very nice," she could hear her Boss say and then she heard footsteps that came closer and then stopped, obscuring her view of the window. Before her was her Boss's waist, a belt, an expensive shirt tucked into even more expensive slacks. Broad hands holding a golf club—a driver.

"You can imagine what this is for, whore."

"Yes, Boss."

One hand balanced the club against the desk, directly in front of the secretary's eyes. Another dipped into the slacks' pocket and withdrew a condom. The Boss unwrapped the condom and slid it down over the handle of the club, retrieved a rubber band from the caddy on the desk and rubber-banded the condom in place, picked up the club, and walked back to the rear of the secretary.

The secretary felt frozen. She did not want the club in her. It looked long and menacing. Her mind raced with what the Boss could do to her insides with it. She might be a tall woman, the secretary thought, but she had a rather small pussy. And her ass...she willed herself to keep her asscheeks spread apart with her hands, but she felt herself tense up, nearly to the point of shaking on the table.

A hand smoothed her lower back, rubbing gently over the cleft where her lower back swelled into her butt, tenderly cupping her asscheeks, soothing her flesh as a trainer would a trembling mare. The hand dipped between her thighs, slipped between the wet-slick folds of her labia, and knowingly rubbed her clit for a few moments.

The secretary felt her body start to relax a bit and surrender to the pleasure. The voice behind her was whispering sweet nothings, and while the secretary listened for words that she had to respond to, she heard none, and let them wash over her, causing her to relax.

"I'm going to fuck your pussy with this club."

"Yes, Master," she responded.

"You want me to, don't you, slut?"

The secretary paused. "Yes, Daddy," she admitted as much to her Boss as to herself.

The club entered her pussy, shocking and cold and hard, the Boss's fingers still on her clit. Her face was on the desk, her hands spreading her asscheeks, her weight on her chest, and she had a hard time pressing into the hand, but she pressed nonetheless. Despite the ungainliness of her position—or perhaps because of it—despite the fact that anyone from any office tower could see her illuminated in this position—or perhaps because of it—she felt intense pleasure rush through her, the club so hard that she clenched her pussy muscles around it. Once more, she could nearly smell her cum, her orgasm shimmering before her, a pulsating pleasure cloud, fulsome and ready to release.

The hand stopped, the club withdrew.

"I'm going to fuck your ass now."

"No, Sir," she said, starting up, almost before she realized it. "Please. Don't."

She felt a hand on her head, felt her hair yanked and her neck snapped back. She felt the warm breath of her Boss on her cheek, heard the voice menacing, no longer dispassionate in her ear.

"You will get fucked in your ass," the voice said. "You want it. Tell me you want it, slut."

A pause. The secretary's breath came raggedly. "No," she gasped.

The hand pulled her farther back by her hair, craning her head uncomfortably. Another hand grasped a nipple between a cruel forefinger and thumb and pinched.

"You will get fucked," the voice repeated. "You want it. Tell me you want it, you dirty whore."

Another pause. A lifetime of pauses and the infinite eternal moment that stretches through the barest flicker of time. The sound of two humans breathing ragged and taut, a palpable susurration of battling wills.

Her body slumped slightly. "Yes, Boss," the secretary's voice was small and acquiescent. "I want you to fuck my ass."

She heard herself being called a good girl, she felt herself being pushed into her previous position, she felt her hands being placed onto her ass, her own fingers pressing into her buttcheeks and spreading them.

She felt something cold splatter on her ass. She felt the slow pressure of the golf club handle entering her ass, pushing slowly, inexorably, blindly past her sphincter. She felt it glide in, in, into her ass. She felt the pain.

And then she felt the glimmer of pleasure.

"So beautiful," her Boss said from well behind her, standing, the secretary guessed, far enough away to watch the club penetrate her ass, watch her asshole slowly and, almost against her will, open up for it.

A hand crept between her thighs, slipped onto her clit, and began rubbing. Rubbing and rubbing as the club entered her ass, paused at its apex, and then again as it was almost all the way out of her. The secretary felt the club's flanged tip brush past her G-spot in each movement, the pleasure-laden pain of fullness and the pleasurable near-absence.

She felt herself very close to coming. She had to hold on not to come. The hand on her cunt was rubbing so well and so effectively. She felt her body wanting to drop down down down into orgasm, to collapse upon itself shuddering and inexplicable there on the desk, but she dare not.

"Would you like to come?" The Boss asked, the Boss knew—

the Boss always knew when she wanted to come.

"Yes, Master," she moaned, nearly inarticulate, pleasure-pushed almost preverbal.

"Push down," said the Boss, "push against my finger, push against the club, push down as hard as you can, whore."

"Yes, Boss," she moaned, pushing, willing her pussy to reject the orgasm, to expel it out of her, and as she did, she felt it swell, and grow, this tremendous wall, and swell, like a tsunami, and she gushed, a slick of girl cum spurting out of her, drenching the hand of her Boss, and pooling on the acrylic carpet protector beneath her.

She collapsed on the desk and felt the club being gently removed from her ass. She felt the cool blade of a pair of scissors slicing off her stockings and the packing tape binding her legs to the desk. She felt hands grasping her and pulling her up off the desk, holding her, and she felt her Boss's lips on her own.

"That was a good orgasm, wasn't it?" her Boss asked. The secretary nodded weakly, more vulnerable now than she had been before, splayed and impaled on the desk.

"Very good," the Boss said and kissed her tenderly. "Now get on your knees and thank me properly." The secretary dropped to her knees, pushed the thought of her undoubtedly pissed-off waiting boyfriend out of her mind, unzipped her Boss's pants, pulled them down, her panties too, and happily buried her tongue in her Boss's wet, aching, and swollen pussy.

"Very good," the Boss said. "Very good work...."

BANDANNA KISS

Moxzi Lantana

I was barely out of Evanston, about to ride around Salt Lake City, when the smell and feel of the air changed and dark clouds filled the sky. It's not a great idea to be on a Harley when heat lightning and high winds break loose. I could read the clouds enough to expect hail and heavy rain along with lightning. The rumble of my Harley was a whisper compared to what thundered in the sky.

I put away my sunglasses and zipped my leather jacket, tucking in my red bandanna that kept my neck from sunburning. I squinted to see as far ahead as I could, hoping to spot a rest stop. An air horn sounded as a custom-painted sleeper tractor pulling a flatbed trailer with a wrapped load passed me. I was surprised to see it wore the same charcoal and silver metallic paint and similar black pinstripes with silver leaf in flame designs as my Harley. It had to have been painted by the same artist. I raised my arm to salute only to see a woman driver smiling at me.

She pulled in front of me and over enough to look back at me again in her side mirror. I smiled at her but then saw a tie-down flap loose in the big wind that blew across her rig just before it shoved me a few inches toward the side of the road. A piece of her load looked askew and a tarp flapped loose.

I zoomed up beside her cab, pointed back to the trailer, and signaled for her to pull over. Unfortunately, there wasn't a good place to stop on the interstate.

The truck driver used her cell phone and then looked over to me and pointed ahead. I gave her thumbs-up and slowed to keep an eye on her load from the other lane. Several miles ahead, she pulled over where there was a shoulder barely wide enough. I stopped to help.

It sure was a pleasure to watch her climbing on the trailer. She was tall, about an inch over my five-nine height, and had a somewhat tomboyish muscularity, yet was obviously feminine. Wind whipped her straight dark hair so it flipped and whirled just above her shoulders as she worked.

I felt a strange urge to jump up there and tie her hair with my bandanna but held back. I was surprised to feel I'd want to give in to more urges if I got closer to her. I'm no saint. I've had sex with women in recent years. But I hadn't felt quite like this before.

She shouted down to me, "Have to make it to a truck stop to get the load resettled. Here."

She tossed the end of the tie-down to me and I helped from the ground. I guess it was fair enough, but she sure did her share of looking me over while I got the tie-down reattached and worked the lever to secure the load.

Thunder and lightning startled us both. The storm was closing in fast.

She said, "There's a rest stop a few miles ahead."

I nodded and we both ran for our rides to try and beat the rain.

The rest stop had no covered areas to park under so I parked my Harley close to her rig, between it and another, hoping that would give it some protection against the storm.

By the time I dismounted, the truck driver came jogging around the front of her rig. I was pulling out the cover for my Harley. I guess I had a puzzled expression when she began to unhook my saddlebags.

She laughed and said, "Come on, you and your gear best join me in the cab. The radio says these are killer storms."

Then she paused and gave me a smile so beautiful it was hard to imagine going anywhere but with her. Her eyes were so dark that I couldn't really see the color, only reflections of light. I wanted to volunteer to explore that dark, sure I'd find the treasures of her within those shiny windows to her soul.

She climbed up and put my saddlebags in her cab. I handed my tank bag up to her. More gusts of wind blew in and a few spits of hail came down as I finished securing the cover on my Harley. She shut the door to her cab.

We looked at each other, grinned, and quickly took off running and laughing. We raced to use the restroom and get back to the rig before the storm got too bad.

We almost made it back to the rig before the downpour began. I took off my jacket and put it over her head and shoulders, so she stayed dry above the waist. We ran fast, but I still got soaked all over before we made it into her truck.

The sleeper cab was roomier than I expected, yet made intimate closeness unavoidable. She pulled out beach towels to sit on and bath towels for drying, then put my jacket on a hanger and wiped it dry. I pulled off my boots and socks and leaned over to dry my hair with a towel. When I glanced up, she was just looking at me, and giving me that beautiful smile again.

She said, "There's really no sense in being shy about this, is there?" Then she unzipped her jeans and slipped them off right in front of my hungry face.

I inhaled the scent of rain and womanly warmth, and wanted to totally absorb both. I tried to keep my cool. Sort of. But she grabbed the hems of my jeans and pulled. What was I to do but unzip and let her tug them off me?

She unbuttoned her work shirt and let it slide off, revealing a camisole with lace trim. Then she looked at me expectantly.

What was this, a stripping game? A piece for a piece? Clothing, I mean, pieces of clothing. Well, I did have choices—the killer storms or sweet torture from this confident femme. I unbuttoned and removed my outer shirt. I liked hearing her breath of pleasure when I did.

Since it was her rig we were in, I wanted to be a respectful guest. But being the butch I am, it was time I began to lead this dance. I took off my T-shirt in a way that flexed my muscles, something that never fails to impress.

She licked her lips and drew her index finger over my chest, slowly making the shape of a big *S* and said, "Be my Superwoman."

That did it. My breasts tingled where she'd finished the *S*, and all parts of me ignited with lust. Yeah, I was willing to rescue this lady trucker, all right.

My feather-stroking of both her arms from wrists to shoulders caused thrill bumps. I slipped the thin camisole straps over her shoulders and began slowly peeling down the lace that led to her cleavage. My hands gently grazed her breasts as I revealed them, then teased her midriff.

Her nipples reached for me as I leaned to pull the camisole over her hips and down off her legs. I massaged her feet, then ran my fingers back up her legs to hook her panties. I quickly whisked them off her. She liked the surprise and gave a sweet moan.

Thunder answered her. We both jumped and chuckled. The storm blew so hard, it shook the cab back and forth. The day outside had turned dark as night. Hail replaced the drumming rain with showers of banging and tapping bits of ice. We shrugged, grateful to be inside together.

She surprised me when I bent over to open one of my saddlebags. Suddenly, she gripped both my buns and kneaded my ass. Her fingers teased between my legs while she stripped off my briefs. I tossed some gloves and dams where we could reach them. When I turned back around to face her, I kept something hidden behind my back.

Her eyebrows bounced up and down, and her grin made her eyes shimmer with glee. I laughed and tried not to blush. This woman had more spunk than any I'd met. But that just made me more determined to be her hero.

I thrust my hips forward and rotated them suggestively. She caressed my belly and mound with her open hand. I turned my rear toward her again, so I could insert the shorter end of my FeelDoe into my pussy, leaving the longer end for me to make love to her. I love the freedom of no harness, not to mention getting some extra thrill inside me while I pump my ever-erect purple cock into another woman. Not that I need any added equipment to give a good fucking.

Curiosity got the best of her before I turned back to face her. She tried to look around me, but I teased her by pulling away to hide my surprise for her. She reached around me from the back and discovered my cock. I thought she might lift us both right up through the roof of the sleeper cab.

"Ooh, the dyke of my dreams—and accessories included!"

We both laughed as we tumbled around in gentle wrestling for who would be on top. I won and straddled her legs, but then raised up on my knees. That way, she could sit up and take my cock in her mouth, if she wanted to. She admired it and me, then swirled her tongue around the tip and sucked it into her mouth. Her stroking all over my lower body while she sucked my cock drove me wild. I caressed her too. I swear she grew more beautiful as our trust and intimacy deepened.

I realized we hadn't even kissed, so I eased my cock out of her mouth. We both tried to go slowly, gently kissing at first, intending to gradually make love. Passion took over. We kissed not only with lips, but with our whole bodies.

Like two wild women, we both quickly moved so that I was between her legs, which were bent and close to her chest. I trembled from holding back, trying to not rush things too much for her, but she grabbed my cock with one hand and guided it and pulled me to her with the other.

She pleaded, "Please, take me!"

So I did. I filled her with my cock, quick and deep, the whole thing in one plunge. She glowed like the best of life had just begun as I was fucking her.

The wind and rain drowned outside sounds, but her moaning and squealing filled the cab. She thrilled me to the core. I found myself wishing the storm wouldn't stop. We sure didn't.

Somehow, she caught me off guard and separated me from my cock, which she kept inside her pussy. Next thing, she was on top of me and had taken my bandanna off my neck. She teased that she would tie me up with it if I resisted. What could I do but surrender?

She began hand stroking and lip kissing me all the way from my neck to my clit. Then she squeezed my ass, rubbed my belly, and worked her lips and tongue all over my pussy. She didn't stop but worked more magic with her hands, finding all my favorite spots.

I'm sure not one to admit doing any squealing, but she might tell a different story. I will admit that I wondered whether she often drove through Wyoming and nearby. I considered how frequently I could get away on a ride so we could meet up.

We made love throughout the storms. We didn't stop until her cell phone rang maybe half an hour after the day had turned sunny again. She hung up her phone and looked at the clock. I knew she had to get back on the road, get her load resettled, and try to make up some time. She looked like she wanted to find a way to stay longer.

I did too. But I kissed her softly, hugged her close, then swatted her rear to get us moving. While we were getting dressed to get back on the road, I realized we hadn't even given our names. I wondered if I should just leave it that way. I couldn't be sure how she would want it left between us after such a passionate leap as we'd taken, but I still found her irresistible.

First endings are always a little awkward. I decided to leave my business card tucked between her bed sheet and pillow, hoping she'd find it in the evening and give me a call.

Outside, I uncovered my Harley and loaded my gear while

she checked over her rig. When she stopped beside my Harley, she looked like a dream come true in fresh denim and jersey and my red bandanna.

"My name is Moxzi Lantana," I said as I hugged her one more time.

She whispered, "Kylie," and kissed me on the cheek.

I took a breath but stopped short of asking for her phone number. Did I see her eyes tearing up? I couldn't be sure.

So I only said, "See you on the road sometime, Kylie."

She jogged around the front of her rig and I mounted my Harley. Both our rides rumbled to life about the same time, but I waited and let her leave first. Figured it wouldn't hurt if I followed her until she got to a truck stop that could fix her load.

Less than twenty miles down the road, the signs indicated the exit she would take. I considered stopping, but didn't want to make her feel pressured. I hoped she'd use my phone number after she'd found my card.

We were a half mile from her exit when she waved to me to pull up beside her cab. I did and saw her arm stretched out, holding my red bandanna out the window. She shook it at me, like I should grab it. So I pulled closer and stood up on my Harley and reached. She let go of it as soon as I grabbed for it and blew me a kiss. I caught both.

I stuffed the bandanna in my pocket and waved to her as she turned off the highway. I rode for another hour or so before I stopped for gas and food. The setting sun was hot on my neck, so I reached into my pocket for my bandanna. My cell phone bumped my knuckles and again, I wished I had asked for her number. Her scent on the fabric made me want to taste her and touch her again.

I got back on my Harley and looked at the highway, kind

of hoping to see her rig rolling by. But there was hardly any traffic.

When I stretched out my bandanna to fold it for wearing, I saw something dark on one edge. I held it up in the light.

Written in black laundry marker was, *Kylie Demarest 1-555-142-4673.*

I entered the number in my cell phone and tucked the bandanna back in my pocket. I'd make sure Kylie and I were tucked in together again soon.

FLIPPING THE SCRIPT

D. Alexandria

When Quinn walked through the door that Friday evening, her eyes widened with surprise before my hand forcefully grabbed her by the neck, holding her still as I slammed the door shut. Instinctively, her light brown eyes clouded over with anger from pride, but she remained silently still, her lips pressed into a thin line, nostrils flaring as she breathed heavily, and I knew if she could, she'd throttle me in an instant. But of course she wouldn't.

"Good boy," I said softly, my own eyes filled with amusement over seeing her struggle to act accordingly. And no amount of pride or anger could hide the flash of pleasure that crossed her face at hearing my words.

My free hand quickly went to her pants, unzipping them, and I reached inside, inwardly smiling because she had remembered my request before she left for work that morning and must have strapped on in the car.

"Nice and hard for me, huh?" I said as I pulled her dick out, holding it firmly. I watched her tremble, knowing I was stroking it. I stepped closer, my lips to her ear. "Boys like you are always hard, isn't that so? Always fucking horny like you don't know better."

"No..." she started to say, then she stopped herself, and I knew her heart sank as soon as my head started to shake. Unless she had permission, I never wanted her to speak.

"Knees," I said simply, and like a good boy, she got down.

"Follow me." I walked into the living room, knowing she was crawling behind me. It wasn't what I had planned, but I knew it would give her the chance to take in the view of me since I hadn't instructed her to keep her head down.

Unlike other submissives we've met, I'm not required by Quinn to dress in special costumes for our play. Tonight, I wore a blue satin sleeveless top, calf-length black-and-white pinstripe skirt with a slit up the back to my knees, and black open-toed, three-inch heels. My hair was pulled into a tight twist, and my makeup and jewelry were minimal. This was the look she loved most on me, and how I used to dress before I stopped working when we decided to have a family. She preferred the conservative look and I loved her for it, since I couldn't see myself wearing corsets or those PVC suits.

When I reached the living room, I moved to the sofa and sat down. Quinn crawled around to face me, remaining on her hands and knees. I gave her a stern look before crossing my legs, the top foot hovering a few inches from her face.

"Stand and undress."

I could see her tense as she rose to her feet, but she quickly removed her work shirt and pants, tossing both beside me on the sofa. When she was finished, she stood before me wearing nothing except for her boxers and the strap underneath, the dick still poking through the flap. This was the only clothing I permitted her to wear, since she sometimes couldn't deal with seeing the leather that bound her dick to her.

"Good boy." My eyes met hers, and she looked relieved. "Knees."

She was back down, this time knowing to keep her back straight and her hands clasped behind her. I watched her, relishing in the knowledge that I had her to myself for the next two days, although she didn't know it yet. The kids were at my mother's for the weekend, so I had free rein to torture and enjoy her at my leisure. I reached out and gently caressed her cheek, a move that made her body shudder and she actually dared a smile. But it was quickly gone when I grabbed her hair, snapping her head back so I could look down at her. At the same time my other hand had closed around one breast, pinching her nipple.

"I am in the mood to torture you, boy, and you have no choice but to accept it, because it pleases me." I gently licked my lips. "Do you understand?"

Her face was surprisingly calm as she nodded.

"Smart boy," I leaned forward to press my lips to hers, but stopped about half an inch away. I could feel her breath and knew she could feel mine. We mirrored the deep desire to feel what a kiss would do to us right now, but I was the only one who could attempt it. I parted my lips more; breathing hot air against hers, before I quickly ran my tongue along her bottom lip, then her top, coming full circle. I was about to pull my face away, and she sensed it, pushing her face toward mine, and our lips touched.

Despite the fact that the kiss sent shivers all the way down to my toes, I pulled my face away before my hand shot out and connected with her cheek.

Quinn gasped from shock, but couldn't fully react before my hand was on her neck for the second time that night, squeezing tightly. I could feel myself growing wetter at seeing her struggle to breathe under the pressure.

"Now, we both know you know better than that."

She opened her mouth to speak, but I heard nothing as she cast her eyes downward, remembering I hadn't given her permission.

"Since we both know that you know better, I have to assume that you did that deliberately; blatantly disobeying me. And disobeying me only hurts you, my boy." My other hand was again on her breast, my nails now biting into her nipple. "And it's a shame. I was so looking forward to a sweet torture"—my lips were at her ear, and I whispered softly—"and then letting you fuck the living daylights out of me. But since you want to be a little punk, thinking you can do whatever you want, you lose out tonight, my love."

I let her go, and then leaned back against the sofa, instantly lifting my left leg and planting my foot in the middle of her chest. I still had on my heels and knew the point was biting into her skin, but she remained still.

"You still think you're running things, don't you?" I asked accusingly.

She squared her jaw in response.

"What, you got something to say, little boy?"

Her eyes flared, but she kept her mouth shut.

"C'mon now, baby, we both know the truth, despite what you tell your boys." I pressed my heel in and she winced, gritting her teeth.

"Take it off," I said softly.

She took my foot in her hand, slipping off my shoe, and carefully rested it on the floor. She removed my other shoe, before placing my bare feet back on her chest. This time I pressed harder, forcing her to lean back a few inches. I made her hold that position for a few moments before I lifted my foot to her mouth, brushing the tips of my toes against her lips. I heard the growl of arousal from deep in her chest, and I smirked at her.

"Open wide. Let me see your tongue."

Quinn parted her lips, and as soon as I saw her tongue, I ran my toes across it, making my pussy pulsate from the tickling sensation. I pushed three toes in her mouth and she quickly closed her lips around them, sucking gently.

"Good boy." I pulled my skirt up to my hips, lifting my right leg and spreading wide to reveal my bare pussy. Her eyes were glued to my hands as I lowered them. One hand parted my lips, while the other dipped into my slit, getting my fingers nice and wet. I watched her face as she watched my fingers toy with my throbbing clit. I gasped at first contact and her eyes lifted to mine for a moment, showing slight frustration from not being able to touch me herself. But lust won out because she couldn't keep her eyes off my slit as I masturbated, her tongue expertly teasing the tips of my toes as she continued to suck.

Damn, coming was definitely not going to be hard tonight. I was being rather brazen with my movements, wanting to draw it out as much as possible, tugging on my clit until it was standing upright and practically begging for more attention. But as soon as my fingers touched my hole, there was no way I could ignore it. I was so wet that I was able to slide two fingers inside myself with ease, and the growl in Quinn's chest grew louder.

I was now moaning loudly, the sounds of my wet pussy echoing throughout the room, and I knew full well this was driving her insane. So of course I had to push her a little more, right?

"So, where was I? Oh, right, your punk ass. This could be you right now, if you weren't so disobedient," I told her, having to force my voice to be steady. "I bet you're missing the feel of my pussy tightening on your fingers, huh? You wish you could just tear into me, and pound me like I want you to...."

She closed her eyes for a moment, and I watched her body tremble.

"I don't even know why I deal with your ass," I continued. "All I wanted was a good fucking and look at me, having to fuck my damn self because you can't control your actions—"

I slapped her cheek hard. Quinn's eyes popped open full of raw lust and pleading, but I didn't care. I knew it was getting her off as much as it was tormenting her, and she'd have to handle it for as long as I wanted.

"You keep your eyes open and watch me do what you, for some reason, can't." My voice was threatening and stern and she knew to do as I said.

As she forced her eyes back to watch, I slid my hand behind the pillows beside me, pulling out my favorite, hot-pink, six-inch dildo. I could almost feel the need she had to touch me, as the head of the dildo lowered to my hole. I quickly entered myself with the toy, and couldn't have suppressed the groan that escaped me even if I tried. Quinn is the type of lover who doesn't give you the chance to get used to her dick once she has it in. So I pushed myself and started sliding the dildo in and out of my wet pussy, gaining speed quickly. Quinn's eyes were so wide, her mouth working feverishly on my toes. Since she was a natural voyeur, I knew that as much as she wanted to be fucking me herself, watching me do it was just as fascinating for her.

"You wish this could be your dick pounding me like this, huh?" I asked her as I started to fuck myself harder. I was using so much strength that my arm was starting to ache, but it felt too good for me to stop. "No matter. I'm probably fucking myself better than you could anyway, so maybe it's good that you fucked up the way you did."

Ahh, that pushed a button. Her eyes grew dark but she held her control, and I was rather impressed. I kept fucking myself for a few more minutes, enjoying the sight of Quinn visibly having to restrain herself, before I decided I wanted to give her a true punishment.

I pulled my foot away from her mouth as I slowed my hand, giving myself a few more thrusts, then slowly pulled the dildo out of my pussy. I could see the mild disappointment on her face from having to give up my foot so soon, but also the look of anticipation of what I had planned for next. I kept my face solemn as I looked at the dildo, which was dripping with my juices. I turned it around, placing the butt end at my pussy, and then closed my legs, pressing my thighs together, trapping the dildo. I then looked up at her.

"Suck it."

Her body grew rigid, and the look on her face showed her surprise at my words. Oooh, I'd hit a nerve. This was the perfect way to put her in her place.

"C'mon, boy," I said, my voice gaining strength. "Suck my dick."

There have been times that we've hit obstacles like this. The first time I slapped her, the first time I cuffed her to the bed and she realized she was helpless, or the time I demanded she finger herself in front of me. But this was one act that struck her like no other. This time I was seriously testing her studhood. And for a split second, I wondered if this might be the line and she'd use her safeword.

It was a struggle; I could see it in her eyes, and I instantly knew I had struck gold. I could practically feel the turmoil she was going through at my calling her out on what probably was a desire she had locked away for who knows how long. She had two choices: either claim it and explore it with her wife, or deny something that she was so curious about. I was silently begging her to just claim it, because if I was the one initiating it, she had to know that I felt it was okay, and she and her masculinity were safe.

And just when I thought she was going to use the safeword, and I'd have to go to Plan B, she took a deep breath and moved. I watched her stare at the dildo with caution, before she eventually lowered her head. When she paused a few inches away and I saw her tremble, I placed my hand on her head, pressing her closer. She finally parted her lips, and with grand satisfaction, I watched my dildo start to disappear. I kept the pressure on her head until she had swallowed about half, then held her still, just enjoying the sight of it. I knew this was hard for her on many levels. The idea of sucking a dick period was bruising her ego, plus, damn...I was having her suck a pink dick at that. That alone would offend any stud, regardless of how stone she was. But I also knew that this seemingly taboo act would turn her on like nothing else I'd done.

"That's my boy," I said softly, my breathing ragged from arousal. I raised my hand enough to let her back off, but before the head could escape her mouth, I pushed her back down, just as she would have done to me if the script was flipped. We kept this up a few more times until I was sure she had the rhythm. I relaxed against the sofa, just enjoying the feel of the butt of the dildo grinding into my clit in an almost painful way. Each time she slid her mouth down, I imagined her on my clit and quivered. I started lifting my hips, pushing more of the dildo down her throat. To me, this was amazingly sexy. Never had overpowering her felt so electric, knowing that for my pleasure, she'd go this far. There weren't many femmes who would ever experience this moment, and I was enjoying it to the fullest. I was going for broke now, fucking her mouth at a steady pace, and Quinn was bracing herself by holding on to my thighs. The dildo was sliding in and out of her mouth so fast it was a blur, and watching her cheeks work so hard at sucking was getting to me too much. I was ready to cum.

I sighed loudly as if I was bored, pulling her head off the dildo and then tossing the toy aside. As soon as she straightened herself, my foot was back on her chest, and I forcefully pushed her hard till she fell on her back. My movements were quick, and in a moment I was straddling her stomach, looking down at her.

"So, tell me," I said, bending my head to lick across her lips, tasting my juices. "How does it feel to suck a dick, boy? I bet you liked it. I bet that as soon as it touched your lips, your dick got fucking harder, didn't it. Answer me."

"No..." she began to say, but I silenced her by putting a finger to her lips.

"If you lie to me, you'll be severely punished."

Her eyes were practically begging me, but I didn't care. This was going to be my triumph of the night.

"Say it." My slippery pussy was sliding against her bare skin, and I knew the feeling of it was driving her crazy. All I had to do was move lower for both of us to be happy.

But she was silent, her eyes still staring into mine, and I could see the realization hit her that I wasn't going to give her what we both wanted until she made this sacrifice.

"SAY IT!" I growled.

Her eyes closed. "I...I liked sucking your dick." Her body got flushed, and her nipples looked so painfully hard. The confession was turning her on more than I had hoped.

I smiled, but still didn't move. "Louder."

Only a slight pause this time. "I liked sucking your dick!"

"Oh, that's my boy." I pressed my lips to hers, pushing my tongue into her mouth, and she practically sighed from the reward. I captured her tongue, sucking on it hard, as I reached for her dick, maneuvering my pussy above it. As I sank down on it, we both moaned.

"Is this what you needed?" I panted as I rocked my hips. "You needed your dick in me, huh?"

"Yes!" she gasped.

I sat up, knowing the pressure from the harness would press against her clit. I slowly rotated my hips, and she watched me, eyes dancing. As I rode her, I unbuttoned my blouse, tossing it and my bra aside, and I started to pinch my nipples. She was biting her lips, her hands resting on my thighs, and I decided to allow the contact, because I needed it as much as she did.

I placed one hand on her stomach, getting my balance as I quickened my hips, feeling my orgasm starting its ascent. My other hand disappeared behind me, and I felt inside the leg of her boxers for her pussy, making her gasp.

"You looked so amazing sucking my dick," I told her. "I think I'm gonna enjoy having you do that often."

"Oh, god."

"What, Quinn? You don't like hearing that you're gonna be sucking my dick whenever I want? That your femme got you like that?" I reached to feel her pussy, already soaking wet, and quickly pushed two fingers inside her, and she groaned loudly.

"Oh, shit..."

"You're my boy, you hear me? And as a good little boy, you will always do what I say. And if I want you to suck my dick, you will do so, understand?"

"Yes."

"What will you do?"

She was now thrashing beneath me, her own orgasm threatening to break. "I'll suck your dick whenever you want me to."

"And why?"

Our eyes locked; mine encouraging, hers finally submitting.

"Because I...oh, my god..." Her body started to shake.

"C'mon, Quinn, why? Why do I got it like that?" I gave a hard thrust, forcing her body to move along the carpet.

"Because I'm your boy!"

"God, yes..." I said and fucked her dick harder, the feeling of her wet pussy tightening around my fingers as she came sending me over the edge, and I screamed as I came as well. But I wouldn't let up, sliding up and down on her dick until my body gave out and I collapsed on top of her.

Quinn's arms enveloped me, and I pressed my face into her soft neck, happily breathing in the scent of her sweat mixed with her cologne. After a few moments I was able to talk again, and I asked, "You okay?"

"Yeah," she said, despite the fact she was trembling. But I

felt her lips on my forehead. "Thank you, baby."

I raised my head so I could meet her eyes, seeing complete relaxation there, and it warmed my heart. At moments like these I realized I loved her so fiercely there was nothing I couldn't do for her.

I kissed her lips. "No, little boy, thank *you*."

THE BREAKING POINT

Lucinda L. Flanary

Jill waited silently in anticipation. Her blindfold was doing the job it was intended to do.
She could not see even the slightest evidence of
daylight in her bedroom. Her lack of sight made
her hyperaware of every sound and touch. She
could hear the gentle hum of a vacuum cleaner,
perhaps Mrs. Gardner in the apartment next
door? A gentle breeze and a slight knocking
sound came from the ceiling fan above. She
was thankful for the cool contrast to her warm
perspiring skin.

The unyielding chair beneath her was another
small comfort. There was so much uncertainty
in her current situation, that even something as
seemingly innocuous as the solidity of the chair
that she was tied to gave her some relief. She
licked her lips, suddenly thirsty, but she did not

dare say a word. She was unsure if Kat was in the room and even the smallest sigh escaping her lips could command a slap across the face. Just the thought of Kat's beautiful hand leaving its imprint on her face gave her a new burst of wetness between her parted thighs. But this was a game, and Jill was determined to win at all costs and any sign of weakness was a loss in her book.

A small bead of sweat was making its way down her forehead to disappear beneath the blindfold. She could feel its sister droplets sliding down between her breasts. Her heightened sensitivity made her aware of everything, including the footsteps approaching down the hall. She did not need her eyes to picture Kat wearing the long, black vinyl boots that had the studded turned-down cuff midthigh. That image was burned in her brain like a brand burned on cattle. The sound of those heels clicking was music to her ears. The footsteps stopped in front of her and she felt Kat's presence. It was as if someone had put a wall of heat between Jill and the moderate breeze of the fan.

She felt a gloved finger trace her lips and blaze a trail through the perspiration from her chin, down her neck, between her breasts, across her stomach, and straight down to the crotch of her panties. The finger pressed the damp material between her swollen lips and rubbed it around to create some friction. *Oh, god! Don't moan, whatever you do, don't moan!* Jill thought.

She stifled her sigh of pleasure somewhere in the back of her throat. The glove traced the leg band of her panties, then slipped beneath the fabric. Jill shuddered as the leather found all of the evidence it needed to prove that she was enjoying this sweet torture. A finger slowly slid into her pussy. In and out it moved, and Jill knew that Kat was delighting in watching her try to keep her hips from thrusting to the rhythm of this welcome intruder.

Kat bent down to kiss and lick Jill's lips, her other hand placed gently but firmly around Jill's neck, forcing her head back. Kat could feel her deep swallows as she tried so hard to retain that ever so important sense of control. But how much control could Jill have, bound with her arms at her sides and her legs spread? The reaffirming of Jill's vulnerability gave Kat a power surge that made her even more determined to break the other woman. Jill was hard to crack, but not impossible. Theirs was a slow dance, and tonight, Kat was determined to lead.

She removed her hand from its home between Jill's legs. Kat straddled her defenseless partner and sat on her thighs facing her. She ran her hand along the back of the chair, creating a slight vibration that sent a chill down Jill's spine. Her fingers slithered through the long, brown hair and yanked Jill's head back, making her scalp ache. A wet and salty pair of leather-clad fingers forced their way into her mouth. "Suck it like it was my fucking cock, you little cunt!" Kat hissed through clenched teeth.

Jill obeyed, trying to lick and suckle at the fingers that she knew were covered in her own wetness. Kat shoved the fingers in and out of her mouth more violently, almost gagging her. Jill hurried her pace trying to keep up with Kat's thrusts. "Yeah," Kat cooed, "now, that's what I like to see...my little princess responding to *my* needs. That's it, baby girl, you lick those fingers clean after they've been in your little pussy."

Jill imagined the smirk on Kat's face as she looked down upon this tied-up girl with no choice but to give head to her captor. Finally, the hand pulled away from her violated mouth and her hair was released from the tight grasp. Jill's head was tingling from the blood rushing back into her scalp.

She was distracted by the slight pain and had not realized

that Kat had walked away until she heard the sound of something being dragged across the room. Furniture maybe? She didn't have to wonder long as she heard Kat climbing onto something beside her, and felt Kat put her hands on her shoulders as she steadied herself. Her imagination was going into overdrive trying to figure out what Kat was about to do to her. A mental picture began to form, as she smelled the familiar scent of Kat's pussy hovering only inches above her face. Yes, Kat had moved something on either side of the chair and was now standing above her with her legs spread and her crotch poised for Jill's tongue to please.

"Put your fucking tongue out here, princess, I got a surprise for you."

Jill followed Kat's instructions, sticking her tongue out as far as she could to receive the shaven sex of her tormentor. Kat's juices flowed freely over her face and slid down her tongue. She lapped feverishly at the hard little pearl buried deep in the folds of Kat's pussy. She felt those gloved fingers part their owner's lips, so that she could gain better access. Kat began to breathe more heavily and a couple of low moans escaped and created a melodic call for Jill to go harder and faster. Kat began to ride her face, bucking and calling out obscenities, riding her tongue and pumping up and down and back and forth.

"Oh, shit, yeah, baby…. Ahhhhh, that's it you bitch, eat that pussy…make me cum all over your face…fuck, yeah, FUUUUUCK!!"

Kat's legs trembled and she had to brace herself by squeezing her thighs around Jill's head. She climbed down and composed herself for a moment before slapping Jill's face. "You are such a dirty girl," she teased. "Good, wholesome, clean girls do not eat pussy like that! No, they lick gently and delicately and take their time. But you, you ate like a greedy little whore! You enjoyed licking me and making me cum in your filthy mouth, didn't you?" Kat slapped Jill again, this time across the other cheek. Then she grabbed the crotch of Jill's panties in her fist and pulled them down to her knees. "Oh, and big surprise! You got your panties soaking wet with cum! Did you cum when you ate my pussy? Did having your soft, pink tongue in my twat make you cream yourself?" She slapped Jill's mound with her hand then pinched her nether lips. Jill bit down hard on her bottom lip, but refused to give Kat the satisfaction of crying out. "Well, I have a little cleansing ritual for dirty girls...."

Kat left the room and Jill's mind began to race. "Cleansing ritual"? What could that mean? A bath? Washing her mouth out with soap? The first seemed too easy and the latter too harsh, so Jill sat uneasily for what seemed like an hour, just squirming in her chair, awaiting Kat's return.

Finally Kat was back, and she busied herself untying the nylon cording that held Jill in the chair. "Get up!" she barked, and Jill stood up. Before she could even enjoy her moment of freedom, Kat had swept her hands behind her back and bound them once again. Jill entertained the idea of using the safeword out of fear of the unknown, but quickly dismissed it. She knew that Kat would never hurt her and the most likely outcome of this new game would be her own orgasm. And besides, so far she was winning.

Kat led her down the hallway and into the bathroom. Jill could hear the jets running on their whirlpool tub and deduced that her "cleansing" would be nothing more than a soothing bath, but she had no idea how wrong she was. Kat positioned her, standing facing the door with the tub to her left. Jill could hear some rustling and movement at the edge of the tub. She felt Kat's still gloved hand reach around beside her and pull her forward, then push her down so that she fell over. She realized that Kat was sitting on the edge of the tub and she now had Jill bent over her lap, panties still around her knees and her upturned ass exposed. Jill was still okay with this; she thought that she could keep her composure through a spanking as long as it was just Kat's hand being used against her backside. She braced herself for the first blow, but it never came; instead she felt her asscheeks being roughly spread apart and Kat's gloved finger putting a sticky gel around her asshole and then inside. Jill broke out into fresh beads of perspiration. Kat noticed her trembling and tightened her hold on her ass.

"It's all right," she soothed, "this won't hurt a bit, but it will teach you a lesson. Good girls...clean girls, are humble girls. They are not greedy and selfish." Kat continued to work her lubed finger in and out of Jill's puckered anus. She reached over and clicked open the cockstop on the enema bag. Jill's buttocks clenched at the unfamiliar sound. If nothing else, Kat knew that she had the element of surprise in her favor. She drained a small stream of the warm water across her wrist to check the temperature and to release any air in the tube. Then she spread Jill's cheeks wide apart and inserted the nozzle slowly. She noted Jill's gasp and was pleased. She squeezed the other woman's cheeks back together tightly around the tube and continued to work it in a little deeper.

Jill had heard the click of the cockstop, but the sound and the following actions did not fully register in her mind until she felt the warm liquid filling her gut. She had to admit that it was not an altogether unpleasant sensation, but still a hot blush rose in her cheeks and she was sure that Kat heard her cry of surprise when she began administering the enema. She felt Kat's hand reach down between her legs and rub her clit. She was an expert at bringing Jill to orgasm. Her skilled hands rubbed in a gentle circular motion. Jill felt the hot tears welling up in her eyes and spilling out under the blindfold and down her cheeks. The warm water was working its way deeply into her, and she could already feel the pressure building, giving her stomach that overfull feeling. The discomfort contrasted with the pleasure rising up from her cunt. It was radiating from her clit and slowly spreading to the rest of her body.

"That's a good girl," she heard Kat whispering above her. "Cum for me, sweetheart. I want you to enjoy this as much as I do." Kat continue to stroke her clit and murmur encouragement about how good she was doing. She knew that Jill had taken almost all of the enema, and she was worried that she would not cum before she had to release the water. Finally, she felt the little tremors of orgasm from her little princess. She noticed that her own thighs were soaked from the intermingling of both of their juices. Kat clicked the cockstop back to stop the flow. She massaged Jill's backside for a few moments before carefully removing the nozzle from her anus.

"Do you feel like you need to go to the toilet, honey?"

Jill silently nodded, and Kat helped her to her feet. Jill turned her back to Kat and waited to be untied as her need to eliminate was becoming more urgent. "Kat, untie me so I can go," she said. She was clenching her sphincter as tight as she could to avoid an accident and was not amused with Kat's little delay.

"No, honey, this is part of the lesson."

"Kat, please don't," Jill began to weep openly as she pleaded for privacy. She finally had no choice but to let Kat assist her to the toilet. She told her to lean slightly forward to help with the elimination. Kat rested Jill's head against her stomach and rubbed her hair as Jill cried during the whole embarrassing ordeal. It took a while and there was some minor cramping, but finally Jill had finished.

"Can you untie me so that...you know, I need to..." Jill could not even finish her request that she be allowed to wipe herself. Her shame had brought on a new round of sobbing. The utter humiliation gave her an arousal that made her sick. It seemed impossible that someone who owned her own business and had put herself through college could not even wipe her own ass...and the worst part was that she was getting off on it!

As Jill sat with her pity and her self-analysis, Kat was getting a warm, soapy washcloth ready. She went back to where Jill sat, stood her up, propping her own foot on the edge of the toilet, and bent Jill over her knee. Then she began to clean Jill's backside. More tears spilled from Jill's obscured eyes as Kat lovingly washed her. Once Jill was cleaned up, Kat untied her and removed the blindfold, revealing a room glowing with candles and a lovely bubble bath waiting just for her. Her red and puffy eyes had been expecting the harsh lighting that normally illuminates their bathroom, but Kat had thought of everything. Now she helped Jill into the tub and bathed her tenderly, shampooing and conditioning her hair, rinsing it with the handheld shower wand.

After her soak, Kat dried her with a fluffy towel and held up a soft, new robe for her to slip into. She led her back to the bedroom and lit some candles as she asked Jill to disrobe and lie down on her stomach on their bed. She did as she was asked and was delighted when Kat picked up a bottle of scented oil and straddled her back. It was an amazingly relaxing massage from neck and shoulders all the way down to her feet. Just as

Jill was about to fall asleep, she felt Kat's warm breath above her upper back. It led to a trail of licking and kissing and nibbling down to her ass. Kat gently parted her cheeks once again and lovingly licked around her recently traumatized anus.

The light flicking of her tongue soon became the thrusting and probing of an appendage that wanted to once again violate this sacred area. Jill raised her bottom up and met each thrust of Kat's hungry mouth, slipping her own hand between her thighs to play with herself. She marveled at how wonderful it felt to have her ass eaten. Her orgasm was long and violent and it left her wanting to share that pleasure with the one who had introduced it to her.

Jill fell forward, pulling away and turning to spring upon Kat. She tackled her and held her down while her hand searched out her wet cunt. Jill thrust two fingers inside Kat and used her thumb to tease and rub her clit. As Kat called out from pleasure, Jill began to whisper her plans of reversing their roles. She told Kat that soon it would be *her* tied and blindfolded and lying across Jill's lap. She told her how she would lube up a probing finger and force it into her tight ass before replacing it with the hard plastic nozzle. She promised her that she would fuck her with the nozzle as the water flowed into her, that it would be like Jill cumming in her ass endlessly. Kat began to shudder with her climax as Jill described the impending scene.

The two lay as one mass of tangled lips and limbs, basking in the aftermath of their newfound mutual pleasure. They were just about to fall asleep when Kat tilted her head toward Jill's ear and whispered, "I won!"

THE CHRISTMAS GIFT

Thea Leticia

I show up at my Daddy's doorstep with a plate of cookies I made just for him. I've stolen a nibble or two but I don't think he'll notice; they're so pretty and sparkly on the striped platter. He lets me in and gives me a hug. I can't help but sigh and give a little happy shudder in my tummy when I see that he is wearing my favoritest leather pants, the ones that are almost too tight and make me feel a little bit dirty. Don't tell.

He thanks me for the cookies after brushing some crumbs off my pretty velvet shirt. "I see they were yummy," he says.

"Mmmm!" I giggle. "Where's my prezzies?"

"I think you got coal."

"Nope. Where's my prezzies?" He laughs that yummy laugh when I stomp my high-heeled foot and hold out my hands for treats.

"Okay, fine silly grrrl, they're under the tree. Where else would prezzies be?"

The living room smells like pine and cinnamon and party. I see a bunch of presents under the tree all wrapped in sparkly peppermint striped paper with lots of ribbons and bows. I sit patiently at his feet in front of the tree waiting to be told where to start.

"This looks like it has your name on it."

The label says, *To my bestest good baby grrrl ever.*

I giggle and shake the box. Inside is the most perfectest, prettiest little girl bear with purple boots and a purple raincoat and I love her. I climb up on Daddy's lap and hold up my bear for kisses. "Thank you!" He kisses my bear on the nose and strokes my hair, making me giggle.

He laughs. "That's it? That's all you wanted, no more prezzies?"

"More!"

I get bubble baths and lotions and pretty pens and just when I think I'm all out of prezzies to open and have happily stuck a candy cane in my mouth, he goes to his room and comes back with two more packages. "These presents are kind of for Daddy," he says and I giggle.

In a pretty gift bag is the cutest lacy nightgown, except parts of it are see-through. My Daddy is a perv, how about yours?

I'm about to go change when his hand gently stops me.

"Change here," he says as he crosses his strong legs in his yummy leather pants. He closes the blinds and the drapes and nods for me to strip.

I like stripping for my Daddy. I know just how to do it too. He likes it when I start at the top, so I let my hair loose and shake it out till it cascades down my back. He is grinning at me, which is all the encouragement I need. I slide my velvet shirt off and fold it neatly. I'll never forget to do that part after the spanking I got the first time I tossed my clothes to the side. Well, sometimes I "forget," but today I want to be good for him.

"Help me, Daddy?" I can hear him breathe hard when I sit on his lap so he'll unfasten my red Christmas bra. His fingers have the clasp undone but not before I manage to wiggle against him, just the way he likes it. And I like it too; I love being on my Daddy's lap. It is the best place in the world. I stay there as I take my bra off, slyly rubbing against him in a naughty way that makes me blush. I stand in front of him and slowly lower my skirt over my hips while he watches. I bend all the way down, my hands on the floor showing him my pretty red and white panties and slowly I get back up with a giggle, lower the panties, and stand there. I peek at Daddy behind my shoulder, and I can tell I'm doing it right. He has that look in his eyes that means I'm in all kinds of good trouble.

I pull the nightgown over my head wiggling till it's in place. It's red and white striped, and the feathers on top tickle me, making me squirm. Then I step into the tiny panties that have a bow in the front. "These don't cover very much, Daddy!" I giggle and strike a pose.

"Pretty?" I ask him with my hand on my hip.

"Beautiful," he answers in a husky voice as he licks his lips. "The perfect present for Daddy."

I blush and stand there letting him admire me and waiting to be told what to do.

He hands me the other package with a smirk that makes me feel dirty.

"I can tell you are thinking naughty thoughts, baby grrrl,"

he tells me as he motions me closer. I stop at his feet and look down.

"Aren't you?" he asks me in a firm voice.

"Mmm-hmm," I answer in a small voice. My heart is pounding and I know he's right; I want to be naughty, and I'm excited and scared of what he has in mind.

"Open it."

I carefully unwrap the present, trying to hide the slight tremor of my hands. I giggle a little as I hear the box rattle. I open the box cautiously and gasp as I catch a glimpse of leather. I pull the gift out and find a leather harness complete with a purple cock attached. I look up at Daddy with my eyes wide, holding the leather uncertainly, blushing and stammering, unable to ask.

He laughs heartily at my reaction and leaves me there, at his feet, uncertain, then without a word he motions me over with his eyes and I obey.

He runs his hand up my thigh as I stand awkwardly holding the harness and trembling. His touch makes me gasp. He reaches up and takes the harness from my hands. Sliding his hands over my hips and across my belly he fastens the top strap. His fingers tickle my inner thighs as he fastens the straps at my hips. I stand still, shivering slightly, blushing and uncertain.

I look down and a bright purple cock is poking out from under my sexy nightgown. Daddy calls me to his lap, and I sit nervously. He brushes my hair aside and nibbles on my neck. I close my eyes and whimper softly.

He whispers in my ear, "You've been such a good grrrl for me; I thought you should learn to fuck your Daddy."

I can feel my heart pounding furiously, I can feel my body

trembling, and I know I have to answer but my voice catches in my throat as I manage to say, "Yes, Daddy."

"How does that make you feel—the thought of fucking your Daddy?"

I'm so nervous my eyes are bright, and I shiver and answer with a moan I can't hold back.

He laughs, satisfied with my answer.

"Up."

I lift up off his lap somewhat gracelessly and blush at my own clumsiness.

He leads me to the bedroom and has me lie back on the bed. My heart is pounding as I watch him take his clothes off. He peels off his sexy leather pants revealing that he wasn't wearing anything underneath them. I moan on the bed as he approaches me naked. I'm dressed in my cute baby doll, and my Daddy is completely naked throwing me off completely.

"You like the way your Daddy fucks you, don't you?" he asks me as he drops to the bed and runs his fingertips over the gauzy fabric.

"Yeah." I stammer and blush. "A lot."

"Well, your Daddy wants you to make him feel that good. Do you think you can do that, babygrrrl?"

He reaches down and touches himself, bringing his wetness up to my lips. I moan and suck his finger into my mouth closing my eyes. My Daddy tastes so good, and he hardly ever lets me taste him. I revel in the moment and lap at his finger with hungry tongue.

"Yes, Daddy," I manage to whisper when he extracts his finger from my mouth with a chuckle.

"You're going to be a good grrrl for me, aren't you?"

I nod breathlessly.

"Would you like for your Daddy to ride you? Would you like it if I took your pretty purple cock?"

My moans are more insistent as I answer, "Oh, yes, Daddy, please."

I look up as he straddles my body, watching me and smirking.

"You are not to move unless I tell you to. Understood?"

"Yes, Daddy."

He lowers his body onto my cock and I can feel the pressure as he puts his full weight on my crotch, feel myself quiver as he growls deliciously.

"That's a good grrrl," he murmurs as he looks down on me.

"Eyes open," he orders and I groan. His breathing quickens, and I can feel him rocking against me as I watch him sliding up and down on my purple cock.

I can barely fight the urge to move my hips, and I feel myself dripping onto the bedspread.

"Mmm, that's a good grrrl," he repeats, moaning huskily. "That feels so good. Do you like being inside your Daddy?"

I try to answer and keep my eyes open, and my hips involuntarily rise of their own accord to meet him. I realize what I've done and blush and groan.

He pinches my nipple hard through the thin fabric.

"I thought I told you not to move. Do you want me to stop?"

I groan and whimper, "Oh, no, Daddy! Please don't stop. Please. Please. Oh, please don't stop. Please." I can feel myself tearing up at the thought.

"Then don't. Fucking. Move." His voice is cold and his body slams down on me hard as he moans.

I can feel his arousal, feel the impact of his body on my clit, feel the driving urge to move my hips, and I'm breathing harder and faster from the effort of not moving.

"Good grrrl," he says through gritted teeth. "Tell me how much you like it."

"Oh, Daddy, I love it, oh, please don't stop! Please. Oh, it feels so good, oh, god yes." My words disintegrate into moans and gasps. Each rough movement of his body echoes on my clit and makes me whimper and moan.

"You want to move your hips, don't you?"

My arms are above my head and I want to touch him so desperately.

"Yes, oh, yes please."

"Do it." Two words that meet no resistance as my body reacts to his command.

My hips rise to meet his, and I can feel myself driving into him as I moan. I can feel him close to coming and my own building heat which he taught me to recognize, and all too often to stop.

The pace quickens and he growls, leaning down to bite my neck hard.

"Such a good little grrrl," he whispers in my ear. "You want to come, you naughty little thing, don't you?

"Oh, yes."

The driving rhythm of his pressing against me is bringing me closer each minute.

"Your Daddy is going to come all over you," he tells me and I whimper. "You may come as well."

I moan as I feel his orgasm building, and his sharp moans signal his release. He drives his body into me furiously as I feel a scream bursting out of me, struggling not to move my hands, struggling not to grab him to me, moaning as I feel him coming hard against me, growling ferociously, trembling with the power of his body.

I close my eyes as the powerful orgasm takes me over from head to toes, and he rolls off of me gently. I groan at the sudden loss of his weight on me, feeling suddenly cold, denied of his warmth. He reaches down to undo the straps with nimble fingers and orders me to raise my hips so he can remove the harness from my body. His fingers brush gently against my soaking wet panties making me groan and shudder. He smiles as he puts a blanket over me.

He smoothes back my hair and murmurs, "That's a good grrrl."

He kisses my forehead. "You've made your Daddy sooo happy. You made him feel so good, babygrrrl."

I can feel my eyes tearing up as he continues to stroke my hair lovingly.

"What a good grrrl. You tried so hard not to move, I know that was hard."

I nod tearfully.

He showers my face with soft kisses, letting me breathe in his scent as I close my eyes and feel my body become relaxed and warm.

"You're such a good grrrl," he whispers in my ear. "You've pleased your Daddy so much."

I snuggle up to him, greedily seeking the comfort of his warmth.

"Thank you, Daddy," I whisper.

"Did you like your presents, babygrrrl?"

I smile and answer quietly, "Mmm-hmm."

And for a few minutes I float away quietly in my Daddy's arms, knowing that all is safe in the world. I love presents. Don't you?

BLADE, INK, STEEL

Sharon Wachsler

To the Skin

Too early, no sleep, on Ella's arm, all's black.
Buzzed on java shots, skittering heels stick in
cracked linoleum, I stumble, catch a wheez-
ing laugh far left. Ella shoves me onto a chair,
quick unlocks one cuff, yanks my wrist to
the armrest. *Click, click, click* it closes, and
swift she does the other. Seat clanks up like
a dentist chair. Ankle shackles ratcheted to a
bar below.

Ella jerks off my blindfold. In sudden flickering fluorescence, dented metal mirror exposes
my waxy skin, red-lined eyes. Ella drops into
a rocker, nods to coughing tough crushing
out her cig in the dim. Tar-fingered stranger
slouches over, scissors in one hand, clippers in
the other, fists the chestnut hank hanging from

my nape to ass. "Nuh!" I toss my head, sick rises at the *snick, snick, snick* of quick blades.

"Good we've got that ball gag in, eh, Sweet Pea?" Ella smirks. "I'd be so disappointed if you didn't appreciate Gen's work."

Sweet Pea. I purple: gentle, dainty taunt. If I could spit it, those words—not my hair—would be on the floor, ground into the grimy vinyl.

Gen bows me. Clippers devour vanity in jagged arcs, tears canyon between cheeks and nose. Then she sits to watch.

Ella stalks up, jacks my skirt to my hips, lifts Gen's shears, with a flick she fillets my panties, tosses the scissors, and pries me apart. Scooping my severed braid from the floor, she fans it up my thighs, tickling it against my pulsing cunt, bristles sharp and soft—too light. I jut toward the tease.

Laughter. "What, no tears now?" Ella feeds the dark shock inside me, brown ponytail swirling my cunt, silken ends whisper at pussy lips. I strain at the restraints, loose a whimper. She snakes it out, glistening with cream, smears my cheeks, chin, nose with my reek. Lazing, she puts the twist between her teeth, sucking like a cigar. Nods to Gen: "Tastes like a cunt."

Then Gen's back, cutting relentless. Wielding a razor, scrapes my scalp.

The scratching distracts me as Ella throws my damp hank in my lap, releases a wrist. "Unbraid it," she says. Shaking, my fingers finish, she reclasps the wrist.

She licks her lips to suck the end again, flicks her Zippo, flames the tip. Brunette spider's threads curl quick like spent filament. She drops it in a chipped glass dish as it opens into charred gray dust.

I sit transfixed till Gen spins me, holding a second mirror

behind. The front's still a blunt cut, but from nape to crown the back's a quarter-inch except the stark letters carved to the skin, not even stubble there: *E L L A ' S*. I quiver as Ella uncuffs me to run my hands over her name. Over and over and over. ELLA'S. Over and over.

Flipping Gen ten bills, Ella grins, "Get lost for twenty." Pumps the chair low, unzips her jeans to unleash her dick, my mouth. I reach, one hand finds her cock, the other fingers my scalp, and suck her: heaven. Now I know, Samson should've kissed Delilah's dick.

Tight and hot I blow till her stained fingers push mine away. She rakes me with blunt nails and I feel her brand—the razor burn.

In the Skin

Ella recuffs and gags me, frees my feet, flags a cab, herds me onto vinyl. Dizzy with possession, I rock, thighs squeezed, rubbing my scalp against the seat, reading it like inverted Braille. Vise-gripping my wrist, she snarls low so the driver's not wise, "Trying to get off?" Slicks two fingers under my skirt and into me. I gasp, arch to get her deeper.

Slap, slap! She smacks the Plexi. "Next Seven-Eleven."

Cab swings wide, and Ella jerks out of me and cab. My yelp muffled, I shiver in the empty. Back, she cradles cherry soda and yogurt, releases my mouth, strawing the drink. "Suck like it's mine." She squeezes her crotch. I gulp the sweet while she tumbles the yogurt. "How would you eat yourself?" I lap the spoon.

Low, "You're too in your head. I'm getting into your body." I moan. "Know why it's all cherry? Cuz I'm gonna bust yours all day, Sweet Pea."

The dairy sours. I choke it down, open for the gag. "Good." Then, "Here!" she hollers. Cabbie jams to the side, Ella's pulling me out before I read the signs. Inside, walls crawl with arms, backs, necks, lined, linked, inked. I skitter back, but Ella's palming my skull. "What do you say?" She rubs: *ELLA'S*.

"Tina!" she belts.

A juicy olive femme dances in, hands her a drawing. "Beauty, eh?"

Ella pats her ass. "Perfect."

Tina swings to her table. "Hop up!" She caresses it. Ella hoists me.

Tina smiles, lays paper in my lap, talking as she traces a lithe stem branching up, delicate fronds unfurling. "These two little blossoms will be white," the tattooist says, pointing a red-tipped finger. "The leaves, stem, and pods will all be green of course. Sweet, eh?"

They turn to me. I freeze. All I see: that tender vine.

"So," Tina lays down her pen. "Read and sign this—consent, liability, notice of safety practices, et cetera." I see the exit, my chance.

Ella rises, steps toward it.

I scribble, fitful, my signature illegible. Ella pivots, flashes "Lay down." Casual, she flicks my skirt back, baring me. "It will fit?"

Crimson, I cringe. Tina frowns, "Don't you want this?" Motions to my mouth. "Better take that out."

I look down, try to catch Ella's eye, but she's turned, tracing her name in caps on a scrap, a big apostrophe *S*, gaze lazing to the door.

Tina touches my face with a lacquered nail. "Hon, you're

the one who'll wear it. You gotta love it." I swallow the lump, nod, let myself fall limp as Ella walks over again.

Tina unwraps gel and razors. "Great," she says, beaming. "The stem'll start here," a red-tipped finger touches above my thigh, "avoid the crease, leaves and flowers curling up…." Finger arcs my mound. "A pod hanging on each *labia majora.*"

Ella sits to the side, I press my head into the table to feel the empty places, tasting pools of magic cherry Kool-Aid in my mind. Watch her watching Tina shave me smooth, transfer the pattern. I slip into the *slick, slick, slick* and Ella's eyes.

Then a million burning needles break my skin. The stabbing switches on and off with soothing swipes. Lidocaine cream, I learn later, makes it such a pure pain, tides of cool and hot rocking me. A minute, ten, a hundred, endless—wipe, burn, wipe, burn, holding still, exposed, exquisite. The searing juices my cunt, heat rising pungent past Tina's needles.

Four hours gone: I'm drunk on pain, Ella's triumph, Tina's rhythmic *swipe, sting, swipe, sting* as she wipes away black and green and white—and red so beautiful, can't believe I'm setting it free.

I'm desperate for Ella's dick, tongue, thumb, touch. Finally, Tina flashes glass at me. In the mirror, I'm transformed: Ella's tender cunt.

Through the Skin

Aftercare words blur as Ella pays, pushes me into a back-room chair, sits on its counter. Blissed, I eye Ella's dick, try to tickle my clit. Slaps my hand—"Lucille!" she bellows.

Billy-Idol dyke ambles in, gleaming metal beads.

Another paper. I sigh, sign, smiling. Unbutton my top, finger a nipple.

"She tweaking?" 'Cille frowns.

"Nah—endorphins. New tat." Ella lifts my skirt. I squirm forward, giving blondie a good look. She chuckles.

"You'll oversee aftercare?"

"What do you think?" Ella jaws.

"A'ight," 'Cille raises palms in surrender. "But take *that* out."

Ella scowls, releases my mouth. "Lean back, Sweet Pea," *sotto voce*. Ceiling swirls. She motions to 'Cille.

"Here," Ella touches my uninked, inside labia.

"Oh." I tilt toward it.

"And here."

"Aye-ah." I wriggle.

Lucille shakes her head, looking down at me. "I can't do this if you don't hold still."

"Ella touched me," I explain.

"Christ." Lucille slops coffee on her T.

Ella looms. "I'm chaining you. Don't move."

I nod, peaceful.

Astringent tingles my clit hood. Fantastic lights dance, but I statue. Purple pen dots, Ella and 'Cille eyeball angles, tilt, peer.

Then red-hot pinwheels fire left, clean pain—just a taste— the pulling, fishing-line fine, until the tug, when I think I might come, but it's not enough. Again the pierce, this time right, I bite back my cry. Sweet hurt, tickle, tug. Tightening, fastening clasps, that pinching has my hands gripping, Ella's tongue circles her lip.

Hand glass held below my open lap. "Here." Two tiny steel hoops, each gold-beaded, gold links hanging between. My pearl, pulsing pink, draped in gold.

Ella stealths to me, slipping her littlest finger under, tugs feathery. My eyes roll.

From her pocket Ella spins a new ring: thick gold band, a long strand dangles a clasp. "You'll heal, then who owns you, Sweet Pea?"

I make my mouth an O. Ella slips the ring between my lips. Kingly, she holds her hand out to be kissed. I slide the ring down her fourth finger like unrolling a rubber, tasting the metal tang, licking her underside's wrinkles.

We kiss. Ella takes me home.

BENEATH THE CARPET IS THE FLOOR

Anna Watson

The park ranger tells me she's put in for a transfer. She's craving forest, she says, enough salt spray, enough sand-logged condoms snagged out of the dunes, enough trying to educate the public about sandpipers and their nesting needs.

"It's your job to educate the public," I say. *And me,* I think, *what about me?*

"Down with sandpipers," she says, "up with spotted owls." She wants to go to Northern California and leave me and my beach shack behind, just when our fucking was reaching what I can only refer to as new heights.

Now, for instance. She stops talking and snaps her fingers, pointing to a spot by her right boot. I drop in an instant, hearing myself murmur in my head, *Assume the position,* which is on my knees, legs spread, hands upturned and balanced lightly on my thighs. Back straight, tits out, head slightly lowered, eyes downcast. I read about it in a book, and the first time felt silly, but that low hum of pleasure in her throat made it all okay and now I do it without thinking. Not thinking is the key, actually.

I feel her hand on my head, rough and gentle at the same time, exactly the way she'll absentmindedly rub a dog's head, one tied up outside a store, for example. She rubs my head, then she reaches back and grabs a fistful of hair, yanking my head up until I'm nose to dick, taking in the bulge in her uniform pants, unable to look elsewhere.

"Like what you see?"

"Yes, Sir!" And I like what I hear, the way her voice deepens when she's topping me, the desire bleeding through.

"Tell me what you want to do."

"Sir! I want to suck your dick, Sir!"

She pushes my head back down and lets go of my hair. "Oh, that's imaginative," she sneers. "The girl wants to suck my dick. Suck your dick, Sir!" She mocks my trembly, eager voice, and I blush, tears rushing to my eyes.

"I can do better," I whisper, settling back into position.

"Hmm." She moves across the room and I can hear her unzipping her bag. That black leather bag. Sir's bag. I feel a rush in my cunt and I make sure my back is straight. I can't help breathing faster and there's an itch on my cheek but I don't scratch. She's back, lifting my chin with the butt of the small whip. I'm looking at her manhood again, tears spilling from my eyes.

"I'm giving you another chance," she says, sounding bored.

"Thank you, Sir!" I hesitate, unsure if I should go ahead.

I am intensely embarrassed and am starting to sweat. I know exactly what I want to say, but getting it out is almost unbearable. I know I have to. I can't.

"I'm waiting." She taps my chin with the whip butt and I gasp.

"Sir!" I can always say that, and I have said it in so many ways, screaming it when I come, gasping it when she beats me, sobbing it when she holds me. "Sir!" I force myself to continue, "I want to bring my face right up close to your fly, Sir, but not quite touching. I want to breathe on your cock, Sir, so you can feel it through your trousers, and then I want to slowly put my lips there, Sir, I want to feel it pressing against my mouth, the sweet weight of it, I want to move my lips up and down, Sir, get your trousers wet, bite a little, Sir, use my tongue, and then…"

She stops me by putting the butt of the whip across my lips. I risk a look up at her and she's smiling.

"Good girl," she says, then frowns to see me looking. She lets the whip drape lazily across my back and sighs. "How can a good girl be so bad? Lie down!"

I'm on my stomach before she's even finished giving the command, with my lips as close to the tip of her boot as they can get without touching. I am safe here. A friend once wrote in a poem, "Beneath the carpet is the floor," and I never feel the profound and simple truth of that more than I do when I am prostrate before Sir. Forever. I could lie here forever.

She shifts her boot so the tip is between my lips. "This is my dick," she says, and I am busy immediately. Her dick, she's letting me pleasure her dick. My pussy is wet and my tits hurt, squashed under me. I push with my toes to get a little purchase and she rocks her boot in my mouth, demanding more,

as much as I can take. I open. I am hers. I breathe and suck
and lick, sand from the beach mixing with my spit, the leather
taste, the polish, no, the primal salt of her dick.

When she finally pulls away, I am breathing hard, spit running down my chin, mouth sore and filled with grit.

"Look up," she orders, and I tilt my head to see she's unzipped her trousers and is cupping herself through her shorts.
"Do you want me to fuck you, little girl?" She strokes herself.

I can hardly believe my luck. "Yes, Sir!" I say as smartly as I
can through my swollen lips.

She steps on my head, forcing it to the floor. "I'm considering
it." She twists her boot back and forth like she's grinding out a
cigarette. I can feel my hair tangle and pull. She presses hard,
one final time, then walks off.

"Panties down, ass up," she says and then she's gone, the screen
door slamming. I know where she's going—down to watch the
breakers as she smokes. I used to hate the smell of cigarettes. I
used to have a big NO SMOKING sign up on my door.

I pull down my underwear and decide to leave them shack-
ling my ankles; she didn't tell me to take them off, just down.
I flip up my skirt and hunker down on my elbows, getting
my ass as high as it will go. It's uncomfortable and hurts my
elbows and knees. I wish she would come back. I wish I could
just lie on the floor again. I'm cold. What if someone comes
by? I know I'm not allowed to move, my cheek itches, my
back is starting to hurt. Sir. I concentrate on Sir, the breeze
catching the smoke from her cigarette and carrying it away,
her eyes on the sea; maybe there's a seagull out there, getting
lunch. Then I stop thinking, or rather, I just think about the
floor. How it's holding me up. How solid it is. How much I
can count on it to be there.

The screen door slams again and she is standing behind me. She stands there for a long time, observing, every now and then making adjustments with her boot. Panties off. Ass higher. Knees farther apart. Chest closer to the floor. That's right.

I allow myself to think I'm going to get fucked. My pussy softens; my mouth is dry from panting; I listen as hard as I can, straining to hear the rip of a condom package, the unzipping of her trousers. Everything is very still.

Then there's the sound of something coming through the air, and in my dazed state, I don't recognize it until the cane has caught my upper thighs so hard I fall forward, scraping my cheek on the rug. Right away, I'm sobbing. I haul myself back up and she mutters something, then the cane is falling on me like the breakers, no relief, no stopping, just pounding and pounding. I can't take it. I do take it. I hardly notice when she brings the cane to my lips—I kiss it distractedly, weeping more softly now, and it hurts so bad. Did I say thank you like I was supposed to, or did I say, "Don't leave me"? Sir doesn't comment. She's got a soft shammy cloth and is wiping me down like a horse who's just had a hard run. Then she snaps her fingers and I'm back on the floor, pressing my burning cheek into the rug, slowly, slowly, letting myself relax. Sir is gentling me, and I smile secretly into the rug.

"You've been a very good girl," says Sir, still stroking me with the soft cloth. "But surely you remember there was some behavior from last week."

I tighten up again; she feels it and laughs. "Get up."

I push myself onto my knees. My entire back, my ass, my legs throb and burn. "Show me your breasts," she says, then turns away to get something out of her bag. I kneel there with a breast in each hand, offering them to her. She comes back and quickly dresses one nipple in a clamp with a weight hanging from it. She sits on the couch with her legs spread and snaps. I stand in front of her and she takes the breast without the clamp into her mouth, tonguing the nipple so sweetly. She lets me stand there for a long time as she eats my tit, every once in a while reaching over to pull on the weight. I am moaning and writhing; she reaches around to slap my ass and I am immediately quiet and still. She slowly unclamps my nipple and I can't hold back a yelp. Her mouth is hot and wet and she takes my sore nipple roughly, deftly clamping the other nipple now. She goes back and forth like that, back and forth, for a long time, until my breasts are a mess, until I can't believe they've ever been an erogenous zone. Finally she takes the clamp off and I start to relax a little. When she pulls the snakebite kit out of her pocket I start to cry. "I can't, Sir! I can't!"

She cocks her head and raises an eyebrow. Her lips are plump from sucking. "No?"

I can't stand not to please her. Still crying, I hold out my breasts. They feel as if a car has run over them on a gravel road. She nods, then puts the kit to one nipple, pumping it until I'm seeing stars. I sway and she releases the pressure, lifts off the kit, and puts her mouth there, her teeth. Then the other nipple. Back and forth. I can't stop crying. I am hers. I am trying so hard to be good. Through my tears, I can see her look of pleasure as she pinches first one nipple, then the other, the snakebite kit forgotten beside her. She has her tools, but I know she prefers skin on skin, the strength of her own body, flesh against flesh. She snaps and I am on the floor, flooded with relief. She rests her boot on my head, rocking it back and forth.

"Whose girl are you?"

"Yours, Sir!" I say so loudly she laughs.

"Well, perhaps for today. Now roll over and show me your cunt. Keep your eyes closed."

I whimper as I obey, eyes squeezed shut. I get onto my back so I can spread my pussy for her the way she taught me, legs wide, ass lifted, lips peeled back. I hate this position and I especially hate it when she makes me touch myself. But that doesn't seem to be what she has in mind. At last, I hear her opening a condom, the small kissing noises it makes as she rolls it onto her dick. As sore as I am, my pussy is still ready. I still want it. She is pleased with me, she has to be. I took it all so well. I outdid myself. I smile another secret little smile. I allow myself to think that maybe this time, I'm going to get to come. I allow myself to think that now Sir will never leave me.

ABOUT THE AUTHORS

D. ALEXANDRIA (d-alexandria.com), a Jamaican descendant, unapologetically wallows in perversion while residing in the Boston area. Published in the *Best Lesbian Erotica* series, *Ultimate Lesbian Erotica 2006*, and under the pseudonym Glitter in GBF Magazine and Kuma2.net, she is currently penning her first collection of black lesbian erotica.

RACHEL KRAMER BUSSEL (rachelkramerbussel. com) has edited more than twenty erotic anthologies, including *Glamour Girls: Femme/ Femme Erotica; First-Timers: True Stories of Lesbian Awakening; Up All Night: Adventures in Lesbian Sex; Yes, Sir; Yes, Ma'am; He's on Top; She's on Top; Caught Looking; Hide and Seek; Crossdressing; Sex and Candy;*

Rubber Sex; Spanked: Red-Cheeked Erotica; Naughty Spanking Stories from A to Z 1 and *2;* and the nonfiction *Best Sex Writing 2008.* Her work has been published in more than one hundred anthologies, including *Best American Erotica 2004* and *2006, Chocolate Flava 2, Everything You Know About Sex Is Wrong, Single State of the Union,* and *Desire: Women Write About Wanting.* She hosts In the Flesh Erotic Reading Series, is senior editor at *Penthouse Variations,* wrote the popular "Lusty Lady" column for the *Village Voice,* and has contributed to *AVN, Bust, Diva,* Fresh Yarn, Gothamist, Huffington Post, Mediabistro, *Newsday, New York Post, San Francisco Chronicle, Time Out New York,* and *Zink.* In her spare time, she blogs about cupcakes at cupcakestakethecake.blogspot.com.

JEAN CASSE is a San Francisco writer who collects religious icons. She has been published previously in *Best Women's Erotica 2007.*

DYLYNN DESAINT (dylynndesaint.blogspot.com) lives with her partner in the Southwest. An avid people watcher, Dylynn finds inspiration for her stories in everyday life and on her annual treks to the busy streets of New York City. Her work has appeared in *Purple Panties: An Eroticanoir.com Anthology, Iridescence: Sensuous Shades of Lesbian Erotica,* and *Best Date Ever: True Stories that Celebrate Lesbian Relationships.*

LUCINDA L. FLANARY grew up in the mountains of eastern Kentucky. She has always been inspired to write, especially erotic short fiction and poetry. She has recently completed her first book of poetry and is working on a follow-up edition. She is currently living a small town Midwest life, but aspiring to fulfill her New England dreams.

Shanna Germain (shannagermain.com) believes love takes many forms, and always arrives on wings of some kind. Her work, erotic and otherwise, has been widely published in places like *Absinthe Literary Review, Best American Erotica 2007, Best Bondage Erotica 2, Best Gay Romance 2008, Best Lesbian Erotica 2008,* and Salon.com.

Victoria Gimpelevich (vocalminority.wordpress.com) is an evil (vegan) lesbian from San Francisco. She puts herself through college by modeling, writing, massage therapy, and other random stuff. She enjoys sex, punk rock, kittens, and cookies. All of her erotic writing comes from thorough research into the subject.

Sacchi Green writes in western Massachusetts and the mountains of New Hampshire. Her stories have appeared in a hip-high stack of books with inspirational covers, including multiple volumes of *Best Lesbian Erotica, Best Women's Erotica,* and *The Mammoth Book of Best New Erotica.* She has also coedited three anthologies of lesbian erotica, *Rode Hard, Put Away Wet; Hard Road, Easy Riding;* and *Lipstick on Her Collar,* with a fourth, *Girl Crazy,* in the works.

Nairne Holtz is a Montreal-based author whom the *Globe and Mail* has identified as a "writer to watch." Her first novel, *The Skin Beneath* (Insomniac, 2007), won the Alice B. Lesbian Debut Fiction Award and was a finalist for Quebec's McAuslan First Book Prize. She is also the coeditor of *No Margins:*

Writing Canadian Fiction in Lesbian (QPress, 2006), which was short-listed for a Lambda Literary Award.

MOXZI LANTANA rides and writes mostly from the sultry American South, but loves to travel. She has won writing awards and been published in print and on the Internet in various venues. Her projects include novel length and shorter fiction when she is not distracted by a woman. Good thing she is a quick writer.

THEA LETICIA is a Latina queer high femme switch with a passion for adjectives, transgression, hard-packing butches, and social justice. Having discovered her queerness and kink thanks largely to some very naughty erotica, she has a strong commitment to making butches wet with her own paradoxical fantasies. When she isn't busy baking daddies cookies, Thea is an activist, educator, writer, and performer.

ZAEDRYN MEADE (zaedryn.com) is a queer butch writer whose erotica has been published in *Penitalia: Collegiate Erotica*, *Best Lesbian Erotica* (2006 and 2007), *Secret Slaves: Erotic Stories of Bondage*, and *Love at First Sting*. Born and raised in the rainforest of Southeast Alaska, she now lives in New York City.

EVAN MORA is a recovering corporate banker living in Toronto who's thrilled to put pen to paper after years of daydreaming in the boardroom. She now subscribes to a "have laptop will travel" philosophy, and can often be found in coffee shops and downtown parks writing erotica and working on her first novel.

Whether it's erotica or more mainstream queer fiction, JODI PAYNE (jodipayne.net) prefers to read and write about real women with real flaws living real lives. Her lesbian work includes 2008 Eppie finalist *For Better or Worse* and several short stories including "The Good Life," published in Torquere Press's hot lesbian anthology, *Under this Cowgirl's Hat.* Jodi lives and works in the Northeastern United States with her partner of seven years and their family.

RADCLYFFE is a retired surgeon and full-time award-winning author-publisher with more than thirty lesbian novels and anthologies in print, including the Lambda Literary Award winners *Erotic Interludes 2: Stolen Moments* edited with Stacia Seaman and *Distant Shores, Silent Thunder.* She has selections in multiple anthologies including *Best Lesbian Erotica* (2006, 2007, and 2008), *Best Lesbian Romance 2009, Caught Looking: Erotic Tales of Voyeurs and Exhibitionists, Hide and Seek, A Is for Amour, H Is for Hardcore, L Is for Leather,* and *Rubber Sex.* She is also the president of Bold Strokes Books, one of the world's largest independent LGBT publishing companies.

JEAN ROBERTA teaches English in a Canadian university and writes in several genres. Her stories have appeared in approximately sixty print anthologies, including several editions of *Best Lesbian Erotica.* Three of her articles are included in the reference work *LGBTQ America Today. Obsession,* her collection of erotic stories in diverse genders and genres, is available from Eternal Press (eternalpress.ca).

TERESA NOELLE ROBERTS turned her curiosity about other people's sex lives into a career. Her erotica has appeared in *Best*

Women's Erotica 2004, 2005, and *2007, Ultimate Lesbian Erotica 2007, Lipstick on Her Collar, Missionary No More: Purple Panties 2, The Mammoth Book of Lesbian Erotica,* and many other publications. She also writes erotica and erotic romance with Dayle A. Dermatis as Sophie Mouette. When not writing, Teresa spends too much time deciding what to wear.

LISABET SARAI (lisabetsarai.com) has been writing and publishing erotica since 2000 and has three novels, two short-story collections, and two erotica anthologies to her credit. Her stories have appeared in more than two dozen collections including the past three years' editions of *The Mammoth Book of Best New Erotica.* Recently she began ePublishing with Total-E-Bound, Eternal Press, and Phaze. Lisabet also reviews erotica for the Erotica Readers and Writers Association and Erotica Revealed.

TAWANNA SULLIVAN is the webmaster for Kuma (kuma2.net), a website that encourages black lesbians to write and share erotica. Her work has appeared in *Longing, Lust, and Love: Black Lesbian Stories; Iridescence: Sensuous Shades of Lesbian Erotica; Spirited: Affirming the Soul and Black Gay/Lesbian Identity;* and *Purple Panties.* She lives in New Jersey with her civil union partner, Martina.

Finding herself uninspired to write her doctoral dissertation, CHELSEA G. SUMMERS began writing her award-winning blog, pretty dumb things, in March 2005. Since then, her work has appeared in *Penthouse, GQ, Scarlet,* and *New Woman* magazines, as well as in erotic anthologies edited by Susie Bright and Rachel Kramer Bussel. Currently, Chelsea is working on a memoir about her life in men. Having gleefully abandoned the world of academia for that of writing, Chelsea lives and writes in glamorous New York City.

LINDA SUZUKI works in Washington, D.C. as a writer of erotica. Secretly, she dreams of leaving it all behind to pursue her true passion—which is to write technical manuals for the federal government.

JESSICA SWAFFORD (jnicole58@hotmail.com) is a queer femme dyke artist, recently returning to Asheville, NC, by way of San Francisco. She is working on two sci-fi queer smut novels. She has been a professional dominant, a Daddy, and is currently a teenage boi in femme drag. She loves butches. This is her first publication.

SHARON WACHSLER (sharonwachsler.com or sickhumorpostcards.com) lives in rural New England with her partner and service dog. Her erotica has appeared in *Best American Erotica* (2004 and 2005), *Periphery*, *Bed*, *Lipstick on Her Collar*, and many other places. In 2006, the Astraea Foundation named Sharon an "Emerging Lesbian Writer" in fiction. She is the founder of *Breath & Shadow* (abilitymaine.org/breath), the first cross-disability literary journal written and produced exclusively by people with disabilities.

ANNA WATSON is an old-school femme mom who lives with her two sons and her butch Beau near Boston, MA. Her passion for writing smut often gets subsumed by the daily marathon of baseball games, hip-hop classes, and science fair projects, but she does her best to keep sending out stories. Look for more butch/femme sexcapades in the two previous *Best Lesbian Erotica* anthologies, as well as in *Fantasy: Untrue Stories of Lesbian Passion*, on the Steamy Audio website, and forthcoming in the drag king anthology by Suspect Thoughts Press. In keeping with the computer age, she maintains a blog at queer-today.ning.com, putters about on butch-femme.com and mad-femmepride.com, but is generally completely overwhelmed by the Internet and would prefer to just read a good book (or write one). She would like to thank Karen Friedland, who wrote the poem mentioned in her story.

ABOUT THE EDITORS

JOAN LARKIN (joanlarkin.com) is the author of *My Body: New and Selected Poems*, which received the Publishing Triangle's 2008 Audre Lorde Award, and editor of *A Woman Like That: Coming Out Stories by Lesbian and Bisexual Writers*. Her books include *Cold River*, which received a Lambda Award, *A Long Sound, Housework*, and *Sor Juana's Love Poems* (translated with Jaime Manrique). Larkin cofounded Out & Out Books during the feminist literary explosion of the '70s, coediting the groundbreaking anthologies *Amazon Poetry* and *Lesbian Poetry* with Elly Bulkin and *Gay and Lesbian Poetry in Our Time* with Carl Morse. She lives in New York.

TRISTAN TAORMINO (puckerup.com and openingup.net) is an award-winning author, columnist, editor, and sex educator. She is the author of four books: *Opening Up: Creating and Sustaining Open Relationships*; *True Lust: Adventures in Sex, Porn and Perversion*; *Down and Dirty Sex Secrets*; and *The Ultimate Guide to Anal Sex for Women*. She is a columnist for the *Village Voice* and *Hustler's Taboo*. She is the creator and original series editor of *Best Lesbian Erotica*, which has won three Lambda Literary Awards. She runs her own adult film production company, Smart Ass Productions, and is currently an exclusive director for Vivid Entertainment. For Vivid, she directs a reality series called *Chemistry* and helms its sex education imprint, Vivid-Ed, for which she has written, produced, and directed several titles including *The Expert Guide to Anal Sex*, *The Expert Guide to Oral Sex 1: Cunnilingus*, *The Expert Guide to Oral Sex 2: Fellatio*, and *The Expert Guide to the G-Spot*. Tristan has been featured in more than two hundred publications and has appeared on CNN, HBO's "Real Sex," "The Howard Stern Show," "Loveline," "Ricki Lake," MTV, Fox News, the Discovery Channel, and on over five dozen radio shows. She lectures at top colleges and universities on gay and lesbian issues, sexuality and gender, and feminism, and she teaches sex and relationship workshops around the world. She lives in upstate New York with her partner and their three dogs.